2 -

D0425996

|1(7

Hoare and the Portsmouth Atrocities

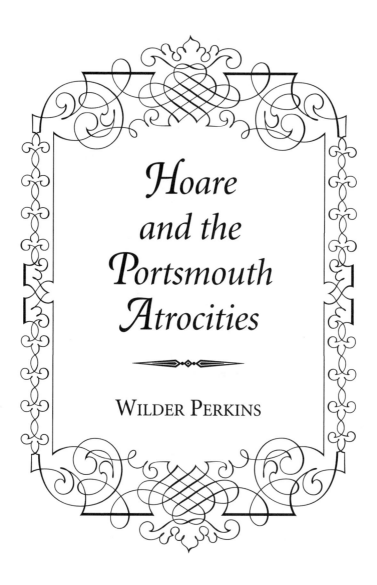

Hoare
and the
Portsmouth
Atrocities

WILDER PERKINS

THOMAS DUNNE BOOKS

ST. MARTIN'S PRESS ❧ NEW YORK

THOMAS DUNNE BOOKS.
An imprint of St. Martin's Press

Library of Congress Cataloging-in-Publication Data

Perkins, Wilder.
    Hoare and the Portsmouth atrocities / Wilder Perkins.
      — 1st ed.
      p. cm.
    ISBN 0-312-19283-5
    I. Title.
    PS3566.E6914867H63   1998
    813'.54—dc21   98-22255
                                        CIP

First Edition: December 1998

10 9 8 7 6 5 4 3 2

Hoare and the Portsmouth Atrocities

Chapter I

⟫◆⟪

$\mathcal{B}$ARTHOLOMEW HOARE and Eleanor Graves first met on the east reach of Portland Bill, across two sprawled bodies. It was late on a gray afternoon in mid-June of 1805—Trafalgar year.

The week before, a water hoy, returning empty from supplying the ships on the Brest blockade, had brought in *Scipio*'s launch. *Scipio,* 74—a seventy-four-gunship of the line—had not been reported since she departed Plymouth five weeks ago, bound for that same Brest blockade. The launch was awash, empty, charred in places, badly mauled. *Scipio* had been well-found, well manned, and there had been no adverse weather on her presumed course.

The condition of the lonely launch had shouted "explosion" to Hoare. Moreover, he had had a brief encounter in May with the contents of an oddly well-made keg. The keg, of the small, ten-gallon size known as an "anker" to the vintner trade, had been picked up by a Coastguardsman on a country roadside near Corfe. It might have been poorly packed on a pony; the pony might have escaped from a midnight caravan;

1

the caravan might have belonged to one of the region's flour-ishing smuggler gangs. Whatever the anker's provenance, its contents—strange pieces of clockwork—were far more inter-esting to His Majesty's government, and to Hoare, than mere brandy would have been.

Caught in the narrow grooves between the anker's tarred staves he had found grains of a fine grayish sand, of which he had kept a sample. The anker had been officially spirited out of Hoare's possession and taken off, he believed, to London. It was when he put together the two bits of information—the anker's contents and the ruined launch—that he had placed his suspicions before Sir George Hardcastle, Port Ad-miral in Portsmouth. An hour later Hoare had set off westward on a wearisome fourteen-hour day of tacking down-Channel in his own little pinnace-yacht *Inconceivable,* bearing the sand with him.

He had landed last night in Lyme Regis and had spent most of the day conferring with old Richard Dee about where the anker might have come ashore. Old Dee, Hoare had learned a year or more ago, had sold his fishing boat and gear when his aching bones got the better of him and on the pro-ceeds had retired to an overturned barge on the western out-skirts of Lyme. Here he had taken up the subject of *sand.* He claimed to be able to tell the source of any handful of sand, provided it derived from any beach between Land's End and Dover.

Hoare had found himself hard put to it to understand Dee. To his ear, the Dorset dialect comprised nothing but *z*s and *oo*s. The man sounded like a giant obsolete bee. Moreover, since a spent ball had crushed Hoare's voice box at the Glori-ous First of June and old Dee was quite deaf, Hoare's remain-ing whisper of a voice was useless.

To communicate at all, then, he had had to dredge up an interpreter. Young Mary, the oldster's granddaughter, had had some schooling; she could pick up Hoare's whispers, relay them to her gaffer, and interpret his buzzing replies. Hoare felt indebted to her, although finding even her milder accent hard to understand at times.

He had begun by testing Dee's reported gift, using sand specimens whose provenance he knew and which he had brought along in tiny apothecary's vials. He had wholly failed to catch the old man out. Hoare had even set Dee a trap by combining dead-white sand from the Conqueror's landing place at Pevensey with a blood-red grit that he had collected on the beach below the cliff at Goonhilly Downs during a recent passage from Cornwall. Dee had peered at the pink mixture, rolled it between thumb and forefinger, smelled it, and cackled.

"Gaffer says, 'Ye'll not gammon Dickon Dee that easy,' sir," young Mary said. When the sand master went on to tell Hoare exactly where he had picked up both moieties, Hoare had to admit his feeble ruse. As penance, he had bought the old fisherman a second pint before offering him the specimen that he really wanted him to identify.

"Buzz. Ooo. Zuzz."

"He says: 'Now you'm goin' to tell me you didden pick her up on way past Weymouth,' sir," the girl said. " 'But you'll be wrong again. That there sand be from off easterly side of Portland Bill, she be.

" 'Halfway up the Bill, where the tide sets shoreward,' he says."

This time, Hoare had taken Dee at his word. After tipping young Mary and buying the old man his third pint, Hoare had hoisted his lanky self back aboard *Inconceivable* and cast off from Lyme's stone pier.

Today, the westerly wind was wet, raw for the season. Little spits of mixed rain and spray carried across the Bill to sting Hoare's face. Before taking her back up-Channel to her berth in Portsmouth's Inner Camber, he would collect another bit of sand from the spot old Dee had named and see for himself how well it matched his sample. While there, he would snoop a bit to see if any interesting flotsam besides the well-made anker had drifted ashore there.

Now as close to his goal as guesswork permitted, he slipped into *Inconceivable*'s bows and lowered her kedge, deep enough to hang below her keel as a makeshift lead. The tide might be making, but he had no wish to ground her tender bottom on the knobby cobbles whose round tops crowded out the sand hereabouts like so many black grinding teeth.

It was now that Hoare first saw Eleanor Graves: a short woman in brown, her brown hair blowing across her face in the spray-laden gusts. She rose from behind an overturned shallop, to face two tinkerlike men with long cudgels who were approaching her along the beach at a purposeful trot. Fifty feet from her, and the same from him, Hoare could hear their jeering voices.

Putting two fingers into his mouth, Hoare blew a piercing whistle. The attackers paused. Then, seeing they had only one man to contend with, one turned to await Hoare's landing while the other continued his purposeful advance.

The woman reached back. In her left hand she held a sling—*a sling!* She twirled the ancient weapon underhand as if she were heaving the lead in a man-of-war's chains and slung a rock at her leading assailant. It struck him full in the forehead; he dropped, his legs twitching like a pair of gaffed salmon.

The other attacker stopped in his tracks. This was his mistake, for now the woman took a full step toward him and let fly another rock. She threw it this time, using her right hand and not her left. She must have hit her target in his nose or mouth, for Hoare saw him clap both hands to his face and heard a choked cry of pain.

Inconceivable grounded with a soft crunch at the feet of the two men. Hoare pulled the tiller from its straps to serve as a makeshift quarterstaff and launched himself over her bows at

4

them. There was no need; the two were in no condition to fight on.

"Davids two, Goliaths zero," whispered Hoare to himself, and stepped up the shingly beach toward the woman in brown.

She had already whipped out a length of spun yarn from a coil hidden somewhere about her person and had bent over to secure her first target. The cold rage in her face changed to welcome on seeing Hoare's naval coat, and she finished knotting the man's limbs together in a neat cat's cradle behind him. "Well met, sir," she said, and cut another length of spun yarn. "Would you mind . . . ?" She handed him the second hank.

The woman would not be able to hear his whispered reply over the louder whisper of the soft surf, so Hoare simply nodded and turned to and triced up the other.

"I am in your debt, sir," she said in a clear contralto voice, "for coming to my rescue, even though I appear to have managed by myself.

"To whom am I indebted, may I ask?"

Even standing erect, she had to tilt her head back to look up into Hoare's faded gray eyes, for she could have been little more than five feet tall. Her figure was sturdy, if not plump; she reminded Hoare of an assertive partridge. Her piercing eyes were brown. There were a few gray streaks in her coarse brown windblown hair.

Hoare reached into an inner pocket of his coat and drew out several pieces of paper. Selecting one, he handed it to the brown woman with an apologetic look and a bow. She read it just loudly enough to be heard over the soft, pulsating rumble of surf.

" 'Permit me to present myself: Bartholomew Hoare, Lieutenant, Royal Navy. My deepest respects. That I am not speaking to you is not a matter of intentional discourtesy but is due to my inability to speak above a whisper.' "

Unlike many strangers, the brown woman did not now assume that because Hoare was all but dumb he must be deaf to boot, for her next words were neither shouted nor spoken with the exaggerated care the unthinking use with infants and other incompetent persons who cannot talk back.

"I am Eleanor Graves, sir, wife of Dr. Simon Graves of Weymouth. I know he will add his thanks to mine for coming to my defense against this cowardly attack."

One of the bound bodies on the shingle, the man she had struck in the nose, had already struggled to a sitting posture. He was hunched over as far as his bonds permitted, dripping scarlet steadily onto the shingle between his leather breeches.

From Mrs. Graves's behavior, she and Hoare might have been meeting at a Bath cotillion instead of over their two victims on a cold, wet September beach.

"Now, sir, what shall we do with these rogues?" she asked.

For his answer, Hoare pulled out a set of wax tablets, of the kind the ancient Romans used, and wrote: "My boat—to Weymouth?"

"Excellent," she said. So, between the two of them, they dragged their cocooned captives across the shingle to *Inconceivable,* attached them to a handy-billy, and hoisted them aboard. They heaped the rogues out of the way but within sight, just aft of her companionway.

Hoare subjected the two men to a quick search. Other than a miscellany of miserable personal effects, seaman's sheath knives, two mason's hammers, and three guineas a man, Hoare found only the cudgels and a length of tough, thin line. He tossed the cudgels over the side, sequestered the hammers, the knives, and their sheaths, and appropriated the line for *Inconceivable's* small stores. He handed the guineas to Mrs. Graves.

Without any apparent concern about soaking her skirts, Mrs. Graves helped Hoare heave the pinnacle off the beach. She then took the hand he reached down to her, sprang aboard, and got out of his way. He trimmed the flapping sails, returned the tiller to its straps, and set a course alongshore toward Weymouth. It was not far.

His passenger sat silent in the tiny cockpit, facing him. Hoare realized she understood the futility of trying to converse with a stranger when she could not hear his replies. Unlike the few other women he knew, she seemed comfortable enough without speech passing. But as *Inconceivable* drew into the dock behind Weymouth's breakwater, she spoke.

"Do you know this harbor, Mr. Hoare?"

The town and the slopes behind it gave enough of a lee so that Hoare thought he could make himself heard. He cocked his head and shrugged. "Yes, but not well," he whispered. "I'll welcome local knowledge."

"If you do not choose to continue your voyage tonight— and I hope you will not—you may wish to rest at the Dish of Sprats. Over there to the left of where you are aiming now, this side of St. Ninian's Church. That's the steeple you can see."

Mrs. Graves might not know her nautical terms—she said "left" like a landsman, not "port" like a seaman—but her directions were clear all the same, and Hoare eased his helm to suit.

"Will you hold the tiller for a moment while I take off sail?" he whispered.

She heard the whisper. She hesitated for a moment, then grasped the tiller ahead of his hand, lightly at first, then with increasing assurance.

"So, so," he said. He stepped forward around the captives' surly bodies and dropped *Inconceivable*'s jib onto its club, lashing it in place with its own sheet. He uncleated her main halliard and brought it aft with him to the helm.

"I'll take her now, ma'am," he said. "I'll be dropping the mainsail in a heap, so you should edge over to the rail."

Hoare thrust the tiller smoothly to starboard. As *Inconceivable* luffed up, he waited until she had just enough way left to make the harbor's sloping shore and let her tall mainsail go with a run to drop on top of the prisoners, together with the boom. He left them there for now, one muttering in a dazed voice. The little yacht's keel grated on the shingle once again, and she came to rest, listing slightly to starboard, while Hoare gave the mainsail its own rough furl and propped it in a pair of jeers.

He locked the cabin hatch and hopped ashore to offer Mrs. Graves a hand down. She took it—more out of courtesy than of necessity, Hoare thought—and leaped nimbly down in her soggy skirts to stand behind him, looking back at *Inconceivable*.

"We might turn our captives over to the port guard?" she said, half-inquiringly.

"Or the Chief Constable," Hoare suggested. "Whichever is less likely to be their drinking companion." While not actually acquainted with Weymouth's guardians of the law, he knew that all along Britain's beleaguered south coast the lawman and the unlawful were often as close as a virgin's thighs.

Mrs. Graves's laugh was an odd throaty gurgle. "Of course. Sir Thomas Frobisher, then. It would be . . . what, three o'clock?"

Hoare nodded.

"Then he will be at the Town's Club—as will Dr. Graves, in all likelihood. Come."

She took Hoare's arm and directed him to a building facing the new esplanade below St. Ninian's. It was a large house, which Hoare thought could have belonged to a leading merchant of the town.

"The Club's house once belonged to a prominent merchant of the town," she said as if reading his thoughts. "But he fell on hard times, and a cabal of other leading citizens clubbed together to buy it and make it their meeting place. To be away from their wives, you know."

Hoare laughed. The breathy little noise, according to the

waspish wife of a fellow officer, sounded for all the world like an angry butterfly.

The pale, leathery steward of the Town's Club must have seen Mrs. Graves coming, for he opened the massive door himself.

"Why, Mrs. Graves!" he cried. "You must have gone wading in the sea—and in this wet weather, too! Come in to the fire in the Strangers' Room, and make yourself comfortable while I call Dr. Graves!" He bustled ahead of the brown woman and Hoare, stirred up the sea-coal fire in the grate, and was about to leave them to toast in front of it when Mrs. Graves called after him to ask if Sir Thomas was in the house. He was.

"Ask him, Smith, if he would be so kind . . . And perhaps, too, you would send a man to Dr. Graves' home for my maid. He should tell her to bring my olive twill gown and a cape to me here at the Club."

The fire's growing warmth was welcome.

Mrs. Graves looked up at Hoare. "If you were not present, sir, I would be hoisting these poor skirts to warm my person directly."

"If you wish, ma'am, I shall be happy to withdraw and leave you to your privacy."

"I wish no such thing," she said. "That would be poor return indeed for your services."

"What, ma'am, may I ask, took you to the beach under Portland Bill?" Hoare whispered.

"Stones, Mr. Hoare."

"Stones, ma'am? For use as missiles?"

"Only incidentally, as needed. Ever since I was a child, I have had a fondness for the remarkable shapes and colors of sea-washed stones. They dwell in flat pans filled with water, to keep their colors bright.

"I patrol Portland Bill quite regularly, for the local urchins who collect stones elsewhere—sometimes from under my very nose—remember the old Saxon belief that the Bill was once the druids' Isle of the Dead and shun it.

"Dr. Graves has sometimes chided me for taking up a whole room of our house for my collection. But 'tis a small room in a large house, I remind him, and he need not begrudge me the space.

"After all," she added musingly, "we have no children of our own, and my stepchildren are long since wed and fled . . . or dead. In any case, the weather has been foul for a week, and I was feeling housebound. So I went for a walk. That is all there is to it."

"You are Dr. Graves' second wife, then?"

"His third, sir. His first gave him two sons before dying of a consumption, and his second gave birth to stillborn twins before dying from loss of blood. Then he lived alone for over twenty years before we were joined together. Sir Thomas, by the by, claims to stand in lieu of uncle to me, having given me away to my husband two years ago."

Mrs. Graves's speech was interrupted by the entry of a personage who could only be Sir Thomas Frobisher himself. Squat, bandy-legged, and puffy, Sir Thomas had a wide mouth and goggling tawny eyes. He peered suspiciously at Hoare, then turned to Mrs. Graves.

"Eleanor, my dear! What have you done to yourself now?" he cried. "And what have you brought us this time?" he went on, returning his critical glance to Bartholomew Hoare as he stood, plain in his wrinkled Navy coat, wide, loose seaman's trousers, and wet, coarse buckled shoes.

"Permit me, Sir Thomas, to introduce Lieutenant Bartholomew Hoare of the Navy, who has just rescued me from an unknown fate," Mrs. Graves said.

" 'Hoare,' eh?" Sir Thomas said. "Well, sir, I'll have you know I am a baronet—*and* a knight. Which of us takes precedence, eh? The . . . er . . . lady of the night or the hereditary knight? Eh?"

Hoare knew from old this reaction to his name. It was predictable from old, and he had learned how to avert most of the hostilities that could otherwise follow. "You, of course, sir. Myself, I am merely Bartholomew Hoare—at your service, now, or anytime." He accompanied his whisper with a cold, gray stare. He also made his leg to the man of superior station.

"Frobisher is a famous name in history, Sir Thomas," Hoare continued. "Have I the honor of addressing a descendant of Sir Martin Frobisher, discoverer of the famous bay of that name?"

Sir Thomas's equivocal look showed he was now of two minds about Bartholomew Hoare. On the one hand, Sir Thomas was pleased at the implied compliment to his ancestry; on the other hand, irritated at being addressed in such a strangely confidential whisper and suspicious that *someone*— surely not Mrs. Graves—was making game of him. Was he, head of the Frobishers, risking a challenge to his standing by being asked to meet a whispering man with an obscene name? Even when, in a few words, Mrs. Graves explained Hoare's disability, the baronet's air tilted only slightly toward the affable.

"Yes, Mr. . . . er . . . *Hoare,*" he said. "While the name Frobisher goes back as far as the Conqueror and even beyond, my ancestor Sir Martin Frobisher was the first to bring it into prominence. A century later, of course, Charles II granted the baronetcy to the first Sir Charles, who was my fourth or fifth great-grandfather.

"Since then, the family which I have the honor to head has been prominent in Dorset society. Indeed, the Frobishers are received at court as a matter of course, and each of the eldest Frobisher sons is knighted upon reaching his majority, also as a matter of course. So, you see, we are twice-a-knight men."

Hoare was about to burst into one of his silent laughs when he realized Sir Thomas was in deadly earnest, so he turned his laugh into a breath that he hoped indicated proper admiration.

11

"As a matter of fact," the knight-baronet went on in a nasal, patronizing voice, "I expect to attend the investiture of my only son—young Martin, you know—the next time he accompanies His Majesty to our little city. He is a captain in the Foot Guards, of course."

Guardee the young Frobisher might be, Hoare told himself, but he would remain undubbed for some time if his knighting must await the King's return to Weymouth. These days the poor monarch, self-isolated in Kew for months at a time, seldom even came to London; he would hardly make his way back soon to his former favorite watering place.

"Tell me . . . er . . . *Hoare*," Sir Thomas said. "From whence does *your* family derive?"

"They were Orkneymen originally, sir, and we still consider ourselves such, even though my father has bought a small property near Melton Mowbray."

"What say? Speak up, man."

"The Orkneys, sir." To continue at top whisper Hoare had to strain his maimed throat. He felt himself being brought by the lee. The man must know that an attack on his handicap, unlike an attack on his name, was hard to deal with. Sir Thomas was being gratuitously offensive.

"D'ye hunt, then, . . . er . . . *Hoare?*"

"Not as a regular thing, Sir Thomas."

"Hmph." Sir Thomas began to look about him for something more worth his attention than a disheveled junior naval officer with an obscene name who could not speak and who did not hunt.

It was then that Hoare succumbed to temptation and reacted with a sally that was to cause him considerable subsequent grief.

"Of course, sir, my father is MB of our neighborhood's battery."

"Battery, sir? Battery? 'MB'? What's an MB, pray? And what has a battery to do with huntin'?"

"You know about falconry, surely, Sir Thomas?"

"Of course. Obsolete now, but a perfectly acceptable avocation for the nobility and gentry."

"Well, sir, we Hoares and our like-minded neighbors in the Northern Islands have trained bats to hunt game and retrieve it."

He paused, gasped, and continued.

"We find that bats, being creatures that nurse their young, are far more intelligent, and more easily trained, than falcons of any species. (Gasp.) They are, in fact, as clever and responsive as the Skye terriers our fellow islanders to the south have taken up so avidly, or the herds of Shetland ponies our neighbors to the north employ to keep down the auk population."

Pause; gasp.

"We fly our nimble little fellows in the dusk, of course. It makes for very good sport. My father, having made himself a skilled flederman, was appointed Master of Battery for our little neighborhood hunt. Hence the 'MB.'

"Should you find yourself in Leicestershire, sir, I believe he could promise you an excellent evening in the field."

Hoare heard a smothered sound from Mrs. Graves. He also saw that, while he might not have gained the knight-baronet's respect, he had at least captured his interest.

"What d'ye hunt with 'em, then?" Sir Thomas asked in a reluctant croaking voice.

"Flies, sir. We feed them to our frogs."

By good fortune, Sir Thomas's reaction was cut short; Dr. Simon Graves wheeled himself into the Strangers' Room.

Dr. Graves looked to be in his late sixties; later, Hoare was to learn he was seventy-four. At one time, he would have matched Hoare's height and build, but now he was confined to a peculiar light chair of wicker, bamboo, and ash. The toroidal supplementary wheel outboard of each primary wheel made a continuous handle by which the doctor could roll himself about with his still-powerful arms. Hoare had seen crude, heavy versions of similar invalid's chairs, but this one, light yet obviously strong, was a work of art.

The doctor's wife introduced the two and went on to describe to her husband and the knight her afternoon's affray on the beach. She belittled her own role and exaggerated Hoare's—but not too effusively—and concluded, "So that is how Lieutenant Hoare and I became acquainted and why he is here. I am most grateful to him, my dear."

"As am I," the doctor said in a surprisingly powerful baritone. Hoare thought he could remember what his own voice had sounded like before the Glorious First of June; he thought it had been much the same.

Sir Thomas would allow Dr. Graves to say no more. "But you mean to say there are two rascals tied up aboard your yacht . . . er . . . *Hoare?*

"Why," he added, "I must have 'em taken in charge immediately. I'll have her boarded and relieve you of 'em. Where does she lie?"

Hoare told him and granted permission for Sir Thomas's men to board *Inconceivable* and remove her cocooned cargo.

"And what's her name, sir?"

"*Inconceivable,* sir."

"*What?* Are you attempting to gammon me, sir?" Sir Thomas's eyes opened wide.

Hoare shook his head emphatically. He had been here before and knew his lines.

"No, indeed, Sir Thomas. I also call her *Insupportable,* or *Molly J,* or *Dryad,* or *Serene,* or *Unspeakable.* I change her name according to my mood of the moment. I keep several trail boards below and face the spares into the bilges for a cabin sole."

He paused to breathe.

"It makes no difference to *her;* she answers to none of them. She just answers her helm, and very well, too, at that."

Sir Thomas decided not to take umbrage after all, but his

laugh—unlike those of Dr. and Mrs. Graves—sounded more than a trifle forced. "Very good, sir, very good! That way, you can bemuse Boney. But what brings you down-Channel in these difficult times?" Those goggling eyes suddenly turned shrewd.

Speaking slowly to conserve his whisper, Hoare explained no more than his need to consult old Dee.

"Of course; the psammeophile," Dr. Graves said. "We know him well."

" 'Psammeophile,' sir?" Sir Thomas asked.

"A Greek neologism of my own, Sir Thomas," the doctor said. "A lover of sand."

Sir Thomas returned his attention to Hoare. "May I inquire the nature of your present duties . . . er . . . Hoare?"

"They are miscellaneous, sir. I am at the beck and call of Sir George Hardcastle, Port Admiral at Portsmouth; my visit to Lyme was in connection with one of them." Without saying so, Hoare did his best to indicate that this was as much as he wanted to say about his mission. He must have succeeded, for Sir Thomas turned to Mrs. Graves.

"But, Eleanor, what could have persuaded you outdoors in such weather, and what could have brought your attackers out on your trail?"

Mrs. Graves disregarded the first part of Sir Thomas's question and suggested that the second part would best be answered by the culprits themselves. Then Smith, the steward, appeared at the door to announce that her Agnes had arrived in the chaise and was waiting for her in the kitchen with a valise of dry clothing, so she excused herself and withdrew.

Sir Thomas, in his turn, made his apologies to Dr. Graves, but not to Hoare, and departed to send a file of capable men to unload *Inconceivable's* passengers, leaving the other two gentlemen to entertain each other at the fireside.

"I observe you have suffered an injury to your larynx, Mr.

Hoare," the doctor said. "There must be a story attached to that. Would you enlighten me?"

As briefly and modestly as he could without seeming secretive, Hoare described how a spent musket ball had crushed his larynx, leaving him unable to speak above the hoarse whisper he was using.

Hoare went on at Dr. Graves's request to show the aids he had developed for communicating when his whisper could not be heard. His Roman tablet went unremarked, but then he withdrew from his pocket a silver boatswain's pipe hanging from a black silk ribbon like a quizzing glass and began to play for the doctor a few of the shrill calls he used when making his wishes known to those persons—servants and other subordinates—whom he had trained. He went on to a seductive whistled rendition of "Come into the Garden, Maud," which was self-explanatory. He concluded with the earsplitting whistle through his fingers that he had developed as an emergency cry. When this brought Mr. Smith to the door in alarm, the doctor shook his head and laughed softly.

"Ingenious," he said. "Dr. Franklin would have admired your solutions."

"You knew Dr. Franklin, sir?"

"Yes, indeed. In fact, we corresponded from time to time. His loss to our kingdom when the Americans won their independence was not the least we have suffered through His Majesty's mulishness. I often wonder if the King's madness was not already at work in '76."

Hoare could only agree. "I met many rebels during that sad, fratricidal war," he said, "and came to respect not a few on both sides."

He did not add that his sweet French-Canadian bride from Montreal had died in childbirth while he was at sea in '82, over twenty years ago, leaving an infant daughter in Halifax whom he had never seen. Antoinette's family, ever resentful of their daughter's marriage to an *anglais,* had snatched the babe back up the Saint Lawrence, out of her father's reach.

"If you would care to meet another American, sir," the doctor said, "Mrs. Graves and I have engaged Mr. Edward Morrow to dine this evening. If you do not plan to attempt a return to Portsmouth tonight, we would welcome your presence, too, at our board."

Hoare had begun to protest that he was not clothed for dining in company when Sir Thomas returned to the Strangers' Room, frowning. His men had stuffed one of Mrs. Graves's assailants into the lockup in the cellars of the town hall, with two drunks and a poacher. The other—apparently the leader—was still senseless. Sir Thomas's men had untied him and locked him into a separate cell until he awoke or died.

Sir Thomas refused Dr. Graves's offer to attend the man. "You would find it difficult to negotiate the narrow stairs down to the lockup," he said. "Besides, Mr. Olney, the surgeon, is medical examiner for the town, as you know. He would take it quite amiss if he were to feel himself overlooked. I know you will understand, sir."

Accepting this small rebuff, the doctor returned to the matter of Hoare's evening dress. "You and I are much of a size," he observed. "Mrs. Graves, I am certain," he said, "would not object to your appearing at her table in a pair of my breeches. I shall send a pair to you at the Dish of Sprats immediately upon my return home."

On Dr. Graves's suggestion, Hoare then instructed one of the Club's servants to take a room there on his behalf.

By now Mrs. Graves had changed into dry clothing and rejoined the others. On her husband's behalf, she refused Hoare's offer to lift the doctor into the waiting chaise. It was clearly a matter of family pride: a Graves needed no stranger's help. So Hoare watched as she and the maid Agnes formed a seat with their crossed hands, slipped them under the doctor, and flung him into the air. He gripped two handles on the chaise with his powerful old arms and swung himself into its seat. He reached down and drew his wife up beside him.

The maid Agnes attached the wheeled chair behind the chaise by an ingenious metal latch and reached up to her master. The doctor drew her, too, into the chaise and clucked to the cob between its shafts; the chaise and the chair trundled off in the light rain. Hoare was oddly sorry to see it go, glad to know he would be seeing the Graves couple again.

Chapter II

WHEN A watchful manservant ushered him into the Graves drawing room that evening after a long walk up the cobbled High Street, Hoare saw two other guests had preceded him. Mrs. Graves introduced him to the lady, naming her as a Miss Austen, a friend visiting from Bath. Like every properly schooled gentlewoman, Miss Austen sat her chair as if it were an instrument of torture, her long back well away from the support it offered the slovenly. Save for a pair of piercing, inquisitive dark eyes, her appearance was even less remarkable than Mrs. Graves's. Hoare made his leg and forgot her.

The gentleman was another matter. He was of his height, and heavier. He might be a seasoned thirty or a well-preserved fifty; Hoare could make no closer guess. His figure was foursquare. Above his ruddy lipless face and low forehead sprang long, coarse black hair, which he wore clubbed in the old style. The skin was drawn as tight over his broad cheekbones as it would have been over the knuckles of a clenched fist. But for the eyes, as gray as his own, Hoare could have mistaken him for one of the Red Indians he had seen in the streets of Halifax.

"Lieutenant Bartholomew Hoare . . . Mr. Edward Morrow," Dr. Graves said, nodding to each in turn. "I hardly know which of you takes precedence over the other, so I hope the affronted party will bear with the insult."

"Our host tells me you have visited the New World, sir," Morrow said.

"I have, indeed, sir," Hoare replied, "and I regret the parting of our two countries more than I can say."

"Why, our two countries are still one, Mr. Hoare; at least they were when I last heard from Montreal." He pronounced the town's name in the English manner.

"I beg pardon, sir; I had understood you to be American," Hoare said.

"And have the king's loyal subjects north of the Saint Lawrence no right, sir, to call themselves American? After all, some of us came to America before the Yankees did, while my mother's ancestors were already standing on their native shores to welcome the first European invaders. A welcome which, by the by, many of both peoples lived to regret."

Hoare felt his ears burn. He had meant no offense. Was this formidable-looking man intent upon a quarrel?

"Peace, Mr. Morrow, peace," Mrs. Graves said. Her putty-colored silken gown flattered neither her coloring nor her figure. Perched erect as she was, on a round, squat, cushiony hassock, she looked even more like a partridge than she had that afternoon. A partridge at home at the foot of her pear tree, Hoare thought, keeping her eggs warm.

"You are certainly the person present who is most entitled to the honor of being an American," she told Mr. Morrow, rising from her nest. She left no eggs behind her.

"Mr. Hoare," Dr. Graves said, "I have a request to make of you. Would you permit me to auscult your throat?"

"Aus . . . ?" Hoare had never heard the word before.

"I beg pardon, sir. I detest the parading of professional arcana, as I fear so many of my calling are wont to do. Simply put, as I should have put it in the first place, I would like to listen to the noises your throat might produce when you try to speak. May I do so?"

Hoare could not endure the prurient prying with which some people approached his handicap, but Dr. Graves was his host and obviously a man of talent as well as years, and he felt obliged to agree. He said so.

"Good," Graves replied. He wheeled himself nimbly over to a mahogany stand at the far end of the room, selected two devices, and wheeled back.

"Now, sir. Perhaps you would be so kind as to loosen your kerchief and bend down? Or, on second thought, since Mrs. Graves has conveniently vacated her tuffet, you could take her place on it."

Hoare obediently cast off his neck cloth and sat on Mrs. Graves's tuffet. It was still warm from her posterior.

"Very good," Dr. Graves said. One of his two devices was an eighteen-inch tapered cylinder of polished leather with a flare at the smaller end. Mildly flexible, like a tanned bull's pizzle, it might almost have been one of the speaking trumpets used by serving officers of better voice than his own.

While his wife and Mr. Morrow watched, the doctor applied one end of the cylinder to the scarred spot over Hoare's distorted voice box and said, "Breathe, please."

Hoare breathed.

"Say, 'God save the King.' "

"God save the King," Hoare whispered.

"Now, sing it."

"But I can't sing," Hoare protested.

"Pretend that you can, sir."

Hoare tried. He produced a squawking sound that resembled the call of a corncrake, blushed, and shook his head.

"Very good," Dr. Graves said. He sat back in his wheeled

chair. "Now I would like to presume on your kindness for another experiment," he added. He set the tube down and fitted the other device onto his own forehead by a soft leather strap, which Mrs. Graves tightened around his head. This object was a mirror. To Hoare, it resembled the mirrored inner surface of a slice from a hollow sphere, a concave mirror with a round hole in its center.

"Open your mouth, if you please, and lean forward. Very good."

Dr. Graves drew the device down over his head further, adjusting it so that Hoare could see an eye peering at him through the hole.

"Now sing. Do not trouble yourself with the words; just attempt to sing, 'Aaaah,' with your mouth open."

Hoare uttered another macabre squawk, and the doctor sat back in his chair.

"So . . . so. Very good," he said as Hoare coughed and coughed. "Or rather, *not* very good, I fear. You may replace your cravat, sir."

"Would you now tell me, sir, what this is all about?" asked Hoare as he complied.

"Well, sir, it was partly an inexcusable curiosity on my part and partly a hope that I might be able to help you recover at least part of your speaking voice. Enough, perhaps, for you to shout commands at sea. You see, I have a special interest in abnormalities of the singing and speaking voices."

Hoare drew a hopeful breath. It was the loss of his voice that had put him on the beach in the first place, for no deck officer can issue audible commands in a whisper. Its recovery could mean his return to sea, perhaps even to the post rank his affliction denied him. It was his dearest wish.

"Well, sir? Your verdict?"

"The vocal cords are, I fear, displaced in your case, in a manner that none of today's surgeons have the skill to repair. I had thought perhaps Monsieur Dupuytren . . . but no, probably not even he. Besides, Dupuytren is French and would hardly wish to offend his Emperor by releasing a talented officer to battle against his own Navy. Moreover, the cords are badly atrophied. I am surprised that you do not have difficulty in swallowing. I am sorry."

"Thank you just the same, sir," Hoare whispered.

"It would have been a small return for your having saved Mrs. Graves' life today," the doctor said. He looked up at his wife and put his hand over hers, where it rested on his shoulder. He handed her the mirror and the tube.

"I am most interested in that tube, sir," Mr. Morrow said. "You have not shown it to me before. Will you demonstrate its use to me now?"

"Certainly. Its most common application is in listening to the beating of the heart. Monsieur Laënnec—an old friend but another Frenchman, I fear—invented the thing so he could diagnose diseases of the heart and lungs more precisely. Being an *amateur* of instrument making, as you know already, I have made some small improvements upon his invention. Let you try it, first upon me, and then upon Mr. Hoare, if we can oppress him once more. Then you in turn shall submit to the ordeal, if Mr. Hoare, too, is minded to try the tube."

"I should like it above all things," Hoare said.

"I shall be satisfied to watch," Mrs. Graves commented. Miss Austen concurred with a nod.

"But first," said Mrs. Graves, "I see Agnes hovering in the doorway. I believe she wants to tell me Mrs. Betts says the soles will be getting cold. We must not upset Mrs. Betts, so let us defer the demonstration until after our dinner. Will you, Mr. Hoare, be so kind as to escort me into the dining room while the doctor follows us and accompanies Miss Austen with Mr. Morrow?"

As his host rolled his chair into the adjoining dining room, Hoare overheard him murmur, " 'Jack Sprat could eat no fat, his wife could eat no lean . . .' "

Miss Austen spluttered and Hoare suppressed a grin, but he heard no reaction from Mr. Morrow.

"I was noting the appearance of Mr. Hoare and Mrs. Graves as they preceded us," explained Dr. Graves in a normal voice. "Does not the contrast between their two figures remind you of the old nursery rhyme?"

"Of course. Ha ha," Mr. Morrow said dutifully. There was something puzzling here, Hoare thought.

As they discussed the soles, Mrs. Graves, with occasional interjections by the subject, explained to Hoare that Mr. Morrow was the son of an English fur merchant who had settled in Montreal after the cession of Quebec by the French in '63, and thrived. Morrow senior had taken to wife the daughter of a Cree chief, which explained why the son looked as if he would be more at home beside a campfire in the North American wilderness than at the Graveses' board.

But Edward Morrow, the son, had preferred civilized over savage life and, upon inheriting his father's small fortune, had returned to the homeland of his forefathers. He now owned one of the lesser marble quarries on the Purbeck Downs behind Weymouth, had become a justice of the peace, and was hob-and-nob with Sir Thomas Frobisher.

Hoare heard this with polite attention, but he was far more interested in something else. He turned to his hostess.

"How, Mrs. Graves," he asked once her husband had carved the roast, "did you learn to sling and to throw a stone with so deadly an aim?"

"Brothers, sir, brothers—and no mother," she answered. "Three brothers: one big and wise beyond his years, one a bully, one a weakling. Gerald was an everlasting torment to little Jude and to me, until Jack taught me, at least, how to defend myself and poor Jude against him. Fortunately, my two hands are equally skilled; I can write well enough with both—simultaneously, as I will show you after dinner if you wish—as well as I can sling stones or throw them. Jack drilled me and drilled me until, one bad winter when Father was away and times were hard, I fed the family almost entirely with the game I brought home."

Hoare saw that Mr. Morrow was at least as interested in Mrs. Graves's tale as he himself was but puzzled. Evidently Morrow had not heard the details of her exploit that afternoon. Hoare disclosed them.

"It was truly astonishing, sir," he concluded. "I would not care to have our hostess as an enemy—not, at least, if she had a stone or two to hand."

"Your tale would have impressed my mother's tribe," Mr. Morrow told Mrs. Graves. "Any brave would have given much in trade for a wife who could defend herself the way you did. I am surprised, in fact, that you did not faint."

"I am sure you flatter me, sir," she replied in a voice that told Hoare, at least, that she was no such thing. "And, as to fainting, what earthly good would that have done? Except for Mr. Hoare's opportune arrival, it would have left me completely at the mercy of the two thieves, or ravishers, or whatever they were.

"You know me better, Mr. Morrow," she concluded, and changed the subject to the safe, popular issue of Lord Nelson. Everyone knew the hero had left England's shores to comb the Atlantic in search of Villeneuve. Did Hoare believe the Admiral would succeed in catching his Frogs at last?

In reply, Hoare could only offer the usual banality—that once Nelson found his quarry, he would sink his teeth into him like a proper British bulldog and never let him go.

True enough, Hoare told himself, but the hero was wont to hare off after his enemy in the wrong direction, which often made his fleet slow to find his Frenchman. Once found, of course, the foe was doomed.

While carrying on this conversation with his hostess, Hoare could not help hearing snatches of an interchange between the other gentlemen. It had an odd, probing quality, one

25

more suited in Hoare's opinion to political (or even personal) opponents.

"I have told you before, Morrow," Dr. Graves concluded rather testily, "that I am a physician and a natural scientist, not a manufacturer. You must seek elsewhere—Mr. Hunter's establishment, perhaps, in Pall Mall. Under the circumstances, of course, I cannot recommend any of the Continental makers."

As he had been taught to do, and to avoid the appearance of eavesdropping, Hoare now transferred his attention to his right-hand companion. "Have you and Mrs. Graves been acquainted for long?" he asked.

"We were dowds together, in Bath," Miss Austen said dismissively, "but she came off to Weymouth and left me in Bath, to dowd it in solitude."

"In solitude, Jane? Nonsense," Mrs. Graves interjected. "A solitude interrupted by—let me see—your mother, father, sister, and heaven knows how many nephews and nieces? Let us have no more appeals for sympathy."

Miss Austen laughed a bit ruefully. For the balance of dinner she had nothing to say. The occasion being informal, the ladies did not leave the gentlemen but joined them over the Stilton and the nuts. When these had been defeated—"destroyed in detail, like so many Frenchmen and Spaniards," Dr. Graves said—Mrs. Graves led Miss Austen and the gentlemen back into the drawing room, where Agnes had set out the tea tray. Dr. Graves delayed in the doorway a moment and drew Hoare aside, apparently to address him privately.

"My earlier levity about my own wife and her figure took you aback, I believe, Mr. Hoare. Let me reassure you. I recited that snatch of nursery rhyme on purpose. I must come to know Mr. Morrow's heart better, in the philosophical sense rather than the medical. My little test showed he lacks at least that sense of the ridiculous, the willingness to be amused at even his own follies, that Mrs. Graves and I—and you as well, I saw—share.

"As to Mrs. Graves, she is not only a formidable person. That you have already learned for yourself. She is a truly kind, loving, and tender soul, though she would heatedly deny she has a soul at all. She is truly my better half, and we love each other dearly."

With that, Dr. Graves signed to Hoare to wheel him into the drawing room. When Mrs. Graves had served up the first dishes of tea from her tuffet, her husband doffed his own coat, the better to demonstrate Monsieur Laënnec's device, and invited his guests to follow suit.

Hoare noted a distinct difference in the sounds he heard in the other men's chests. The Canadian's heartbeat sounded like the man himself—sturdy, brisk, strong, deep. While the old doctor's heart was also steady and strong, he could hear in the background a soft, rustling, almost musical sound. Hoare said as much to Dr. Graves.

"Yes, Mr. Hoare," the doctor said. "That is one of the few benefits of advancing age. One commences to make a soft music within one's self. It is generally a very private music, of course, so only a few besides the musician are privileged to eavesdrop upon it."

"That is why I chose to stand aloof from this particular parlor game," Mrs. Graves said. "I permit no one but Dr. Graves to listen to the sound of *my* heart. It belongs to him."

"Mr. Hoare appears to have an excellent watch," Mr. Morrow remarked after his turn with Dr. Graves's listener. "It ticks four times for every one of its owner's heartbeats."

"From my experience, that would be about correct for a timepiece of high quality," the doctor said.

When the Canadian went on to pose Dr. Graves several questions about how his instrument operated in circumstances that did not involve the human body, the doctor could not enlighten him. So he took out his own watch, set the device against it, and listened with a delighted smile.

"Thank you, sir," he finally said as he handed the tube back to its owner. "Very enlightening. Very interesting. You never showed this to me before." Mr. Morrow was so interested, in fact, Hoare thought, that he was repeating—all but word for word—a remark he had made before dinner.

"I never had occasion to show it you before, Mr. Morrow," his host said gently.

Hoare reminded his hostess that she had offered to demonstrate her ability to write with either hand. She dimpled—the first time Hoare had seen her dimples (there was one at each corner of her mouth, like a parenthesis)—and had him replace the tea tray with a writing desk. From this she drew paper, ink, sand, and two pens—one from each wing of the bird. She began with her right hand.

"Begin your dictation, sir," she ordered.

" 'When, in the course of human events . . .' " Hoare began, and continued reciting.

"Treason, sir, treason!" exclaimed Mr. Morrow as Mrs. Graves began to write down Mr. Jefferson's defiant message to His Majesty's government. She paid no attention to Mr. Morrow but changed hands almost without stopping and continued to write Hoare's words, cack-handed. Looking over her shoulder, Hoare could detect only the slightest difference in her tidy script. He did not complete his recitation but stopped at the point where the recital of wrongs began.

"Now observe, gentlemen," her husband said.

Mrs. Graves took out a second sheet of paper, positioned it beside the other, and continued to write. Both hands moved as one across the paper, somewhat more slowly, but still producing the same uniform strokes.

Finally, Mrs. Graves set her right hand at the left margin of its page and her left at its page's right margin and dashed off the following: " 'I could not love thee, dear, so much, lov'd I not honor more.' "

The lines under her left hand were a mirror image of those under her right.

"Useless, but amusing," Dr. Graves said with quiet pride, sitting back in his wheeled chair. "And a commendable sentiment."

Evidently Miss Austen had been using her long silence to compose a Remark. Now she cleared her throat for attention and began.

"This is a most interesting form of conversation," she said in a high, strained voice. "As with any meeting among relative strangers—I except yourself and me, my dear Eleanor—our talk has consisted mostly of casting agreeable literary flies at one another. If the prey responds with a reference to the same literary source, or with an otherwise appropriate trope, so much the better; the two are now happy to know that they are two members of the same social tribe. If the response is inappropriate, the caster of the fly must release his victim, not only unharmed but even appeased—by compliments, perhaps, which are as unpatronizing as possible.

"A comfortable game, is it not?"

"Yes," said Mr. Morrow flatly.

Hoare found himself hard put to it to relate the evening's conversation to Miss Austen's description of it. A dreadful silence descended on the group. The lady essayed a plaintive smile; she blushed in unattractive patches. Tears appeared at the corners of each eye, crept down each cheek, and dropped simultaneously into her lap.

The silence was blessedly broken by the appearance of the maid Agnes with a message for Mrs. Graves.

"From Sir Thomas, mum," Agnes said.

Breaking the seal, Mrs. Graves read, and the color, already scant, left her face.

"Sir Thomas informs me that one of my assailants has died without regaining consciousness," she said. She dropped the note on the floor before her. "So I have a man's death on these hands."

"In self-defense, ma'am," Hoare said.

Her husband nodded agreement; Mr. Morrow simply raised his eyebrows as if in surprise at her evident dismay.

"Oh, my dear!" Miss Austen cried, forgetting her disastrous disquisition and going to her hostess with arms outstretched.

"Do not pity me, Jane," Mrs. Graves commanded, sitting erect on her tuffet. "I will not be pitied."

Hoare saw it was time to take his leave, and Mr. Morrow offered to join him. Because of the lateness of the hour, the Canadian said, he, too, would be putting up at the Dish of Sprats instead of making his way home, four miles in the dark, up the steep declivity behind the town. They could share a borrowed lantern to light their way.

Once down the ramp leading from Dr. Graves's front door, Hoare turned once again to whisper another word of thanks to the couple silhouetted in the lamp-lit doorway.

"A remarkable couple, are they not?" Morrow said as they walked down the cobbled slope through a light mist.

"There must be more to their story than we heard tonight," Hoare agreed. "For instance, how does one account for the difference in their ages? What of the bullying brother? And what of the twin stepsons she mentioned to me this afternoon?

"Mind the gutter!" he added as loudly as he could, catching Morrow by the arm.

"Thank you, sir; I nearly misstepped," Morrow said. "As it happens, I can enlighten you, for I have known the Graveses since I settled nearby. Dr. Graves has been kind enough to lend me his gifts as the inventor of novel instruments from time to time.

"As to the difference in their ages, I gather you already knew the present Mrs. Graves is the good doctor's third wife. The two stepsons are not twins but both grown and gone, the one a captain on Sir Arthur Wellesley's staff, presently at Aldershot Barracks, the other at Bethlehem Hospital—an aspiring mad-doctor, mind you, not a patient. The twins to which you referred were born of Dr. Graves' second wife; they were still-born, and their mother followed them into the grave within hours, I am told."

By now, the pair had arrived at the Dish of Sprats.

"Pray continue, Mr. Morrow," Hoare whispered, "while we share a nightcap at my expense."

"As to the difference in the ages of the two," Morrow said across a decanter of the inn's muddy port, "after burying his second wife, Dr. Graves apparently expected to die a bachelor. By the time I arrived in the neighborhood, he had become quite prosperous and was well-known in his profession. In fact, it was rumored a knighthood was in the offing, in recognition of his having cured one of the King's horrible sons of a severe stammer.

"Well, sir, only a month or two after we had met, as he was returning from the bedside of a patient on a night much like this, his chaise overturned and pinned him under it. By morning, he was paralyzed below the waist.

"As his recovery was prolonged as well as incomplete, several ladies of the neighborhood took it upon themselves to nurse him in turn. Miss Eleanor Swan, as she was then, was one of them. Her all-round competence evidently attracted the old gentleman sufficiently for him to ask her for her hand. They were married from St. Ninian's two years ago August.

"And that, sir, is the 'happy issue out of all their afflictions' for which we should all pray of a Sunday," he concluded.

"Can you conceive what Mrs. Graves' attackers might have been about?" Hoare asked.

Mr. Morrow shrugged elaborately, almost like a French-man. "I should suppose it was a chance encounter, sir," he said, "and the two saw what they conceived to be an opportunity to rob a woman alone, and perhaps to ravish her. What else?

"Mrs. Graves is a woman of talent, as you saw this evening, but inclined, perhaps, to an unwomanly rashness of behavior.

31

Dr. Graves should have forbidden her to go onto the beach without so much as a manservant to protect her."

Privately, Hoare doubted Mrs. Graves would have been so pliant as to obey any strictures by another—even her husband—on her freedom of movement. But he did not express his doubts to Mr. Morrow.

"You journeyed to Weymouth in your own vessel," Morrow said. "You are a yachtsman as well as a sailor, then?"

"Hardly a 'yachtsman,' Mr. Morrow. And my 'yacht' is a mere made-over pinnace with no pretensions except whatever name I choose for her from time to time."

Morrow laughed. "Yes. I hear that in that respect she is as much of a chameleon as she is a pinnace. *Inevitable,* is she not?"

"Not today, sir. Today she is *Inconceivable.*"

Morrow laughed again. "Did you know I happen to be something of a yachtsman myself?" he said.

Hoare expressed silent surprise.

"Yes. I took it up back in the land of my birth, when I found it convenient to have my own transportation ready to hand for travel between Montreal and Quebec, and up and down the tributaries of the Saint Lawrence, in my fur trading. Now I keep a handy schooner, *Marie Claire,* here in Weymouth and take her out from time to time when so moved. Her crew are all Jerseymen, and exempt from the press, thanks to the protections Sir Thomas has procured for them.

"Perhaps we should match our craft one day soon. A few guineas on the race?"

"One day, with pleasure, sir," Hoare said.

Upon this, the two parted for the night.

LEAVING DR. GRAVES'S borrowed breeches in the care of the landlord at the Dish of Sprats, Hoare set forth down the High Street in the dawn mist to embark for Portsmouth. The town was in great disarray, with heaps of neglected bricks,

Portland stone, and lumber scattered throughout its narrow streets. The King's unheralded decision several years before to make Weymouth his preferred watering place may have thrown the townspeople into confusion but, determined to make the most of it, they had begun a frenzy of speculative building. But His Majesty had apparently dropped Weymouth from his increasingly confused mind, and much of the promising civic beautification had stopped in midproject.

An addicted snoop, Hoare wondered about Mrs. Graves's victim. It was a curious chance, he thought, that the dead man should have been the leader of the two. And who had known this to be the case? He could not remember.

He stopped, turned in his tracks, and climbed up the town hall steps. Common sense told him the town lockup would be in the hall's cellars; that would be the proper location for a dungeon, be it real or fictional. He found it there, guarded by a whiskery turnkey who was sleepily closing a barred door behind him.

"I'm a friend of Mrs. Graves," Hoare told him. "I want to see the man who died attacking her."

"Ye needn't whisper, sir," the guard said, pointing over his shoulder. "Dead as King Charles, 'e be. 'E be right in there, layin' quiet as can be."

Hoare pushed open the door. Below the rough, bloodstained bandage around its head, the face of the corpse was an ashen blue. No one had closed its staring eyes. There were traces of blood around its nostrils and a crust of dried foam around its lips.

Hoare had seen enough men dead of enough causes to know this man had not been killed by the blow of Mrs. Graves's slung stone. He had been smothered.

Thoughtfully, Hoare left the morgue.

"Where is the man we captured with him?" he asked.

The turnkey shrugged. "Dunno, sir. Some men of the town watch took un off just a few minutes past."

Leaving the town hall, Hoare retraced his steps. He arrived at *Inconceivable,* shoved her off, set sail, and set course for Portsmouth. The wind had backed into the east, and once again he could progress only with tack upon tack. He enlivened the trip by selecting a new name for his vessel from among the inventory in her bilges; she had left Portsmouth as *Inconceivable* but would return as *Insupportable.*

It was then he discovered *Inconceivable* had been searched from stem to gudgeon. Hoare had installed a small armory in her forepeak. It included a one-pounder swivel or jingal, mountable into either of two sockets, one of which was set into her bows and the other dead aft; a Kentucky rifle; four pistols; a cavalry saber; a rapier; five grenades; several mantraps; a crossbow with twenty quarrels of various types; and powder and shot for the firearms. At considerable expense, Hoare had equipped the latter with the novel percussion caps.

And now his deadly Kentucky gun was gone.

Chapter III

ARTHOLOMEW HOARE'S father, Joel Hoare, was of Viking stock. Joel brought that good name of his with him when he came south from the Orkneys as an orphan boy, and he had defended it successfully throughout his rise from ship's boy and through the hawsehole to master's mate, thence to post captain.

Both Hoare sons had defended that good name with fists and feet again and again while still in their nonage. Bartholomew's elder brother, John, had been badly injured in such an affray and still limped about the family property in Shropshire, debarred forever from the sea.

Even before Captain Hoare had negotiated his younger son a post as midshipman in *Centurion*, 60, Bartholomew had run a jeering schoolmate through the thigh with a carving knife. Now, more than thirty years later, it was a foolhardy man who mocked that good name of Bartholomew Hoare's; though thus far he had avoided killing a single opponent, he wounded at will with pistol, épée, or saber.

As befitted the descendant of Vikings, Bartholomew was

not only a warrior but also a masterly seaman. While still a midshipman, he had been the sole deck officer in the brig *Beetle* to survive the great tempest of September '81, when a rogue sea swept her quarterdeck clean. That night he led her surviving crew in club-hauling the brig off the roaring rocks of the Isles of Shoals.

Not only that; as young Hoare was working *Beetle* to Halifax under jury rig he had taken a small Yankee privateer by a ruse—her master had drained her crew into his English prizes—and he brought her into Halifax in modest triumph. The privateer had carried specie from one of her captures. Moreover, the navy had bought her up, bringing Hoare the entire quarterdeck's eighth of the proceeds, plus the one-thirty-second share due him as a midshipman—one of the four surviving warrant officers.

Thus, even before being commissioned lieutenant in 1783, Hoare had gained a solid reputation for competence both in the field of honor and at sea. He had also gained what, for a mere midshipman at the bottom of the navy's ladder of success, was a sizable fortune. That amount, £6,127/5/8, paid him by the Halifax prize master, was such a shock to young Hoare that, running counter to the behavior of the typical mid, he invested the entire sum in the Funds and left it at Barclays Bank to accrue in industrious idleness as its owner worked his way up the tedious ladder of promotion.

But the spent musket ball fired from *Eole* on the first of June '94 had put paid to his career at sea. Since any deck officer must be able to hail the main masthead in a full gale, *Staghound*'s captain had regretfully put his first lieutenant ashore, silenced for life, with a letter of high commendation, endorsed by Lord Howe himself. Never since that black day had Bartholomew Hoare gone to sea in anyone's vessel but his own, unless as a silent, frustrated passenger.

By good fortune, Hoare also had influence among the

mighty. Captain Joel Hoare, of course, as a member of Parliament, still carried weight with Their Lordships of the Admiralty, and his Uncle Claudius, brother of Bartholomew's late mother, had married Lady Jessica, eldest daughter of Geoffrey, third Baron Wheatley. It had needed both these connections and Lord Howe's precious letter to find the beached, despairing Hoare a place on the permanent staff of the Port Admiral at Portsmouth.

"And what the hell do Their Lordships expect me to do with a lieutenant who cannot talk?" that officer had asked Hoare as he paced back and forth in front of the stricken lieutenant.

"Can ye speak French?"

"Yes, sir."

"Read books of accounts?"

"Yes, sir."

"Hand, reef, and steer?"

"Yes, sir."

"Hail the fore topgallant?"

"No, sir."

So the Admiral had gone on, firing a question like a broadside every time he passed athwart Hoare's hawse, until Hoare sweated where he stood.

He had evidently passed muster, for the Admiral had him assigned as a general dogsbody, trotting about at the command of either the Commissioner (who commanded the Portsmouth shipyards) or the Admiral himself, as Port Admiral in command of the Navy vessels at the Yard and at Spithead just outside the harbor's mouth. In practice, Hoare spent most of his time slaving for the port's regulating captain—master of the press—and the local masters of the Navy Board, Ordnance Board, Victualling Board, and Transport Board. He ran errands and took on any project that a voiceless officer could reasonably accept. The life kept him out of the countryside where the Hoare family remained; he had found the stink of bilges and the scurry of rats preferable to the stink of cow shit and the scurry of chickens.

As well as becoming intimately familiar from below with the bizarre, cobwebbed workings of the so-called Silent Service, he must have been found useful. For, even though Sir Percy soon hoisted his flag in *Agamemnon*—at sea again at last, leaving the forlorn Hoare behind him on the beach—succeeding Port Admirals had kept him in place, to roll about wherever ordered, aging but gathering little moss. By now, he was forty-three.

Unlike many beached officers—and all too many seagoing ones as well—Hoare kept himself fit. He frequented the *salle d'armes* of Marc-Antoine de Chatillon de Barsac, French émigré and master of *escrime*. Here he worked diligently at perfecting his skill with every weapon that might come to hand, including many that would never see the field of honor, being unsuited to the hand of a gentleman. He also developed a strongly accented fluency in French.

Whenever duty permitted, he wandered England's entire south coast in his odd little yacht. This not only kept his hands and muscles tough from fisting her canvas and heaving on her abrasive hemp but also kept his seamanly skills well honed.

A year or two ago, he had used the guineas won at a lucky run in the Long Rooms to buy the little sloop. As he had vowed upon his being beached, that prize money he had won in *Beetle* remained intact against his all-too-certain retirement as a half-pay lieutenant.

Insupportable had a cabin quite large enough to shelter him and his armory, an occasional guest, a week's supplies, a tiny galley stove, and certain equipment. For while she generally lay in the Inner Camber, just south of Portsmouth dockyard, or traveled about the coast on Hoare's whim, she occasionally carried her master on missions of significance. It was for this reason that Hoare had acquired his just-depleted armory.

Whatever *Insupportable*'s name might be at a given time, Hoare almost always sailed her alone. He had rigged her oddly, with a leg-o'-mutton mainsail, its foot lashed from tack to clew onto a boom and its head reaching the considerable height of her pole mast, and a clubbed forestaysail. She could outpoint any of the clumsy ship's boats and wherries that plied Portsmouth Harbor and give any craft her length half an hour in the Sunday races.

To cut her leeway when working to windward, while retaining her ability to take the ground without damage, Hoare had shipped one of the new, controversial lead-weighted sliding keels. It made no difference to him or to her that the long case in which it nested when raised divided his cabin awkwardly, for it formed the base of a table set fore-and-aft between her two cushioned lockers.

It was near enough four bells of the afternoon watch before Hoare brought his little vessel into the Inner Camber.

NOW, EASING HIS way into her home harbor, he luffed up to check *Insupportable*'s way, cleated a line, and tossed it ashore to a waiting docker. The man caught it with his one hand and dropped the bight in its end over a handy bollard. The two did the same with a stern line. After adding springs and trimming all dock lines to his own satisfaction, Hoare furled main- and forestaysail. He locked the hatch leading below and went ashore by the floating brow, leaving *Insupportable* to snooze lazily in the long shadows of the June evening.

She was as safe here as she would be anywhere in England. Guilford the docker-watchman was alert and sober, well paid by a group of amateur sailors to keep pilferers off their darling yachts. Among these gentlemen, Hoare himself was a mere hanger-on, tolerated for his competence and general courtesy rather than for the depth of his pockets or his obscure lineage.

Guilford knuckled his forehead. "There's a norficer been

askin' for ye, sir. 'E'll be waitin' for ye up to the Anchor," he said.

"The warning's welcome," Hoare whispered. "My little girl could use watering if you have the chance, eh?" He handed the man a shilling.

"Aye aye, sir," Guilford said.

Hoare let himself out of the dock enclave through the barred gate set in its wall and crossed the cobbled Shore Street, bearing to starboard a point or two to make the inn where he lodged. The sign over its open half-door displayed a huge ornate fishy creature with rolling eyes, about to engulf an anchor being cast into the sea by the panicked crew of a galleon tempest-toss'd. The sign's whole effect was quite well suited to the Swallowed Anchor Inn that it proclaimed.

If Hoare's visitor was an officer, he would be in the snug— the private bar to the right of the entrance. So there Hoare went, having adjusted his neckerchief. Upon seeing him, the room's sole occupant rose from his seat and advanced.

"Mr. Hoare?" A half-head shorter than Hoare, the speaker would outweigh him by a full stone. Life had painted him in primary colors. Beneath his carefully tousled corn-yellow hair were bright blue eyes and lobster-red cheeks. Before someone or something had broken his aquiline nose, his handsome face must have broken many hearts among the fair sex. A bit of a naval fop, perhaps, thought Hoare, but probably a man of his hands withal.

"Bartholomew Hoare, at your service, sir," Hoare whispered, taking the other's outstretched hand. "And whom do I have the honor . . . ?"

"Peter Gladden, sir, second in *Frolic*, 22."

"You have a fortunate berth, sir. I have heard good things about your brig."

"She is a fine vessel, to be sure," Mr. Gladden said. "But I am not calling on *Frolic*'s business.

"Will you take wine, sir?" he added.

Hoare smiled and folded his considerable length into the seat across the table as if he were one of those novel American jackknives.

"Happily, Mr. Gladden. But I insist on being host. I live here, after all." Hoare laughed. A young lady of his acquaintance had once described his breathy little laugh as sounding like a kitten trying to blow out a candle.

"The house offers a very nice Canary," he went on. "Can I entice you?"

"Very willingly, sir," Gladden said.

Hoare drew his boatswain's call and blew a soft trill.

"Coming, sir, coming!" came a cheerful soprano voice from the next room. "Just let me finish the sandwiches for you and your guest. You'll be having our Canary, sir?"

Tweet went the call.

"And coffee?"

Hoare looked inquiringly at his guest.

"Later, perhaps," Gladden said.

Tweetle. Hoare stowed the call. "You see, Mr. Gladden," he said, "I have the staff of the Swallowed Anchor well trained. I hope you will forgive me my unkempt appearance," he went on. "I just came across from Weymouth, you see. Aboard small craft I find seaman's trousers handier than breeches."

"I saw you bringing your yacht into the dock," Gladden said. "Odd rig, is it not?"

"Quite unusual," Hoare said. "I saw the Bermuda natives using it in their work boats when *Sybil* called there in ought-one. It struck me as easy for one man to handle, and efficient as well. So when I bought her last year, I copied the rig as best I could remember."

He stopped for breath and then continued, "I have been quite pleased with her behavior ever since. She points closer to windward than any other craft I know."

41

Hoare did not add that, since *Insupportable* had more than supported herself on her winnings last summer, he was now hard put to it to find a match except at impossible odds-on.

A sturdy, pink young woman in a bright blue gown that matched her eyes stepped into the parlor and set a tray on the table between the two officers. It bore sandwiches, glasses, and a decanter of Canary.

"There you are, gentlemen," she said briskly.

"Thank you, Susan." Hoare filled both glasses and raised his. "To *Frolic.*"

"To . . . ," Gladden began in reply, ". . . but how have you named your yacht?"

"Insupportable," whispered Hoare with a smile of anticipation. He had traveled this road before.

Gladden spluttered and nearly spilled his Canary onto his snowy waistcoat.

Hoare went on with the practiced recital he had given Dr. Graves, Sir Thomas, and so many others before them. He ended as usual by saying, "She just answers her helm, and very well, too, at that."

Gladden's peal of laughter was genuine. "So you are commodore of an entire magical squadron," he said. "Hope you have kept your secret from Boney."

"I think I have," Hoare said. "But one never can tell. 'The spies of France are rife among us,' as they say. But, Mr. Gladden, I am sure you have not called on me to investigate my ability to keep the secret of my 'squadron,' as you kindly call her." He paused, eyebrows raised in inquiry.

"No, sir, I am here to trouble you on a matter of justice."

"Of justice, sir?"

"Yes. Although you and I have never met, my surname may be familiar to you. My younger brother, Arthur, served with you at one time."

"Arthur Gladden?" Hoare said. "Why, yes. He was unlucky enough to be assigned me in Lymington for some weeks, to help in the horrid Impress Service . . . *ah.* Of course. Am I mistaken? Has an officer of that name not just been put ashore at the dockyard, under close arrest?"

"I fear so. He is third lieutenant of *Vantage.* You may not know of her; she is newly built and just commissioned."

"Oh, dear. Yes. He is accused of murdering her captain, I believe . . . Adam Hay."

"I fear so," Gladden said again. "And, since *Frolic* happened to be in port, he asked me to be his friend."

Hoare nodded. "His advocate and defender, yes. Naturally."

"But I know nothing about courts-martial, sir," said Gladden. "I'm a seaman, not a damned lawyer. I hardly know how to begin." Gladden's voice rose. "And he cannot have done such a thing, He is a gentle man as well as a gentleman. He hates killing. Father was never able even to get him to shoot. Frankly, he should have taken orders, but Father would not have it. No, he had to become a sailor, just like Father, and just like me.

"It is right enough for me. I like the life. Always have. But for him . . . for him, it has been slow death."

Hoare forbore to remark that, under the circumstances, death for Arthur Gladden might not be so slow after all. To be shot to death in action was a faster matter than dangling and strangling for minutes at some yardarm. The outcome, of course, was the same.

"And what is it you want of me? To undertake your brother's defense in lieu of yourself? As you know, of course, the service doesn't look kindly upon officers who cannot defend themselves before a court-martial. They feel it reflects upon the 'friend' as well as upon the defendant."

Hoare's whisper began to fade. He paused and took a sip of wine before continuing. Even so, the whisper was now a weary rasping noise, nasty to listen to and hard to make out.

"Besides, Mr. Gladden, I find it very tiring to speak at any length. You may have noticed that after a bit I must . . . er . . .

set storm canvas, so to speak, if I am to be understood even in a quiet spot like this. No. If that is what you are seeking of me, I fear I am not your man." Hoare sat back, unconsciously rubbing the scar just above his kerchief.

"But, sir, Admiral Hardcastle tells me you have an uncanny talent for 'untying knotty problems.' Forgive the flight of fancy, but that is precisely what he said."

"I know. The Admiral's secretaries have been known to refer to me as 'the Whispering Ferret.' Quite gothick, it seems to me, but why trouble myself about it? Those pompous, preening pen-pushing pimps would hardly say it to my face, and I need not worry about what they call me behind my back. I have been out too often." Hoare's whisper began to fade again.

Mr. Gladden would be neither diverted nor discouraged. "Admiral Hardcastle also said he would be greatly obliged if you would take poor Arthur's case in hand."

"Admiral Hardcastle said that, did Admiral Hardcastle?"

Admiral Sir George Hardcastle, KB, was currently Port Admiral at Portsmouth, one of the highest and most lucrative posts to which a naval officer could aspire. Bartholomew Hoare's current ultimate commander, he was known as a grim, merciless man.

"Well, sir, that puts a different face on things, does it not?" Hoare said. "Let me think a bit." He refilled both glasses. "Tell you what," he added. "Suppose you carry on officially for your brother. And I shall stand just behind your ear and . . . er . . . *whisper* instructions into it with my foul rum-laden breath as long as you can stand it."

"I should be overjoyed," Gladden said. "How are we to begin?"

"Begin at the beginning," Hoare replied. "Go on to the end, and then stop."

"Well," began Gladden, "on Tuesday last, as Arthur tells me, Captain Hay summoned him to his cabin 'to give an account of himself.' It seems the captain was displeased with the lack of discipline shown by the men in Arthur's division. All waisters, they are; of course, all the crew are new hands—new to *Vantage,* that is, and most of them new to the service. Lumpkins who have yet to see their first anchor weighed. Arthur had to get all of these.

"Even the standing officers are new to the ship and to one another. They have a long way to go before they shake down together.

"Do you—did you—know Captain Hay, Mr. Hoare?"

"Know *of* him, sir."

"Hot-tempered. Greedy. Bullying," Gladden suggested.

"Command sometimes changes a man in disappointing ways, don't you find?" Hoare replied, managing to make his whisper sound noncommittal. "I have also heard," he continued, "that he is—was—a believer in hard, continued practical training, at anchor as well as at sea. And I confess that I agree. After all, the crew of any vessel must be ready to work their ship and fight it, too, night or day, and in all weathers. Should they not have done so as a part of their training in harbor before they face reality at sea and in battle? But I interrupt you."

"In any case," Gladden went on, "Captain Hay made it clear to Arthur that he expected his division to show a marked improvement in discipline and in their performance in the drills to which he had set *Vantage*'s entire crew."

"Which were?"

"As you might expect, they included exercises on deck and aloft—setting up and housing topmasts, exercising the great guns, setting and furling sail, and the like. The men were expected to respond intelligently to emergencies. Arthur tells me the captain took special pleasure in 'killing off' key men—quartergunners and the like—and watching the confusion that resulted. The more confusion, the more wrathful was Captain Hay, and the happier.

"But it was apparently his captain's manner toward my brother that caused the explosion between the two. It seems

45

that Captain Hay was extremely partial to what he called 'drunken lobsters'—lobsters stewed in hock instead of seawater as is usual. I understand he claimed that because they died dead drunk and happy, the creatures ate more tender. His steward had made up a brace of them for his dinner.

"Arthur had reported aft the moment the order reached him. That would have been shortly after six bells of the second dogwatch. We know that, for unfortunately, his arrival in the cabin coincided with the lobsters'. Captain Hay insisted on having his dinner served at six bells precisely.

"As soon as Arthur reported, the captain began to recite a virtual litany of my poor brother's manifold sins and wickednesses. He had failed to report cases of insubordination in his division—answering back, for instance. His gunners were by far the slowest to run out their guns and complete dumb-show firing at anchor, his few topmen fumble-footed.

"The captain accused him of having interrupted his feast on purpose, out of perverse insolence. It was this accusation, I gather, that led poor Arthur to protest his captain's abuse . . . at length. It seems Captain Hay was so enraged at my brother's outburst that he roared with anger, sprang from behind his dining table, and actually grappled with him."

"Dear me," whispered Hoare.

"Here, sir, the stories diverge. Arthur swears to me he broke free by an extreme effort. My brother is not a very strong man. He fled the cabin at a panicked run, not stopping until he had gone the full length of the frigate and reached the heads. Here he was overcome by nausea and a looseness. I am ashamed to say he admits to having fouled his breeches before he could drop them—as indeed I could sense all too well when I visited him in his place of confinement ashore.

"Others of *Vantage*'s people tell a somewhat different story. A quartermaster, one Patrick Lynch, had the watch on the quarterdeck. Lynch says that he heard the altercation, even from two decks below, and that in his opinion it culminated with a shout of pain and not of rage. Yet John McHale, master, was within feet of Lynch and says he heard nothing."

" 'Altercation,' Mr. Gladden? 'Culminated'? The man Lynch sounds more like a schoolmaster than a quartermaster. Were those his very words?"

"Er . . . no, sir. I have not actually spoken with Lynch. That is what I am told he said."

"By whom, sir?" came Hoare's whisper.

Mr. Gladden explained that he had interviewed only his brother and Francis Bennett, Admiral Hardcastle's judge advocate.

"Bennett and I are old friends," Hoare said, "but friendship disappears in the arena of a court-martial."

"Now you see why I welcome your participation," Gladden replied. "I am no barrister."

"Nor am I," Hoare reminded him. "But we shall see. Go on with your story, if you please."

At seven bells, Gladden went on, Andrew Watt, captain's clerk, had entered the cabin with some correspondence that he had been preparing. He found his captain bleeding and breathing his last on his cabin floor. Finding the Marine guard unaccountably missing, Watt had shouted, "Help! Murder!" with all the strength of his little lungs and pelted up the companionway to the quarterdeck to report his news to the officer of the watch. Only then had he fainted.

In his turn, that officer, John McHale, had sent Lynch, the quartermaster, to summon David Courtney, first lieutenant, and left the quarterdeck himself to view the scene of the crime. Here Mr. Courtney had joined him and summoned all the ship's other officers.

Peter Gladden could not tell Hoare exactly how, but word of the altercation between the captain and his third lieutenant came out in no time. Half *Vantage*'s company, it seemed, had been on deck to witness the latter's frenzied flight along her gun deck.

47

"So they took Arthur's sword," said his brother. "Then they sent a signal ashore and, when the admiral ordered him brought ashore, made it so—fouled breeches and all, poor wight. That is really all I know," Gladden concluded.

"Well, we must jump about cheerly, sir," Hoare said. "We have I cannot guess how many of *Vantage*'s people to question, and—" He interrupted himself, "Has a date been set for the court-martial?"

"Thursday, Mr. Bennett told me."

"*Thursday?* Here it is Monday already. We must really stir our stumps, then. I must see if I can persuade the Admiral to postpone—" He interrupted himself again, "My God. I must beg you to excuse me, for I am commanded to the reception this evening at the Admiral's and Lady Hardcastle's residence. I must improve on my appearance as best I may. Let us plan to go aboard *Vantage* tomorrow. Shall we share a wherry out to her, at eight bells of the morning watch?"

"A pleasure, sir. But we shall certainly encounter each other again at the reception, and Mr. Bennett as well."

"Excellent, sir. Let us take him aside, tell him our plans, and enlist his assistance—insofar as his duty permits him to provide it."

Upon this, Hoare saw his guest to the Swallowed Anchor's door. He piped for a bath to be brought to his rooms—using the "Sweepers, man your brooms" call—and withdrew to titivate for the ordeal that gatherings of this kind always inflicted upon his voice and his equanimity.

Chapter IV

———◆———

IN HIS lawyerly black, Mr. Bennett was unmistakable. He stood out, a neat sable blob, among the naval officers' blue and gold and the occasional scarlet brilliance of a Marine. Though no longer a serving officer, he still combined the alertness of a successful deck officer with the stately demeanor of a successful barrister. He looked spruce yet dusty. Peter Gladden was already with him. Both greeted Hoare cordially and joined him in making his duty to his host and hostess.

"So you have got your heads together already, gentlemen," said Admiral Sir George Hardcastle from under huge tufted black eyebrows. His wig might be out-of-date, but on him it looked appropriate. "Good enough, but do not expect good fortune in your endeavors, Mr. Hoare. Afraid your client will . . ." He grunted and went dumb. Lady Hardcastle removed her sharp elbow from her spouse's ribs and smiled sweetly at the accused man's brother.

"So nice to see you here, Mr. Gladden. And how are your dear mother and Sir Ralph?"

So, thought Hoare. That was how Gladden had got the Admiral to lend him out. Gladden, too, had interest among the mighty. "Sir, could I persuade you—," he began.

Sir George forestalled him. "No, Mr. Hoare. Thursday. Half the captains on the court are under orders to Nelson's fleet—that is no secret—and they are itching to get under way. No."

Gladden excused himself to the other two officers and went in anxious search of Miss Felicia Hardcastle, his Admiral's dumpy, spotty, popular daughter. Hoare and Bennett helped themselves to glasses of the punch being handed by an awkward liveried man with the stamp of "bosun's mate" clear on his red, sweating face, and began to circulate.

Hoare listened. It would have been impossible to make his whisper heard over the din of conversation, and he would have had to resort to his Roman tablets, with all the explanations that would have entailed. The most common gossip he heard concerned the rumor that a privateer had sighted a huge French fleet heading *easterly,* less than a day after dipping her ensign to Nelson, who was heading *westerly.*

"He has got himself at cross-purposes again, just as he did before the Nile," said a pale-faced officer. "If only he had as fine a nose for a chase as he does for a battle. A bulldog, not a greyhound, I always say."

"Needs your good nose to show him the way, I suppose," commented a burly bystander, looking pointedly at the pale officer's leading feature. The speaker's own purple face clashing with his scarlet Marine coat, he swayed from side to side as he spoke as if he either were on a Channel crossing or had overindulged in the Admiral's port at table.

"Oh, His Lordship has no need for *my* help," admitted the pale man. "Besides, the Victualling Board tells me I am essential."

"Ah," the bystander sneered as he turned to seek a more

challenging quarry on which to wreak his suppressed rage with the world.

As they wandered the brightly lit, stifling room, Hoare and Bennett could tell where talk had turned to the unhappy event in *Vantage*. There all eyes became fixed on them.

Bennett was intrigued at Hoare's proposed role in the forthcoming court-martial and assured him that before the end of the evening he would prepare a document authorizing Hoare to question any *Vantage* man he might require. They were parting for the moment when a heavy hand fell on Bennett's narrow shoulder. It was the burly Marine, still rocking.

"Here, here!" he cried in a voice filled with truculent, intoxicated good-fellowship. "We can't have secrets being whispered about—not here and now! Make me known to your whisperin' friend, Bennett, eh?"

"Ah, Wallace," said Bennett. "Lieutenant George Wallace of *Vantage* . . . Bartholomew Hoare of the Port Admiral's staff." He made to turn away.

"Whore, eh?" The rocking Marine had found his prey at last. "How much for one time, and how much for all night?" He burst into laughter, only to receive Hoare's standard response to remarks of this kind. The wine tossed into the Marine's face must have stung, for he gasped and spluttered as Hoare whispered, "You may have a free dose, you silly man, tomorrow morning at sunrise."

"You will stand friend for me, Francis?" Hoare asked Bennett as the Marine mopped his face and decided what to do next.

"Of course, Bartholomew," the sea lawyer replied. To Wallace he said in an impatient voice, "Go find a friend, man, if you have one—which I beg leave to doubt—and send him to me here. I want to get this thing over with. We've a busy day tomorrow."

"We'll see how busy you and your Mr. *Whore* are after our

little meetin'," Wallace said over his shoulder as he began to press through the gathering crowd to find a friend to act for him. He looked a bit steadier but still filled with wrath.

"It's very odd," Hoare said sadly, "but I find nothing attracts attention like a whisper."

"Paradoxical," Bennett replied.

"Until tomorrow, then," Hoare said. "I must be off. I have preparations to make."

"I shall be at the Swallowed Anchor a half hour before dawn," Bennett said. He turned to acknowledge the other, younger Marine who bustled up to him, bright-eyed and officious, ready to serve as his fellow Johnnie's second.

HAVING TOLD HIMSELF to wake at four bells in the morning watch, Hoare slept peacefully until then. He donned clean black clothing before leaving the inn in the growing dawn.

At the usual place, a narrow field overlooking the town, the party had to wait while two trembling striplings and their entourage conducted their own meeting.

"I had a few words with your adversary's second," Bennett confided as they stood. "He was unaware of your interesting record until I told him of it. He intended to mention it to his principal."

As Hoare nodded, both boys' pistols went off with faint pops. Evidently, their referee had used his common sense and put half-loads into them. One duelist dropped his weapon and grasped his grazed hand with a yelp of pain; the other puked messily onto himself. Then the embattled youths and their entourage left the field arm in arm, leaving behind an inspiriting scent of burnt powder and a depressing scent of vomit.

The party of Hoare's own adversary arrived in a light carriage as the boy duelists departed. They brought with them a case of matched pistols and *Vantage*'s sleepy surgeon. Mr. Bennett agreeing, the surgeon, a Mr. Hopkin, had also agreed to umpire the affair. The Marines' coats were still a mere gray in the faint light. Mr. Wallace's face was equally gray.

Wallace's second approached the two naval officers, hat in hand. A bit of a coxcomb, Hoare thought.

"Gentlemen," the second said stiffly, "my principal wishes me to say he wishes he had never uttered his words of yesterday evening."

"Does he apologize for them?" Bennett inquired sharply.

"Well, er . . ."

Bennett conferred briefly with his principal, who shook his head and doffed his coat.

"A wish of that kind does not constitute an apology, sir," Hoare said. "With no apology, the encounter must take place."

With no more ado, Mr. Hopkin chose a spot well to windward of the puddle of puke. He opened the case of pistols, loaded both while the seconds watched, and offered the pair to Hoare for his selection. Hoare had been the insulted party, yet the thrown wine had been the direct cause of the challenge, so the choice of weapons was his.

"I see you have both been out before," said Hopkin. Indeed, Hoare and Wallace had already taken position back to back without his instructions. "The parties have agreed to exchange one shot each; the exchange of shots will suffice to satisfy honor.

"I shall count ten paces, after which you gentlemen may turn and fire at will. One . . . two . . ."

At Hopkin's "ten," Hoare turned and took aim in a single move, to see his white-shirted opponent just raising his pistol. He held fire for a heartbeat, and the two shots sounded as one. Hoare felt the faint breath of Wallace's ball pass his head. The Marine grunted, dropped his weapon, and grasped his arse, across which his precious blood was already spreading. Hopkin rushed forward to examine the wound, then rose to confront Hoare and Bennett.

"A clean shot through the right *gluteus maximus*," Hopkin reported. "I declare honor satisfied." He bundled his patient ahead of him into the waiting chaise and departed at a brisk trot.

"Thank heaven. I certainly did not wish to shoot the poor Lobster dead," said Hoare as he and Bennett strolled down the slope to the Swallowed Anchor so he could change his clothes. When he boarded his recent opponent's vessel he wanted to be impeccably uniformed.

"At least he angled himself so I missed one cheek," he went on. "He should be able to shit without too much pain."

"It never occurred to you that *you* might be the one that was shot, then?"

Hoare shrugged.

"I never have been," he said. "I hardly know why."

AFTER A COMFORTABLE breakfast, Hoare and Gladden went out to *Vantage* from the pair-oared wherry they had engaged at the Portsmouth Hard. Had Hoare been the frigate's first himself, he would have had no complaint about her state. Lines were properly flemished down, the guns bowsed up to their ports, topsails given a snug harbor furl.

As *Vantage*'s first, David Courtney commanded her until the Admiralty replaced the late Captain Hay. Mr. Courtney received Bennett's letter and welcomed them cordially enough. Mr. Wallace of the Marines was not about *Vantage*'s deck. He was abed in his tiny cabin, face down, under the surgeon's care.

Mr. Courtney was overburdened with the need to make decisions about stowage, absent boatswain's supplies gone adrift, the disciplining of a distracted new hand, fresh from the plow.

"The foolish lad struck a boatswain's mate," Mr. Courtney said. "Admitted it. 'Strook 'im back, zur,' he told me.

"As you know, gentlemen," Courtney continued, "this could mean death for him. That would not do at all at this early stage of our life together as shipmates—not at all. I must catch Gower, the petty officer in the case, and persuade him to put it about that the blow was accidental."

"Of course, sir," Hoare whispered.

Upon learning his visitors' mission Mr. Courtney, with a routine apology, handed his visitors on to Peregrine Kingsley, second in the frigate. He instructed that officer to escort them to the late captain's cabin and see that any members of the ship's company they wished to question were brought there.

The two stopped on the quarterdeck long enough to quiz Mr. Kingsley. He had nothing good to say about his late captain. Arthur Gladden had been by no means the only officer to suffer from Adam Hay's intemperate tongue. A few days before, Kingsley himself had withstood a half-hour diatribe on his slipshod work aboard and his whoremasterly work ashore. But unlike Arthur Gladden, Kingsley had kept tongue and temper in hand and had escaped undamaged except in his pride.

"He could say what he pleased about me performance as one of his officers," said Kingsley, "but he had no business criticizin' me as a man of parts. Me parts are me own business, damn him," he said. He sounded, Hoare thought, a trifle smug.

Hoare already knew this swarthy, saturnine officer by reputation. He had hired a little sailing shallop that he kept in the same slip where Hoare kept *Insupportable*. Kingsley was known to be a "man of parts" indeed, a ready and randy man with busy privates. He apparently cared nothing for a female's age or her looks as long as she was usable. Many hearts would weep for Peregrine Kingsley when *Vantage* sailed. There was a rumor that one heart in particular, one that should have been devoted to its owner's husband, was heavily smitten. However, the woman's name had not reached Hoare.

Mr. Kingsley had witnessed Arthur Gladden's flight from the cabin and had been one of the fascinated crowd that invaded it when word of the murder spread. That was all he knew, he said. Now, would the gentlemen mind if he deputized an intelligent midshipman to act as messenger for them? Things were a trifle busy aboard *Vantage,* as they may have noticed, and he had ten green gun crews to whip into shape.

The cabin reeked of stale shellfish and old tobacco smoke. Andrew Watt, captain's clerk, was already there, leafing anxiously through the papers littering his late master's table.

"A file is missing," he said accusingly as the visitors entered.

"What sort of file?" Hoare asked.

"The file of Captain Hay's personal correspondence. There were several letters in it: one from Mrs. Hay ashore, several from tradesmen, and one which I could place in no category. The writing appeared to be that of a woman—self-taught, perhaps."

"You are a student of handwriting, Mr. Watt?" Hoare whispered.

"Any man of my trade must attune himself to various scripts, sir," the clerk said. "But I confess I have made a somewhat deeper study of the writing art than most of my associates."

"Interesting," murmured Hoare soundlessly.

Mr. Watt's eyes dropped to his hands.

"Yes?" Hoare whispered.

"I did not read them, of course, except that . . . The one from Captain Hay's wife. I assure you that under ordinary circumstances I would not have dreamed of reading it. I may not be a gentleman, but I try to behave as if I were. It was the enclosure with her letter which caused me to depart from propriety. Frankly, gentlemen, I am no longer ashamed that I did so."

"Why?"

"In my service to Captain Hay, Mr. Hoare, I have occasionally dealt with highly confidential matters—matters so confidential, in fact, that they were recorded in ciphers. Captain Hay entrusted their decipherment to me. The enclosure with Mrs. Hay's letter to her husband was such a ciphered message. I could tell at a glance that it was not enciphered in any way familiar to me. Its presence, and that alone, led me to read Mrs. Hay's letter.

"It was no more than a note. As far as I recall, it read in part as follows:

" 'I found this in his uniform pocket last night. I know the sort of thing it is, and I do not believe he should be in possession of such a thing. But perhaps you gave it to him in connection with *Vantage*.'

"There was more, but nothing of a nature that would bear on this unhappy affair."

"What do you make of that letter?" Hoare asked.

Obviously distressed, Mr. Watt shrugged. "I really do not know what to make of it, sir," he said. "If we knew who '*he*' was . . . but the letter gives us no clue."

As a matter of fact, Hoare said to himself, the letter from wife to husband seemed to imply that "he"—whoever he was—was Mrs. Hay's lover, and known by the captain to be such. Here was an unwanted complication, and a doubly cryptic one at that.

"And the letter from the 'uneducated woman,' Mr. Watt?"

"It appeared to be a threatening letter, sir. She appeared to want money for revealing something to the captain, or perhaps for not revealing it to someone else. I do not know which was the case, if either."

"Well, then, Mr. Watt . . ." Hoare sighed. "Tell Mr. Gladden and me, in your own words, about the events of Friday night."

"I came aft at seven bells, gentlemen, to deliver some dispatches which I had decoded for the captain. There was no guard at the cabin door, so I knocked twice and entered."

"No guard, Mr. Watt? Was it not Captain Hay's standing order to have guards at his door and the spirits locker?"

"Yes, sir. But the Marine contingent was new-joined and may have been a bit confused, I think."

"Unheard of," Gladden said. "Never, never does one leave those posts unmanned."

"Very good, Mr. Watt," Hoare whispered. "Carry on with your story, if you please."

"I stepped directly into a sticky, slippery mess." Mr. Watt's voice trembled. "I found Captain Hay just outside the quarter-gallery. He was lying on his face in a trail of blood, as though he had been struck down near his cabin door. The blood flowed from a wound under his right shoulder blade.

"I knelt down beside him, sir, to see if there was anything I could do. I heard him say something about 'the lobsters,' and then he choked. And . . ."

The clerk gulped but recovered himself.

"He coughed up his life's blood, sir, right across my knees, and . . . gave up the ghost then and there."

" 'The lobsters'?" Hoare whispered. "Are you sure that's what you heard Captain Hay say?"

"That is what I understood him to say, sir. Of course, he was not speaking clearly, and I . . . I was a bit upset. I ran out the cabin door, shouting for help, and reported to Mr. McHale on the quarterdeck.

"Then, sir, I am ashamed to say I swooned and knew no more until I came to my senses as a result of being trampled by members of the crew. I am a peaceful man, sir, and the sight of blood disturbs me greatly. And it has ruined my second-best pair of breeches, which I can ill afford."

"All things considered, Mr. Watt," said Hoare, "you acquitted yourself creditably. You did your duty when it had to be done, and no captain could ask for more."

He dismissed Mr. Watt now, with a request to find the midshipman who was supposed to be serving as messenger boy. Watt had no trouble finding him, for he opened the cabin door into the ear of a towheaded imp in a round jacket. Taking the child by the injured ear, Watt hauled him into the cabin, stood him up, and introduced him to the two officers as Mr. Prickett.

"You are to follow these gentlemen's orders, you young monster, and on the run. D'ye understand, then?" He shook the ear as if shaking his words into it to make sure they were absorbed.

"Yes, Mr. Watt, yes! Don't whang me so!" Mr. Prickett bleated, and began to snivel. He could not have been in uniform long, for when he wiped his nose on his sleeve it caught on the row of buttons placed there precisely to prevent his doing so. He began to weep in very earnest. He looked to be about eight.

"Be kind to him, sirs," said Mr. Watt fondly. "He is very new, and very small."

Wondering about the relationship between Mr. Watt and Mr. Prickett, Hoare again dismissed the clerk. Hoare was sensitive to anything smelling of sodomy.

"Do you know Mr. Watt well, then?" he asked the child.

Mr. Prickett cheered up immediately. "Oh, yes, sir! He was Papa's clerk before he decided to go to sea, and he prayed the captain to take me into *Vantage*! He has six daughters! Papa's a solicitor! *Vantage* is my first ship, sir, you know! I was first aboard, sir! After Mr. Courtney and the captain, that is! I came aboard with Mr. Watt! Isn't she a smacker?"

Hoare assumed the "smacker" the child was referring to was *Vantage*. He wondered if the six daughters were the reason why a "peaceful man," as the clerk had described himself, had decided to join the Navy.

"Indeed. Now, Mr. Prickett," Hoare said, "have you been aboard long enough to know Mr. Hopkin, the surgeon? If so, is he aboard?"

"Yes, sir! He was just telling us men of the gun-room mess about Mr. Wallace's Awful Wound and how it bled!"

"Well, please be so good as to find him, present my compliments, and ask him to favor us with his company in the cabin."

Hoare had Mr. Prickett repeat his orders and found that, while he was apparently unable to speak without exclaiming, he had a good memory, so he sent the lad on his errand.

"WELL MET AGAIN, gentlemen," said Mr. Hopkin upon entering. Like the other officers, he had to stoop to clear *Vantage's* five-foot overhead, so all three seated themselves. "I wish I could say this occasion is a more pleasant one."

"I am of a similar mind, sir," replied Gladden for them both. "But so it is in war."

"I hope your patient is none the worse for his misadventure of this morning?" Hoare asked. "With your permission, I would like to interview him."

"I would not mind, sir, not in the least, provided he is sober enough to talk. I find that the drunker a man is, the faster the work proceeds. The ball passed through only one of Mr. Wallace's buttocks, missing the anus entirely. It cut no important vessels on its way and carried into the wound only a few fragments of his breeches. I probed them out easily, he having had the sense to wear buckskins for the encounter. Leather extracts much easier than fabric, you know.

"To tell the truth, the man's probably better for a bit of bloodletting—a plethoric nature, you understand. And, of course, he now has not one arsehole but two, in case he should mislay the one he was born with."

Mr. Hopkin had no apparent interest in ending his case

history. Hoare ended it for him with a terse request that the surgeon address himself to the matter of his late captain's death.

"It was a simple wound, sir. Triangular in cross section, from a blade thrust into the victim's back on the right side. It slipped between the ribs and slanted to the left and forward as it entered. It nicked the aorta and pierced the left lung. The damaged aorta burst, perhaps as the victim collapsed on the deck, and he exsanguinated through the wound and from his mouth."

"Was Captain Hay's death immediate, or could he have spoken before he died?"

Hopkin looked at Hoare pityingly. "Since he crawled nearly twenty feet, sir, I would expect him to be able to speak a few words. It takes a pig a minute or more to bleed to death, and I'm sure you've heard *their* dying prayers."

Gladden paled.

"Now as to the wound," Hoare whispered. "You say it was triangular in cross section?"

"Yes," the doctor replied. "Or *V*-shaped. Narrow at the base, long on the edges. It was obviously inflicted by the Marine bayonet that lay on the deck halfway between the captain's table and the door. There it is, on the table, under those papers, where I put it.

"The man using the weapon worked it about in the wound before withdrawing it, as though he wanted to be sure to accomplish his fell purpose."

"Not my poor faint-hearted brother," said Peter Gladden. He rose and begged leave to excuse himself and go ashore. "I want to take Arthur a clean pair of his breeches, at least," he added.

"Of course," said Hoare. "Perhaps you would undertake a task for me when you get to shore?"

"Anything."

"Have the watch and the Portsmouth beachcombers keep

their eyes peeled for a discarded Marine uniform coat. It might have come ashore on any of the last few tides, since we are coming up on the spring tides. Either on the Portsmouth or the Gosport side of the harbor mouth."

"A Marine uniform?"

After a pause, Hoare went on. "Lobsters. Captain Hay was dining on lobsters Friday evening, was he not?"

"That's what we are told."

"And the clerk said he overheard the captain say something about 'lobsters' as he died. But no one has even suggested the man was poisoned by tainted lobsters, have they?"

"Not that I know of," said Bennett.

"Then he would have been referring to the other kind of lobster."

"Eh?"

"The other kind of Lobster. Marines," Hoare whispered. "Yes. Find Jom York. He will dig the uniform out if it is there to be dug."

"A Marine uniform. Jom York," Gladden repeated in a bemused voice, rising to leave. "Aye aye, sir. Perhaps you will tell me about Jom York sometime?" he asked.

"Let us meet at the Anchor," Hoare said, "and I shall do so then. We must also question your brother, for there is not a minute to be lost. Thursday is almost upon us."

Upon Gladden's departure but before dismissing Mr. Hopkin, Hoare asked him if he had any notion of why Captain Hay would keep a Marine bayonet in his cabin.

"It's common knowledge, sir," Mr. Hopkin said. "He was in hopes of introducing into the Marine service a hilted sword bayonet of his own design, similar to the 'swords' carried by Riflemen. He kept two bayonets here: a regulation socketed one and one with a grip of his own design. Here."

Without asking Hoare's leave, Hopkin ruffled through the papers on the captain's table and uncovered two bayonets.

They were as described, Hoare saw. Taking them from the surgeon, he inspected them closely.

"This one is clean, Mr. Hopkin, but the regulation one still has dried blood on it. Are you quite sure you did not wipe off the sword bayonet after removing it—as a matter of professional habit?"

Hopkin laughed with ill-concealed contempt. His breath was foul in Hoare's face. "Why should I do a thing like *that*, sir? Every properly apprenticed naval surgeon knows better than to clean off his instruments. Cleaning removes the protective film of blood. 'Wipe it off,' indeed!"

Chapter V

———⊳◆⊲———

$\mathcal{H}$OARE WONDERED what Dr. Simon Graves would make of Mr. Hopkin's views on the maintenance of surgical instruments. After dismissing him with genuine relief, Hoare made a list of the other men he must question aboard *Vantage* today. They included his recent adversary, Mr. Wallace of the Marines; John McHale, master; Patrick Lynch, quartermaster; and Michael Doyle, sergeant of the Marine detachment. He sent Mr. Prickett in search of the three latter; he would go to Mr. Wallace himself.

At the time of their captain's murder, Mr. McHale and the quartermaster had been standing within feet of each other, separated from the crime by a mere two thin decks and adjoining an open skylight into the wardroom just below. Yet the statements of the two flatly contradicted each other. Looking intently at Hoare, Mr. McHale stated that during the time when the murder might have been committed, between six and seven bells of the afternoon dogwatch, he had heard only the ordinary sounds of shipboard life.

On the other hand, Lynch described overhearing an encounter fraught with melodrama.

"The capting begins to roar at Mr. Gladden the very minute I 'ears the door close be'ind him. He calls him hinsolent for interruptin' his dinner, an' lazy an' all like that—I can't remember all the words. Some of 'em I 'eard before, but he used some what I never wants to 'ear used again. Orful, they was.

"He says Mr. Gladden 'ad lorst control of his division an' wasn't supportin' his petty orficers like he orta. He starts givin' Mr. Gladden orders to carry out more hexercises aloft, an' then he starts off with more bad words. Well, then Mr. Gladden pipes up, a-squealin'-like, an' starts a–tellin' off the capting. An' then I 'ears the capting give a roar, and there's a thumpin' and more roarin', an' then I 'ears a scream. It was the captain's death scream, I know for sure, sir. It was orful. It makes me 'air stand on end just to think of it."

"You're no Irishman, Lynch," said Hoare. "You were born to the sound of Bow bells, I think."

"Seven bells, sir. But me da was a Dubliner, me ma always said. Though I don't know 'ow she knew, I'm sure."

"Be that as it may," Hoare said. "You know Mr. McHale says he heard nothing of the altercation you just described."

" 'Alter-what,' sir?"

"Argument. Dispute. Fight, if you will."

Lynch stood on his pride. "I've told you wot I 'eard, sir, and I'll stand by it. About Mr. Mc'Ale's 'earin' I've nuffin' to say." He was as good as his word and would say no more.

Unlike Lynch, Sergeant Doyle was so clearly Irish-born that Hoare was hard put to understand him. He said yes, there was always a guard at the captain's cabin door as well as at the spirit locker. He had placed the man there himself at the change of the watch. Doyle begged pardon for being derelict, but the entire draft was new to the ship and strangers to one another as well as to him, so for the life of him he could not name the man on guard during the time in question. The man was taller than average for a Marine; Doyle did remember that. He was not looking forward to hearing Mr. Wallace on the subject.

But Doyle could also more or less confirm the clerk's statement that there had been no guard at the captain's door when seven bells had sounded. At least none had been visible when Mr. McHale had summoned him to the cabin. And again he was sorry, but in the confusion he had not conducted the muster that Mr. Wallace had ordered as well as he should have, for he had counted off his men to forty at one time and thirty-nine a moment later. He had reported forty to his officer but would not be prepared to swear to the count. He again reminded his listeners that the Marines, like the rest of *Vantage*'s crew, were a new draft and still largely strangers to one another.

"Has a uniform coat turned up missing?" asked Hoare.

Doyle looked at him as though he were a wizard. One of his privates had, indeed, complained about a missing uniform coat. Doyle had cursed the man, docked his pay for its replacement, and had the boatswain assign him to duty as captain of the heads until he could present himself in a new coat.

"Keep on searching for the coat," Hoare said. "Include the bilges and the wings. If you find it, have it brought to me at the Swallowed Anchor by a safe hand. Safe, d'ye hear?"

Hoare now had Mr. Prickett conduct him to the narrow cabin off *Vantage*'s wardroom where Mr. Wallace lay supine, snoring softly in a miasma of used rum.

"Sir! Sir!" cried Mr. Prickett. "Here's Mr. Hoare to talk with you about Captain Hay's murder!"

"Oh, my God," Wallace said. "Hasn't honor been satisfied *yet?*" He tried to sit up in his berth but fell back with a grunt of pain. "Talk away, then, Hoare. I'm at your mercy."

"Just tell me what happened the night of the murder, if you will."

Wallace had nothing to add to Sergeant Doyle's evidence. He had not even been aboard *Vantage* at the time of the murder, although he had returned aboard within the hour and had directed Doyle to muster the men. To Wallace's shame, he was even more ignorant than his sergeant of the men in his detachment. All were new.

As Hoare was about to leave, Wallace cleared his throat.

"I owe you an apology, sir." His whisper was little louder than Hoare's.

"No apology is necessary, Mr. Wallace," Hoare replied. "Honor has already been satisfied."

"I was drunk last night, I confess," Wallace went on. "I was doubly at fault, first for miscalling you and then for mocking your lack of a voice. I did not know, then, the circumstances under which you lost it. I shall not forget your lesson. Indeed, I'll remember it in my gettings up and my lyings down, or whatever the phrase is . . . *unh!*"

Hoare could not forbear his silent laugh, but Wallace was not finished.

"Will you shake hands, sir?"

"Of course."

AT LAST, HOARE could shove off in the late Captain Hay's borrowed gig, under sail. Mr. Prickett was bouncing like a ball in its bows despite the orders of the senior mid at the tiller to bloody keep still in the boat. He had successfully implored his acting captain to let him remain seconded to Mr. Hoare's inquiry.

Hoare directed the midshipman-coxwain at his side to land them, not at Portsmouth Hard, but at the Inner Camber, where he found Peter Gladden again awaiting him in the snug of the Swallowed Anchor. He dismissed Mr. Prickett to the inn's kitchen to be stuffed like a goose under the eye of the pink girl Susan.

Gladden had caught the first mudlark he had seen, gave him Hoare's message to deliver to Jom York, and then called upon his brother in his place of confinement. It was a dark little room in the cellars of Commissioner's House.

"This affair has been death on breeches as well as on post captains," he said to Hoare. "It has ruined the ones your target Wallace was wearing when you shot him, Mr. Watt's when Captain Hay bled all over them, my poor brother's . . . and for that matter," he added, "I hardly suppose Captain Hay's own unmentionables are any the better for their experience the other night.

"But you were going to tell me about Jom York."

"Jom York is the king of the beachcombers of Southampton Water," said Hoare. Hoare himself, he explained, spent his spare time, whether ashore or aboard *Insupportable,* in snooping. He had snooped into the Weymouth Town Hall, with those perplexing results. He snooped into coves, often when not wanted, as once when he had interrupted a clutch of petty smugglers unloading a cargo of casks. It was this that had earned him the trust of at least one gang and had resulted in his being given the interesting anker and then having it taken from him by person or persons unknown. It had been in another cove, of course, that he had encountered that singularly interesting, deadly partridge, Eleanor Graves.

He watched surgeons at their grisly work and listened to them. He interrogated butchers, masters-at-arms, tradesmen, cordwainers, mudlarks—anyone, in short, who had enlightenment to offer him.

Only country folk were immune to Hoare's curiosity. He had no use for farmers. He lumped all herders with beekeepers as men who had dangerous creatures in their power. But even in the countryside he made exceptions for poachers, tinkers, and gypsies.

During one of his snooping expeditions, he explained, he had encountered Jom York, king of the beachcombers, in a slimy little shebeen. Later, Hoare made a friend of the man when he slipped one of his royal henchmen out from the grip of the press. Jom York kept every longshoreman and mudlark, as well as his beachcombers, well under his eye and his large, horny thumb. He extracted his dues of information from all, and from their receivers and fences as well.

It was a long tale, made longer by Hoare's need to use his exhausting emergency whisper toward the end.

"He smells horrible, but he has his uses," Hoare concluded. By now, the two were dissecting a grilled turbot.

"But what about the Marine uniform?"

"As you observed this morning, it is unheard of for a captain to allow his cabin door to go unguarded. The captains right here at Spithead in '97 learned that to their cost, as did Bligh of the *Bounty.*"

"And *Hermione*'s beast of a captain, as well," added Gladden.

"Exactly. And from what we have learned of Captain Hay, he was no man to skimp on proper routine. So I believe that, as Sergeant Doyle avows, a Marine guard *was* posted and that the murderer either enticed him away from his post or did away with him in some way. Or—more likely—the murderer was the Lobster himself.

"And *Vantage*'s sergeant of Marines admits the head count he took that night may have been off by one or even two. And he reports a missing uniform."

Chapter VI

———◆———

WEDNESDAY AFTERNOON, a frightened, fetid wharf rat brought a soggy parcel to the Swallowed Anchor's snug. Susan the pink girl brought both rat and parcel to Hoare and Gladden. Mr. Prickett, who now would let no one detach him from his mute lieutenant, looked with wide, delighted eyes at the smelly things. Both objects, wrapped in oatmeal-colored shoddy, oozed and stank of harbor mud. As between the courier and the packet, only one was the object of Hoare's interest. He dismissed the other with a shilling, and the creature poured gratefully away, carrying its stench with it and singing Hoare's praises discordantly.

Hoare drew his sheath knife and cut the cord binding the parcel. A waterlogged red garment slipped to the floor. He smiled at it as if it were cloth of gold.

Hoare brought the coat's collar up to his nose and sniffed. Then he did the same, first with one of the folded-back cuffs, then with the other. He took a huge white kerchief out of his own coattails and wiped it across the inside of the coat collar where it would have rubbed against the wearer's neck, and then across the cuffs. He nodded to himself and handed the coat to the little mid.

"Take it away, Mr. Prickett," he whispered, "and label it 'Coat found in Portsmouth Harbor.' Put today's date on it. Oh, and take this, too, please."

He handed Mr. Prickett the kerchief. "Label it 'kerchief, with matter removed from Marine uniform found in Portsmouth Harbor, this date.' So, Gladden. We can be practically certain this coat was *not* last worn by one of *Vantage*'s Marines."

"How can you say that?" asked Gladden.

"Work it out, sir. Work it out."

THAT AFTERNOON MR. Gladden escorted Hoare to the place where his brother lay in durance.

Fortunately, the durance faced south, and the afternoon sun poured into it through a small barred window set high in the rough stone walls. There was no need to light the tallow candles flanking the pitcher and basin on the deal table.

In looks, the brothers shared only their wavy corn-yellow hair. Where Peter was shorter than Hoare, Arthur Gladden would have looked him in the eye when he rose to greet them, but for his stooped, scholarly posture. Instead of a bright cornflower blue, his eyes looked faded. Where his brother's face was robust and ruddy, Arthur was lantern-jawed and pallid. He wore clean breeches at last, but the odor of his lapse lingered faintly about him. It was reinforced by the reek of the untended chamber pot in one corner.

"What news do you bring, Brother?" Arthur Gladden asked anxiously in a tense tenor, before Peter could even introduce Hoare.

"None good yet, lad, none bad," Peter Gladden said. "But I have enlisted a wizard on your behalf. Let me make you known to Lieutenant Bartholomew Hoare of Admiral Hardcastle's staff, who has agreed to serve you as counsel on Thursday."

"But I thought *you* were going to stand for me!"

"I am, dear boy, but you know quite well how little I know about all the pettifogging details of court-martial proceedings. Mr. Hoare will back me up with all his experience."

"Hoare. Is that your real name?" asked Arthur Gladden with what sounded like genuine interest.

"Yes," whispered Hoare.

"Oh, you needn't whisper here," said Arthur. "Nobody bothers to listen. In fact, I believe I could walk right out of this place without anybody's stopping me." He paused, as if thinking the idea over, and brightened. "But then they'd catch me, and they'd be sure I was guilty." He sighed.

"*Are* you guilty?" asked Hoare. "And I do not whisper for secrecy's sake but because I cannot speak in any other way. It is a nuisance, I know, but one has to make the best of it."

"No, sir, I am *not* guilty. I admit Captain Hay's outburst made me tremble with anger, which is why I spoke up to him. I realize I never should have done that. But *he* was so angry that he turned purple and laid hands on me, forcibly. That is why I—"

"Fled," said Hoare. "Have you any way of proving what you say, that you grappled with the captain only in order to escape him?"

"No, but I would suppose the Marine guard would speak up for me," Arthur replied.

"Then there was a Marine guard at the cabin door?"

"Of course there was, Mr. Hoare." The prisoner's voice was stiff. "Have you ever known the captain's cabin in any of His Majesty's ships *not* to be guarded?"

For the first time, Hoare thought, the man sounds like a naval officer.

"Who was he, do you know?" he asked.

"A Marine, just a Marine," Arthur replied. "Truly, I don't

think anyone can tell one Lobster from another—except perhaps another Lobster. They're all statues in red coats and heavy boots. Don't you think so?"

Hoare looked at Peter Gladden as if to say, "I told you so."

"As I said," Arthur went on, "there was a Marine on guard when I reported to Captain Hay's cabin. In fact, he opened the door and announced me, just as they always do. Frankly, I did not notice him as I left, since I was pressed by an urgency."

THE MORNING DAWNED bright, clear, and busy on the day of Lt. Arthur Gladden's court-martial on charges of having murdered his captain, Adam Hay. Flotillas of watercraft made their way across the sparkling harbor to converge on *Defiant*, 74, the venue selected by Charles Wright, her captain and president of the court-martial.

Vantage's own vacant cabin would have been the proper place for the court-martial of one of her officers. But both the prominent and the curious were expected; rumor had reached Portsmouth that even royalty might appear. On these grounds and Mr. Bennett's advice, Captain Wright allowed his own life to be disrupted and his own cabin in *Defiant* to be taken over.

On the table behind which the members of the court were to sit, among the quills, inkwells, and sand, lay Arthur Gladden's sword. It was placed athwartships. If the court arrived at a "guilty" verdict, the blade of the sword would face him on his return to the cabin after the court's deliberations.

"Make way!" called a Marine. As the members filed into the cabin along the way cleared for them, the audience rose almost to a man. One guest, a massive figure in admiral's gold braid and the vivid blue Garter ribbon, remained seated in his comfortable chair squarely in front of the court.

"Does Your Royal Highness wish to be made part of this court?" Captain Wright asked.

73

Admiral of the White Prince William, Duke of Clarence, shook his head. The head, which bore a jovial expression, was shaped like a pineapple.

"Gad, no, old boy. Came down to get *away* from court, don't ye know?" The cabin filled with appreciative chuckles. Royal ribaldry, Hoare observed to himself, always amuses.

When the chuckles had died down, Captain Wright read out Admiral Hardcastle's order convening the court-martial, concluding with the words: " '. . . that, on the twenty-first day of June, eighteen-oh-five, in His Majesty's ship *Vantage,* Lieutenant Arthur Gladden did assail and murder his captain, Adam Hay.' "

Recognizing Hoare's lanky figure standing beside the prisoner's friend, Captain Wright raised his eyebrows and interrupted himself. "Does the accused really require *two* 'friends,' sir?" he asked.

"Actually, sir, he does not. The accused officer asked that, as his brother, I stand as friend for him. Both blood and certainty of his innocence required that I agree to do so. However, Mr. Hoare is a far more skilled investigator than I—"

"Mr. Hoare is well-known to me and to others on this court," Captain Wright said impatiently. "But which of you speaks for the accused officer? You or he?"

"I shall do so for the most part, sir, if only because of Mr. Hoare's impediment of speech. And Admiral Hardcastle suggested Mr. Hoare and I collaborate."

"Irregular, but I see nothing wrong with it, nor, of course, with the Admiral's point of view. Do any of you gentlemen?" Captain Wright looked left and right along the table, clearly expecting no contradiction. "Very good," he said. "Now, Mr. Bennett, will you give us your opening remarks? I know you, at least, have no difficulty in speaking up." A soft titter ran through *Defiant's* cabin.

Bennett now outlined the case against Arthur Gladden: how he had been overheard in disputation with his captain;

how Captain Hay had cried out; how Arthur had fled the full length of *Vantage;* how Mr. Watt had discovered his dying captain; and the last words the clerk had heard. That, except for Watt, who hardly had the strength to have stabbed his captain, Arthur was the last man known to have seen Captain Hay alive.

Mr. Hopkin, the surgeon, made the same statements under oath that he had made to Hoare and Peter Gladden. He was followed by the man Lynch. The quartermaster, too, had no more and no less to say than he had a day or two before.

John McHale sounded more evasive.

"And what did you hear through the skylight, Mr. McHale?" asked Mr. Bennett.

"I resent the implication, sir! I am no eavesdropper, especially not upon my captain!"

"Then you are prepared to state—under oath, remember, Mr. McHale—that, at anchor on a calm night, on deck, at your proper post within feet of the cabin skylight, you heard nothing through it? Not even any raised voices?"

"Under penalty of perjury, Mr. McHale?" interjected the junior member of the court, a commander, from his place at the left end of the table.

Vantage's master gulped.

"In the face of what Lynch said he heard, and he well forward of you, leaning against the quarterdeck rail?"

Mr. McHale paused for a thoughtful moment. "Gentlemen, I retract my earlier evidence. Mr. Gladden is a weak man, gentlemen, but an honest one."

From his seat behind the prisoner Hoare saw Arthur Gladden's ears redden.

McHale continued, "He wouldn't hurt a flea, let alone his captain. Why, he hasn't the gumption of a rabbit. His division of men was already well on the way to becoming a very mob because he couldn't bring himself to control them. I pity him. He doesn't belong in the Navy. I do not wish him to lose his life by my doing, on my evidence. But I have my own wife and children to consider."

"Confine yourself to the facts, Mr. McHale," warned Captain Wright. "What, then, *did* you overhear?"

"I heard Captain Hay order Mr. Gladden to put his division through an exercise on the morrow."

"What sort of exercise?"

"Fire drill, sir," said McHale, "followed by a simulated battle against a French frigate on either side. Then, if I knew the captain, he'd declare our mainmast shot away at the crosstrees or the like, kill off all the senior officers, and leave Mr. Gladden to get himself out of it. A hard trainer, sir, was Captain Hay, but a good one.

"I then heard Mr. Gladden cry out at length against Captain Hay. He accused the captain of prejudice against him . . . of being 'unfair,' as he put it. In the middle of Mr. Gladden's outburst, I heard a roar of rage, and a grunt. Then I heard the cabin door close behind Mr. Gladden—"

"How did you know it was Mr. Gladden?" asked Hoare.

Mr. McHale looked surprised. "Why, sir, Mr. Gladden and the captain were the only men in the cabin. And it certainly wasn't the captain that ran out the cabin door."

"And if you believed Mr. Arthur Gladden and his captain to have come to blows, why did you not raise the alarm?"

"I could not be sure of that, sir, not from where I was standing. Besides, there was the Marine guard at the cabin door."

"So you, an experienced sea officer, left it to an unknown Marine private to decide whether or not to raise the alarm. Eh? This will do your career little good, Mr. McHale. That will be all, sir."

Called and sworn, Mr. Watt repeated in essence the story he had told Hoare a few days ago. When the little man arrived at his captain's dying words, the junior member of the court spoke up again. He had been the only one besides Captain

Wright to take an active part in the proceedings. Bernard Weatherby was his name, master and commander in *Crocus,* 20; a man of promise and one to remember, Hoare told himself.

"Frankly, gentlemen, I'm at a loss," Captain Weatherby said. "No one has suggested for a minute Captain Hay was poisoned by one of the lobsters he had been consuming, and Mr. Bennett tells us the captain's steward swears the creatures were alive when he dropped them into the pot of hock. We have no reason to doubt the man's word. Why did the captain talk of 'lobsters' as he was dying, then?"

" 'A babbled of green tomalley,' " someone muttered in the back of the cabin. Someone else tittered.

"Belay that nonsense." Captain Wright's quiet, flat voice brought silence. "Another episode of that kind, and I'll have the perpetrator publicly gagged, even if he's a post captain."

Silence fell.

Mr. Prickett slipped into the cabin and whispered a few words into Hoare's ear. Nodding his thanks, Hoare leaned forward and relayed the whisper to Peter Gladden.

"Having received the court's prior permission, gentlemen," said the latter, "Mr. Hoare asked Sergeant Miller of *Defiant's* Marine detachment to take as many of his men as required and board *Vantage,* where he was to replace *Vantage's* entire Marine detachment for as long as might be required. I also gave Miller certain instructions.

"Sergeant Doyle of *Vantage* has now mustered his detachment in the waist below the break of *Defiant's* quarterdeck. Mr. President, may I ask you to adjourn this court to the quarterdeck?"

Captain Wright caught Bennett's eye and nodded. Arthur Gladden, guarded by his two Marines, left the cabin first, to be followed by his brother, Hoare, Bennett, and the members of the court. Next, His Royal Highness clambered up the companionway to gleam in the summer sun. Behind them all limped Lieutenant Wallace in a pair of loose pantaloons. The lieutenant would see himself damned if he would witness any man of his being grilled by some whispering upstart of a duelist without his officer present to protect him in case of need.

Sergeant Doyle had drawn up *Vantage*'s forty-seven Marines in the waist of *Defiant,* in two facing ranks. Upon catching sight of his officer among the gathering on the quarterdeck above him, the sergeant called his redcoats to attention, and they presented arms with a familiar *clank*. Wallace hitched himself painfully down the larboard companionway into the waist, and took position between the two ranks. From there he looked up at Captain Wright and raised his hat in salute.

"What d'ye want to do now, sir?" Wright rasped at Peter Gladden. "You may as well know these fancy departures from proper procedure do your client no good at all in the eyes of this court."

Mr. Gladden bowed. "By your leave, sir, I would like him to accompany me down the ranks of these Marines. I want him to identify the man who stood on guard outside Captain Hay's door when he reported to the captain on the evening of the murder."

"Very good, Mr. Gladden. You may accompany your bro—the accused into the waist."

The procession made its way down the starboard gangway—first a Marine guard, then the prisoner, then the second Marine, and finally the prisoner's friend and brother. Arthur Gladden walked slowly and gravely along the first rank of lobsters, stopping now and then to peer into a face. He came to the end of the first rank, turned, and walked the length of the facing rank, until he had examined every Marine in *Vantage*'s detachment. Concluding with Sergeant Doyle himself, Arthur looked up at the officers of the court-martial as they stood at the quarterdeck rail.

"He's not here," said Arthur Gladden.

"What d'ye mean 'he's not here'?" Captain Wright barked.

"The man I saw is not one of this detachment, sir. As I think of it now, the man on guard had a most unusual face. The skin had a peculiar coarse, florid quality; his eyes were larger than normal. And his mouth . . . Well, sir, his mouth looked almost painted. Like a mask. I can see no Marine here with those features. I am sorry, sir."

"I have an explanation for that, sir," said Peter Gladden. He spoke on his own, without Hoare's prompting. "However, I must ask that what follows be heard in . . . in . . ." He turned to Hoare for the proper term.

"Yes. *In camera.*"

"If you expect this court to subject itself to still more harlequinades, Mr. Gladden," said Captain Wright, "you will have to convince a very skeptical group of officers, I assure you. Draw nigh, sir—yes, Mr. Hoare, you, too—and explain yourselves."

Thereupon the officers of the court-martial put their heads together to hear the whispered explanation Hoare and Gladden had prepared for them. Considerable head-shaking and protest followed, especially from the fire-breathing Commander Weatherby. At last Captain Wright rapped sharply on the quarterdeck rail.

"Mr. Hoare, Mr. Gladden," he said with some asperity, "I would be happy to let these proceedings run as long as necessary to arrive at a true bill. By doing so, as you pointed out just now, this board would conform with the letter of Admiralty regulations. However, I, like you, am an officer of the Royal Navy. My first duty, like yours, is to marshal all our naval forces as swiftly as may be to the defense of the realm which we serve.

"If, in order that this ship and the five others commanded by the captains on this court may sail with all possible speed to reinforce Lord Nelson, I must hang Mr. Arthur Gladden out of hand tomorrow. I shall do so, sir, be he innocent or guilty.

He will become a casualty, a single casualty out of all too many. But if he dies to let these ships go free, he may save England.

"So this court grants your request to continue these proceedings *in camera* for the remainder of the day, reconvening here tomorrow at eight bells of the forenoon watch. However, at noon tomorrow, if needs must and even if I hang for it myself, I *will* direct this court to declare Mr. Arthur Gladden guilty, adjourn this court-martial, and see him hanged.

"Not a minute later than noon tomorrow, therefore, this vessel and those commanded by my fellow captains on this court will have their anchors up and down in preparation for departure. Do you understand, gentlemen?"

The other captains, Arthur Gladden, and his two friends nodded solemnly.

"Very well. The board will now reconvene below. I ask all unofficial persons to withdraw. Your Royal Highness, will you go or stay?"

"I'll stay, sir," said the duke. "My presence might even save your necks, what what?"

When the observers had left *Defiant* and the board had returned to his cabin, Captain Wright turned to Peter Gladden. "Proceed, sir," he said.

"When I went ashore from *Vantage* after questioning some of the witnesses," said Gladden, "Mr. Hoare asked me to make a request on his behalf of a certain beachcombing party of his acquaintance. In turn, that person made the request known to his own people. The result was this." He reached into the portmanteau beside him and withdrew the vile-smelling Royal Marine uniform coat. Its scarlet dye had bled slightly onto its blue facings.

"This coat was fished out of Portsmouth Harbor on Tuesday night last and brought to me and Mr. Hoare. I know every officer in this cabin will recognize it. Upon examining it, Mr. Hoare found certain substances on its collar and cuffs.

80

I would like to ask him to tell the court about what he discovered."

"What I wiped from the collar and cuffs," whispered Hoare, "was paint, gentlemen, removable paint. I could even smell it over the tidewater smell. Removable paint, or *maquillage,* as the Frogs have it, has a distinctive odor, you know." Hoare paused to fill his chest for his next sentence.

"The man who had worn that coat was wearing *maquillage.* And I doubt that any member of the ship's Marine contingent would own any of the stuff, let alone know how to use it. No, the man we are looking for has to be an actor—an amateur Thespian, if you will. Now who could that be, I wondered, and *why?"*

Hoare interrupted himself again, as if preparing for battle.

"It is in the interest of obtaining the answers to those questions that I asked you, Mr. President, to adjourn the court until the time you set for it to reconvene—tomorrow, at eight bells of the morning watch.

"Finally, I suggest that you will find this evening's performance of Mr. Sheridan's *The School for Scandal* both interesting and instructive."

THOUGH THE ATTENDANTS had long since lowered the houselights and lit the footlights, the curtain of Portsmouth's sole theater had yet to rise. The audience, officers and their ladies for the most part but including a sprinkling of townsmen as well, had begun a discontented murmur. Overriding the subdued babble came Prince William's masthead growl from the royal box.

A dainty person in black slipped out from between the curtains. "In this evening's performance, the part of 'Charles Surface' will be played by Mr. Thomas Billings," he announced. "The part of 'Maria' will be played by Miss Oates." He slipped back out of sight.

81

There was a collective sigh of feminine disappointment, for "Charles," the romantic lead, was to have been played by Lieutenant Peregrine Kingsley, second in *Vantage*. As a new widow, Mrs. Hay, of course, could not now tread the boards in the role of "Maria."

Hoare snapped his fingers. With a nod to his companions to follow him, he eased himself from his place in the back of the theater and left by the main door. He returned by the stage door, where he sought out the person in black. Tonight's impresario, Mr. DeCourcey, looked as if he should be wringing his hands.

"Where's Kingsley?" Hoare asked.

DeCourcey rolled his eyes and shrugged as eloquently as Mr. Morrow of Weymouth. "Who knows?" he said. "Here the man was, as good a juvenile as you could ask for in Drury Lane itself, superb in the part, and he has gone missing."

"He's bit!" whispered Hoare with a wicked grin. He clapped the distracted DeCourcey on the shoulder so hard as to dislodge the quizzing glass from his left eye. Hoare put his head out the stage door and blew on his silver boatswain's call.

There was a tumult and a shouting in the evening streets of Portsmouth. Some men mounted to take up their mission; others climbed into waiting chaises; still others—these mostly the hard men of the press gang—began their search through the late dusk of June for the missing Kingsley.

Hoare withdrew to his post of command in the Navy Tavern, just off the Hard, to await the outcome. To him, among others, came Mr. Peter Gladden and Mr. Francis Bennett and most of the members of the court-martial, including Captains Wright and Weatherby. Mr. Prickett was already in place, his mouth smeared with somebody's jam.

"Well, Mr. Hoare!" Weatherby cried. "Your trap seems to have been well designed. My congratulations!"

"Premature, Captain, but I thank you nonetheless," whispered Hoare, with more than a trifle of envy. He knew very well indeed that, since he would never make post, the only way he could hoist his swab—his epaulette—and earn the courtesy title of "Captain" was to be made commander.

"How did you do it, sir?" Wright asked.

"I'm afraid it was mostly guesswork, sir," Hoare replied modestly. "Guesswork and speculation."

He and the rest of the company rose at the unannounced entry of H.R.H. Duke of Clarence.

"Be seated, gentlemen, please," said Prince William. "D'ye know, if I were ever to succeed to the Throne, I do believe I'd do away with all this risin' for royalty. I've seen too many promisin' naval officers brain 'emselves on the overhead when risin' to give the Loyal Toast."

"Hear him; hear him!" one of the juniors was heard to say.

"Go on with your tale, Mr. Hoare, eh?" Royalty said.

"It was clear from the start, sir, that Mr. Arthur Gladden is no man to kill his fellowman. Captain Hay's killer had to be someone else. The captain's servant? Mr. Watt, his clerk? What motive could they have had? Only the Marine guard could have told us, and he was mysteriously missing.

"That was when I reasoned that the Marine himself was the most likely culprit. He had the means—his bayonet—and the opportunity. He could enter the captain's cabin at any time on the pretext of announcing a visitor or bringing a message. Sergeant Doyle admits he was as yet unacquainted with his men."

Hoare paused to take a long draft of a mild lemonade.

"Yes? Yes?" A small, lean man with a weary face leaned forward impatiently, and Hoare continued.

"This would have made it easy for a Marine, or another man posing as a Marine, to insinuate himself into the post of guardian at the sacred portal. No one would really see him as he stood at his post. As poor Arthur Gladden said to me, 'I don't think anyone can tell one Lobster from another—except perhaps another Lobster. They're all statues in red coats and heavy boots.'

"The only thing missing now was motive. Why would a Marine, a stranger to his captain like all the rest of the ship's company, want to kill the man?

"Then Watt mentioned a missing file. He appears to be a meticulous man and braver than he credits himself for being, and I could not see him as being mistaken in a matter of his profession. Someone had taken the file, then. Why not the captain's murderer? The Marine—or, rather, the pretended Marine?"

He took another draft of lemonade.

"It was then that I launched a search for a Marine uniform coat. I reasoned the murderer would throw it overboard—weighted, perhaps, though I prayed not—rather than hiding it somewhere in the bilges of the ship. Sooner or later some prying member of the crew would find it.

"Now I had a stroke of luck. As I was musing about the killer's description—if not a Marine himself, he had to be able to impersonate one convincingly, and he had, of course, to be a naval man—I happened to see the playbill posted outside my lodgings. And there I saw the name of *Vantage*'s second, Peregrine Kingsley, in the part of 'Charles Surface,' the dashing young blade. There was my man, I was certain."

Hoare's voice now gave out entirely. He fell back upon breathing his words into Mr. Prickett's ear so the midshipman could relay them to the audience, a clear, proud treble stentor.

"This might have explained Mr. Watt's missing file as well. Conceivably, Kingsley could have got wind that someone had sent his captain something so incriminating that he felt he had to filch it, even killing Captain Hay if need be, while doing so.

"He easily abstracted from the Marine detachment the coat which was later found in the harbor. Before donning it, he disguised his face with *maquillage,* leaving unavoidable traces of the stuff on the coat as he did so, and slipped into ranks when Sergeant Doyle mounted the guard. Again, it was easy for him to include himself.

"If I was right, the altercation between Arthur Gladden and his captain gave Kingsley his chance to create a red herring in the form of the hapless young officer. After Arthur fled, Kingsley entered the cabin on some pretext and bayoneted the captain. He switched his bayonet and the one the captain had in his possession, dropped the bloody uniform coat over the side, and disappeared into the anonymity of nighttime aboard a newly manned vessel."

"But all this is speculation, Mr. Hoare," Captain Wright said.

"Precisely so, sir. That is why I had to lay a trap for Kingsley by means of a piece of theater of our own. We continued the court-martial, but *in camera* so that Kingsley was excluded. Thus it appeared to him to be the court's secret that it was now in search of a naval person with acting experience.

"But even secret proceedings will out, as we all know, all too well. I made sure they would, by instructing young Mr. Prickett here to be a trifle loose-mouthed."

Mr. Prickett grew pink, either with embarrassment or with pride.

"Sure enough, the word spread, as the word will, and Kingsley was deceived into believing the law was on his trail. He panicked, as we all know, and fled. That's all, gentlemen."

The room broke into applause and cries of, "Hear him; hear him!"

"Present him, Weatherby."

From where Hoare stood, across the room and surrounded by admirers, he could hear His Royal Highness's quarterdeck command. He saw Weatherby working his way through the crowd.

"This way, if you please, Mr. Hoare. You know the drill, I suppose?"

"Go to one knee and kiss his ring, isn't it, sir?"

"Gad, no. He's a prince, not the pope, and he's incognito besides. Just hat under the arm—like that, yes—and bow in salute. A bit deeper than usual wouldn't do any harm."

Clarence's circle of courtier-officers opened to admit Captain Weatherby and his prize. Hoare made what he hoped was the proper bow. His Royal Highness put out an affable hand.

"Well done, Mr. . . . er . . . Hoare, by Jove. Clever chap, what what? Amazin'. Should you ever be in need of a friendly word, sir, you may call on me. Short of a ship, of course . . . can't have an officer on the quarterdeck who can't make his orders heard, eh what?"

All too true, Hoare thought for the thousandth time, as the nodding circle of sycophants regathered itself around their duke. The small, lean, weary-looking man drew him aside, named himself as John Goldthwait, and asked that he call the next time he was near 11 Chancery Lane in London.

"Present him." With those two magic words from royalty, Hoare's credit account with the hypothetical Bank of Advancement had doubled. His interest had grown by a cubit tonight. But, even so, it could never give him back his voice, put him aboard a fighting ship, and return him to the ladder of promotion.

THE COURT-MARTIAL RECONVENED on the morning of 1 July, another sparkling day, to acquit Arthur Gladden of the charges against him. When Peter bent to buckle his sword belt about his brother's waist, Arthur seized the weapon and flung it out the open window of *Defiant*'s cabin, scabbard and all.

"Bugger your bloody sword, and bugger the Navy, too!" he shouted. "I resign your bloody service, and be damned to you!"

He pushed his brother and Hoare aside, stormed out through the paralyzed crowd, summoned a wherry, and was off before anyone of the court or the ship's company could summon the wit to stop him. They let him go.

Hoare took his place in the line of officers and dignitaries waiting for passage ashore but caught a lift from the friendly Commander Weatherby. He went straight out to *Insupportable* and took her out into the light morning breeze.

As THE SUN was setting two days later, Hoare sat at *Insupportable*'s cabin table, looking down at several trail boards and wondering what he would rename the pinnace today. They had just tied up after forty-eight hours of personal leave, granted by his master of the moment so he could recoup his exhausted whisper.

"Ahoy, the pinnace!" came a hail from the pier overhead. Hoare stuck his head out the companionway.

Peter Gladden was looking down at him. "Glad you're back, Mr. Hoare," he said. "I've been waiting for you since yesterday. I've news."

Hoare climbed out of the cuddy to greet the other officer. "Come aboard," he said. Hoare thought Gladden looked ready to burst.

"Kingsley's dead," Gladden reported as soon as he stood on *Insupportable*'s narrow clean deck.

"*What?*"

"Kingsley's dead. Taken and killed."

"Come below and tell me about it."

Over a mug of neat rum at *Insupportable*'s table, her alternate names brushed to one side, Gladden recounted the details.

As Gladden told Hoare, Kingsley had apparently laid no plan for strategic withdrawal in the event of need, so had simply followed his high-bridged nose into the hills behind Southampton Water. He might have been intending to hide in Sherwood Forest, adopting the carefree life of that greenwood's most famous inhabitant. One of the press took him at a poor inn in Bishops Waltham during the night. He had disguised himself as a drover and, as his Maid Marian, was accompanied by Maud, Mrs. Hay's former abigail. He had in his possession the clerk Watt's missing file and several other pieces of interesting private correspondence. One part of it showed that Kingsley had long been rogering both mistress and maid—although not, apparently, on the same occasions. This, of course, would only make matters worse for them all in the public opinion.

Kingsley's other correspondence, Gladden went on, included several peculiar messages. Admiral Sir George Hardcastle desired Hoare to present himself forthwith, to examine these documents and render his opinion about them. It was to give him this order that for two days Gladden had been lying in wait for him at the Swallowed Anchor.

Meanwhile, until a new court-martial could be convened, Kingsley had been placed under close arrest in the selfsame Spartan quarters formerly occupied by his junior in *Vantage,* Mr. Gladden's brother.

"Well, sir," Gladden said, "this very morning, the sergeant of Marines was changing the guard outside Kingsley's door when he saw the sentry was standing in a puddle of blood. He says his first thought was that it was the sentry's blood and that Kingsley must have attacked him somehow, but the sentry was at his post, just as surprised as his sergeant. He hadn't noticed the blood, it seems. When the two Lobsters opened the cell door, there was the prisoner, stone cold on the floor, with a bullet hole in his head. I hear it went through the back of his head and blew the front of his face clear across the room."

"There was a naughty soul," Hoare whispered, "who had a little hole, right in the middle of his forehead . . . Excuse me. I couldn't help it.

"So *that's* finished," he added—he thought—to himself,

but he had apparently articulated the words, for Gladden raised his eyebrows.

"What do you mean? What's finished?"

"Why . . . why," Hoare said, "the case of the captain and the Lobsters. What else?"

He knew very well that he was prevaricating to the other. What he had meant was that he now had no chance of eliciting from Kingsley the true motive for his stabbing of Captain Hay. Adultery was not uncommon in these circles. As long as it was not open, it seldom resulted in violence. Why, then, had Kingsley decided that he must silence his cuckolded captain?

"Be that as it may," said Gladden. "The Admiral sent me to find you and to ask you to be so good—"

"And this was two days ago? Shit," said Hoare. "Bear a hand, then, will you?"

Between them the two officers snugged *Insupportable* down in no time. Then they dashed ashore to the Swallowed Anchor so Hoare could shift into a respectable shore-going rig. They were on the way out the inn door when the pink girl Susan caught Hoare by the sleeve.

"Your sword, sir! Would you be forgetting your sword?"

She bent, shaking her head and frowning prettily, fastened the useless thing deftly about Hoare's waist, and let the gentlemen go.

"I have other news, sir," said Gladden, keeping up with Hoare's near-trot through the streets of Portsmouth. "My brother is to take holy orders next month."

"Hardly surprising, do you think?" Hoare asked.

"Not in the least." Gladden had already begun to puff. An officer's confined life at sea did not make for a fit body, Hoare reminded himself, however finely it might hone his judgment.

"He wants you to attend his ordination," the smaller man went on. "Apparently, he credits you with having kept him from being strung up for the day at *Vantage*'s yardarm, like a *Bounty* mutineer or a jammed signal."

"Where and when are the hands to be laid upon him?"

"The twenty-first of July, I think he said. Since Bath and Wells have agreed to direct the thing, I imagine it will be in his cathedral at Wells."

Interest or no interest, Hoare thought, Arthur Gladden might never have made more than an incompetent sea officer, but he could well be a decent cleric. Furthermore, his family moved in exalted circles indeed if the occupant of one of England's oldest sees consented to preside at the ex-lieutenant's priesting.

"I shan't be present," Gladden went on. *"Frolic*'s under orders."

"Oh?" Hoare whispered. His belly churned with envy.

"And so, by the way, is *Vantage,* as soon as her new captain has picked his second and third officers."

"Are the pickings his to make, then?" Hoare asked. "Who is he?" Perhaps—just perhaps—the man would be an old friend who would stretch common sense for friendship's sake and take him on as second, or even third.

"Kent," Gladden said. "John Kent. Weatherby's predecessor in *Crocus* just made post. They say he's decided to make his appointments by interview instead of interest. He's sitting on the candidates today, with Sir George."

The procedure was odd, but perfectly proper. Hoare had never heard of a Captain Kent. "A bit of a jump for him, isn't it?"

"Yes. He was slated for *Eager,* 28, but Their Lordships at the Admiralty had to give *her* to Plummer. Then Kent's uncle, Featherstonehaugh, put up such a row in the House that they gave him *Vantage* instead to keep him quiet."

He pronounced the name of Kent's uncle as "Fanshawe," the way he should. With his courtier's ear and his own family's interest, Hoare thought, it would not be long before Gladden himself climbed another rung or two up that tarry, slippery ladder toward post rank.

"A *Plummer* for Kent, eh?" he whispered. Hoare surprised himself at the words. He could not remember the last time he had uttered an impromptu joke. Perhaps it was a sign affairs were about to look up for him.

Gladden raised his eyebrows at his companion and laughed. "Very good, sir! Next thing you'll be saying is that the news of my departure *gladdens* your heart, eh?"

"It does no such thing, my dear fellow. We shorebound bodies will miss you, you know."

"Thank you, Hoare. I hope another, softer heart will miss me, too."

So that was the way the wind blew. Mr. Gladden's pursuit of his Admiral's dumpy, spotty, popular daughter was a serious matter. If he landed her, their joint interest would have him commanding a 74 within two years. Perhaps, then . . . Hoare smiled bleakly.

Once the Marine guard had saluted them into Sir George's offices, Hoare took Gladden's arm gently and turned to face him.

"You've done the task the Admiral sent you on, Peter, and I'm here for my chastisement. Now go; seek out Miss Felicia, and good luck to you—both with your damsel and with your new ship."

"Thank you, Bartholomew. You've been a good friend to the Gladdens. I shall not forget." Mr. Gladden's towhead disappeared down the street. Hoare smiled after him. He had not forgotten what it was like to be twenty-four, well-connected, and full-voiced.

Chapter VII

———◆———

AFTER NAMING himself to the rabbit-faced clerk outside Sir George's inner door, Hoare sought out an out-of-the-way corner in which he could lean without being bothered while he awaited the Admiral's pleasure and, himself unobserved, could observe his fellow officers. He suspected he would have a long, long wait.

Except for a few who, like himself, were present on other business, the gathering outside Sir George's sanctum consisted of eleven hopeful lieutenants, candidates pursuing the two choice spots in the virgin *Vantage*. Each bore his precious, irreplaceable letters of testimonial, some visibly a decade or more old. Each had dressed in his finest and stood as trim as he could; each glared at any rival who came eye to eye. Among them Hoare counted three weary old trots, older than he by ten years or more, and two downy-cheeked youngsters with rows of shiny new buttons on their uniform lapels and cuffs. The other six were run-of-the-mill serving officers, somewhat scarred but, unlike himself, still serviceable at sea. Of the eleven, three were already flushed with drink.

One of these procured a chamber pot from a nearby cabinet and walked toward Hoare's corner, unbuttoning himself as he came.

"Kindly find another pissing place, sir," Hoare said in his harshest whisper. "I do not care to be splashed."

The other started and paused as if deciding whether to take umbrage. Upon taking stock of Hoare's dire aspect, he mumbled an apology and went off in search of a less controversial corner.

Only three candidates for *Vantage* remained when the rabbit-clerk answered a bellowed summons from within, entered the Admiral's sanctum, and returned, looking flustered.

"Lieutenant . . . ah . . . Hoare? Has Mr. . . . a gentleman by that name presented himself?"

Hoare overlooked the expected titters and wove his way through the thinning crowd to the rabbit. "I gave you my name over two hours ago," he said.

"Oh, dear. And now Sir George is *most* displeased. Oh, dear." The rabbit's ears seemed to droop. It hastened to open the door and squeak out Hoare's name.

It might have been early July, but Sir George was frosty. He was wearing his own hair, almost as frosty as the half-wig he had sported at his reception. As was natural, the three others in the room had caught their Admiral's chill. They were a post captain with the single epaulet carried to starboard that signified less than three years' seniority, a languid elegant in a uniform coat like Hoare's own, and a slim, pallid civilian. These must be Captain Kent of *Vantage* and Sir George's flag lieutenant and his secretary, respectively. Hoare felt himself under four pairs of icy eyes.

"If you will excuse me for a moment, gentlemen . . . ," Sir George began, and then, as his companions began to rise, added, "No, no. Please, simply bear with me for a trice, while I deal with this officer.

"Now, sir, you have damned well taken your time in obeying orders. You have kept me waiting, not only for one morning, but for two entire days. This is hardly the behavior of a dedicated officer of the Navy. What do you mean by it, sir?"

"I was afloat until this morning, sir," Hoare whispered, "on personal leave, to recover my voice."

"You evidently require additional leave, then," the captain began, and drew to himself some of the Admiral's chill.

"Mr. Hoare's affairs are none of yours, sir," said Sir George. The captain reddened and subsided.

"And this morning's delay?"

"I presented myself in your anteroom more than two hours ago, sir, within an hour of tieing up."

"Hmmph. Then we'll set your dilatory behavior to one side for the time being. Now, as to the purpose for which I requested your *immediate* presence *two days* ago . . ." Sir George's qualified absolution notwithstanding, he was not going to forget whatever inconvenience Hoare's absence had caused him.

The Admiral began to leaf through the papers lying before him, but the secretary was quicker off the mark. "The papers you were looking for, Sir George," he announced smugly.

"Damme, Patterson, you're bold indeed to decide for me what I am looking for. D'ye think me a wittol?" Sir George took the packet sharply from his aide's hand.

"Here, Mr. Hoare," Sir George said. "You will have been told that the man Kingsley was found shot this morning."

Hoare nodded.

"It is obvious that Kingsley's murder was intended to stop his tongue. Since the story of his adultery with his own captain's wife was already out and the cuckolded man is dead in any case, that can hardly have been the motive for his murder. He must have been privy to some other, greater secret . . . something which justified silencing him so effectively.

"The question, Mr. Hoare, is: what? And whose secret was it? Perhaps these papers offer the answer. I know of nothing else that can. They were aboard him when he was taken. Some of 'em belonged to Hay himself. Some, which I have turned over to his successor, relate to *Vantage's* business. Here are the rest of them."

The Admiral interrupted himself. "I don't believe I have yet made you gentlemen known to each other," he said as Hoare tucked the packet under his arm.

"This officer, Kent, is Mr. Bartholomew Hoare of my staff—more or less, when he is pleased to feel like appearing. Hoare, John Kent, now captain of *Vantage.*"

"Servant, sir," Hoare said.

Captain Kent acknowledged Hoare's stiff bow with a curt nod. He would be unwise indeed to seek a berth in *Vantage,* Hoare decided.

"As I said, Hoare, Kingsley was obviously shot by no accident, but by someone who feared what he might say at his court-martial. I want you to find out who, and what he wanted hushed up.

"To begin with, you are to read, learn, and inwardly digest these papers and give me your opinion of them. Patterson here says some of them look personal to the dead man—and damning. He says that others are in some kind of cipher.

"Take as much time as you need with this, Hoare, but take it somewhere else. Report to me here, at eight bells of the afternoon watch."

IN THE DIM, stuffy match-boarding cranny at the Victualling Office, which he used as an occasional workplace, Hoare had installed a splintered table to serve him as a desk. The place was awkward and uncomfortable, but it was nearby. Here, instead of in the outer of his own two sunny rooms at the Swallowed Anchor, he spread out the papers Admiral Hardcastle had given him.

Some of them would have been part of the missing file that he remembered Captain Hay's clerk, Watt, describing to him some days ago. Mr. Watt had said of this one, for example, that "the writing appeared to be that of a young woman, self-taught, perhaps." Reading it, Hoare could imagine her bent over the paper, tongue pressed between her teeth in concentration as she wrote. The letter hinted to the captain that his wife was not only betraying him but doing so with his own second officer. It could have been written by Mrs. Hay's maid Maud, since the woman had been found in Kingsley's company.

A week ago, Hoare mused, he would have regarded this letter as priceless evidence of Kingsley's motive for murdering someone—Maud, if not Captain Hay. But now, with Kingsley lying murdered himself, it was of historical interest only. Hoare could see no reason for handing it to Captain Hay's widow. Her past sins were no business of his.

The letter that had caused Mr. Watt's *crise de conscience* lay among the others, with its enclosure pinned to it. As Mr. Watt had remembered, it read: "I found this in *his* uniform pocket that night. I know the sort of thing it is, and I do not believe he should be in possession of such a thing. But perhaps you gave it to him in connection with *Vantage*."

Mr. Watt had not recited the rest of the letter to Hoare and Gladden. On reading it, Hoare placed a note at the head of his mental memorandum file: *Question Mrs. Hay.*

The enclosure was written in minute block letters on the thinnest of tissue. It had apparently been tightly rolled for sending, instead of being folded. There was no trace of a seal. It was addressed to "Ahab" and signed "Jehu." Its text comprised several score five-letter words of gibberish.

It was obvious to Hoare, as it had been to Watt, that this was an enciphered message. Knowing nothing of codes and ciphers, he had to set it aside.

Hoare leafed quickly through the other letters in the file

Kingsley had stolen from *Vantage*'s cabin. They were, as Watt had implied, irrelevant and trivial. Most were from tradesmen, although two solicited places for their sons as midshipmen in *Vantage* and one was a plea for funds from an imprisoned debtor signing himself "your devoted cousin, Jeremiah Hay." He turned now to Kingsley's other papers.

Here were three heated, tousled missives in Mrs. Hay's careless script. Why had Kingsley been such a fool as to keep them? Had he, too, had blackmail in mind?

Kingsley's most interesting documents were four messages. Their appearance was identical to the enclosure that had caught Mr. Watt's eye.

The fourth letter was also in a semiliterate hand:

Estem'd Sir:
if you dont wan er usbin [husband] an the LAW to no about them things you bin doin wat no ENGLISH Genelman shd be doin youl bring 20 pouns to the ol plaic [place] sadiday at for bels. COM ALON!!!! I stil got frens an you dont no mor

yr umbl obt servt
J. Jaggery

In this letter, at least, the threat of blackmail was specific. But since Kingsley was no longer alive to be blackmailed, Hoare felt he could as well set it aside—except that the name Jaggery tickled his memory in connection with something unsavory.

He remembered now. Some years ago, a gunner of that name had suffered two broken legs and a mangled left hand in a sea accident. Since a full set of working limbs was as essential to a gunner as a carrying voice was to a deck officer, the lame gunner, like Hoare, had been put ashore. There, interest of some mysterious lower-deck kind had found him a place at the Ordnance Board.

Janus Jaggery had first come to Hoare's attention as one of a ring of petty diverters who generally had odd pieces of nautical gear at hand for the right price. Although Hoare's inquiry had lifted several light-fingered men out of their secure nests ashore and sent them to sea or to Botany Bay, Jaggery had managed to keep his place. Perhaps Hoare would call on him, after all, at the Bunch of Grapes, once he had finished his survey of Kingsley's papers and made his report to Sir George.

This time, as soon as the Admiral's rabbit caught sight of Hoare he hastened to announce Hoare to his master. The rabbit informed him that Captain Kent had made his selections and disappeared aboard his new command.

Within Sir George's sanctum, Patterson the secretary still hovered at the back of his Admiral.

"I shall be brief, sir," Hoare whispered. "Two letters represent two separate attempts at extortion. The first is the maid Maud's weak approach to Captain Hay, while the other is a more sinister approach to Kingsley by one Janus Jaggery.

"Since both targets are dead, the abortive bits of blackmail have become moot, and I would recommend they be disregarded were it not that the man Jaggery is known to me as a questionable character at best. I would like to make sure of his continued good behavior.

"I also want to interview Mrs. Hay. One of her letters to the late captain gives me reason to suspect that he was not unaware of her liaison with Kingsley."

"Go on."

"The papers in cipher are beyond my competence to handle, sir. However, if you wish to investigate them further, as I think advisable . . ." Hoare paused and cleared his throat painfully.

Sir George gestured to his secretary. "Wine, Patterson. The man's dry."

". . . as I think advisable," Hoare repeated when he had wet his whistle, "and yet do not want to refer the documents to their Lordships' people in London, I know of two persons in the area, either one of whom *might* be of assistance."

Hoare had stressed the word *might* with all the power he could put behind his pitiful whisper, thereby losing all the ground he had made with the wine's help. He had to gesture for more. He must, he thought, find some way of carrying a mild anodyne about so that he could better endure extended talk. Perhaps Mrs. Graves's physician spouse would help. Perhaps he would see her redoubtable little person again.

"Whom d'ye have in mind?" the Admiral demanded. "I don't care to have ciphered messages swanning about my command, out of control. And the thing would be lost to mankind within seconds of arriving in Whitehall."

"One, sir, is Watt, captain's clerk in *Vantage*. The other is Mrs. Simon Graves, wife of a physician in Weymouth. Both are talented in matters of handwriting."

"I can hardly issue orders to a doctor's wife in Portsmouth," the Admiral said. "Perhaps you yourself can find a way of consulting the good woman. Take whatever steps you deem necessary—within reason, of course. As to Watt, I shall second him to you out of *Vantage,* if you'd like, until you've used him up or until she sails, whichever is sooner."

"I would find that most helpful, sir." Kent, *Vantage*'s new captain, would damn Hoare blue if he knew him responsible for stealing his clerk just as his frigate was making ready for sea. Well, Hoare thought, damn *him* blue, right back.

"See to it, Patterson," Sir George said. "Have the man Watt report himself to Hoare at his lodgings, prepared to remain there at the Navy's expense until Hoare's through with him or until *Vantage*'s anchor is aweigh. When will you have that cipher sorted out, then, Hoare?"

"I can't say yet, sir," Hoare whispered, and regretted his words instantly.

" 'Can't say,' sir? What kind of an answer is that to give your superior officer, sir? I've had mids kiss the gunner's daughter for less. Someone should have beaten that sort of insolence out of you, sir, before you were handed your commission.

"You've been on the beach too long, sir. You've got fat and lazy, sir, fat and lazy. You've waxed fat and kicked against the pricks. It's past time you were sent to sea."

Hoare's heart leaped. If he could only take Sir George at his word . . .

"I would be overjoyed, sir," he ventured.

Mr. Patterson gasped. For ten heartbeats that seemed to Hoare like as many minutes, Sir George Hardcastle glowered at Hoare from under his heavy brow. The paneled room was silent.

At last, the Admiral's expression became almost sympathetic. Evidently, Sir George shared Hoare's longing to be at sea again.

"I take your meaning, Mr. Hoare," he said. "Perhaps I shall be your Eurystheus and you my Heracles." He paused again as if to assure himself that Hoare understood the allusion.

Hoare did. The gods had sentenced Heracles to undertake certain labors given him by King Eurystheus of Mycenae as penance for killing his own children by the king's daughter, Megara.

"And Patterson here can be my Talthybius," the Admiral added.

The secretary looked sour. Talthybius had been Eurystheus's herald, by whom the king had sent his orders to Heracles. The hero had dubbed him "the Dung Man."

"If you seek your own *Argo*, Mr. Hoare, make sure your good works are such as to magnify you before Their Lordships. Return Watt to *Vantage* when you have used him, if he has not already rejoined her under sailing orders. That will be all, sir."

"Aye aye, sir," Hoare whispered. He made his bow and removed himself.

MR. WATT REPORTED to Hoare's quarters in the Swallowed Anchor as instructed.

"Captain Kent was not in the least pleased to learn that I was to be taken away from *Vantage* at such a crucial time, sir," the man said. "I do not think it wise to repeat his very words. Even he, however, must obey Sir George's explicit instructions."

"I understand, Mr. Watt. Let us do our best to return you to his care as soon as possible," Hoare whispered. "Now, sir, as I recall from our discussion aboard *Vantage,* you are a student of handwriting. Is that really so?"

"I have come to believe, sir," Watt said, "that a person's handwriting reveals not only his gender—or hers, of course—and position in life, but also his character and personality. In fact, I occasionally entertain my friends by describing a person's nature, based on inspecting samples of his handwriting."

"Interesting," Hoare commented. He handed the clerk the folder. "Tell me what you think of these, then."

"This, as you must know already, sir," Watt said, "is the folder that went adrift from Captain Hay's desk. Certain official correspondence was missing and still is—"

"Sir George has sent it back aboard *Vantage,*" Hoare said, "where I am sure you will find it when you return. Go on."

"The remaining correspondence is as I remember it. A letter from the late captain's lady, several from tradesmen, one written—as I think I remember telling you—by a lower-class woman. She is literate but has had little practice in the calligraphic art. It might be the prelude to a demand for money."

"I agree. Thank you. Now, these," Hoare said, handing Watt the other documents found on Kingsley.

"Oh, dear me," Watt replied upon casting his eyes over

Mrs. Hay's steaming letters to her husband's lieutenant. "Oh," he said again as he read. "Oh, my. Oh, dear." He set the letters on Hoare's desk, his lips pressed firmly together and his sallow face pink. "The letters of a lewd woman and a hot one, indeed, sir. One can only be happy that Captain Hay never saw them." He picked up the letter from J. Jaggery. "This is a piece of outright blackmail, of course," he said. "Again, the writer—a man, this time, probably a seaman, sir, or at least a man of the sea—is barely literate. He places a low value indeed on his silence, does he not? And in mentioning the law, does he perhaps advert to some untoward action on the late lieutenant's part, other than the plowing of his master's field?" He looked at Hoare inquiringly.

"One could indeed draw that inference," Hoare whispered.

When he took up the thin pieces of tissue, Watt's eyes brightened. He drew a glass from his bosom and bent over the papers, his pointed nose almost scraping along their surfaces as he studied them.

"Hmm. Not the Caesar cipher," he muttered to himself. "No vowels at all. Probably substituted numerals. Wonder why? A substitution cipher, indeed. Must count frequencies. . . ."

He reached out blindly for a piece of blank paper, found a silver pencil in his coat, and began taking notes to his own dictation. For now, he had moved to another world. Hoare did not want to bring him back from it. He scribbled a message that told Watt that he was to sleep at the Swallowed Anchor that night and tiptoed out of the room.

On his way to Jaggery's lair, he decided to make a detour, view the body of Peregrine Kingsley, late second lieutenant in *Vantage,* and question the newly widowed Katerina Hay.

Hoare was pleased to find that the corpse had yet to be released to the man's relatives—whoever they were. The attendant made no trouble but promptly pointed Kingsley out from among Portsmouth's other recent naval casualties.

"Ball went into the head, like you can see, sir," the man said. "Stopped there, though. Surgeon took 'er out."

Gladden had been mistaken in this detail, then. This was evident to Hoare from the coarse trephining work that had completed the destruction of the late licentious lieutenant's beauty.

"Where's the bullet?" Hoare asked.

In answer, the attendant rummaged about in a drawer underneath the cadaver. " 'Ere," he said at last, handing it to Hoare.

"I'll want this," Hoare whispered.

The bullet, he saw, bore small slightly canted ridges. It was a rifle bullet, then. If so, it could have been fired from a considerable distance. Furthermore, the killing had been done at night. Thus, he thought, the murderer had to have been no mean marksman.

"You'll 'ave to give me a paper, then," the attendant said.

Hoare sighed but wrote two notes, one to himself, identifying the bullet as being what it was, and one to the attendant. Each signed one note. Pocketing his grisly prize, Hoare tipped the man sixpence and went his way.

Captain Hay's relict had not yet moved from the apartment she had shared with her late husband on the second story of the Three Suns Inn. Hoare had seldom patronized the Three Suns; it catered to flag officers and post captains at the top of the list. Even Captain Hay must have been lucky in his prize money, if he could support an extensive stay there.

That the three gilded spheres of the Medici crest that overhung the inn's portal also served to identify pawnbroking establishments apparently troubled the proprietors of the Three Suns not at all. Their establishment was too exalted for any confusion. Hoare would not have been at all surprised to find Sir Thomas Frobisher in residence. It was his sort of place.

The doorkeeper of the Three Suns made it clear that his

masters discouraged the presence of officers below the rank of commander except on Admiralty business.

"You will either admit me forthwith and have me announced to Mrs. Hay," Hoare said at last, "or suffer the loss of your protection, be pressed, and go to sea again. You have five seconds in which to make your choice."

He had several impressive-looking, meaningless documents stuffed in his uniform pocket for occasions like this. He drew one of them out and pulled out a silver-cased pencil.

"One. Two . . ."

The porter fled. "Mrs. Hay will receive you," he said humbly when he reappeared. "This way, please."

Though he had never been introduced, Hoare had seen Mrs. Adam Hay—Katerina Hay—on stage several times. She was a skilled performer, of near-professional quality. Her acting was a trifle florid for Hoare's taste, but she was a favorite among the serving officers. Since she greeted him standing in the middle of the inn's second-best drawing room, Hoare made her his second-best leg.

Katerina Hay was big, blonde and Dutch. As she stood there in tasteful mourning, her opulent lines reminded Hoare of *Oranienboom,* the two-decker from which he had once fled incontinently. He had been first in *Staghound,* 36, then, and it was just before the day his voice had been taken from him. She looked just as dangerous.

"Please accept my condolences, ma'am, on your tragic loss," he whispered.

"You need not whisp—*oh!* Of course. You're Admiral Hardcastle's 'Whispering Ferret!'" Mrs. Hay lost all trace of her formidable mien. As it did on the stage, her accent lent piquancy to her voice. "Sit down, sir, I pray!" With massive grace, she seated herself at one end of a chaise longue and gestured for him to take his place beside her. "Thank you for your good wishes, Mr. Hoare. But let us come to the point, for you must be a busy man with this inquiry of yours." She smiled at him knowingly. "Oh, yes. After your success with *Amazon,* it would be obvious—no?—for dear Sir George to direct you onto the murder of my husband."

Taken full aback, Hoare could only laugh.

Katerina Hay laughed back. "Did anyone ever tell you, sir? Your laugh sounds like a will-o'-the-wisp in one of our Zeeland bogs. So. What do you wish to ask me?"

"I believe—forgive me—that your husband was aware of your relationship with the late Lieutenant Peregrine Kingsley."

Katerina Hay laughed again—somewhat scornfully, Hoare thought. "Of course he was 'aware,' sir. Indeed, he more or less approved of it."

Then, if the husband of Kingsley's mistress already knew of the affair, what had been Kingsley's motive in killing him?

"Do not look shocked, Mr. Hoare," Katerina Hay went on. "My husband and I remained fond of each other. But Adam had long since become incapable, and I . . . I am a full-blooded woman."

Had she moved an inch or two along the chaise?

"Then that explains the reference in this letter to 'he' or 'his.' You knew your husband would know whom you referred to."

"Exactly, Mr. Hoare. My husband may have condoned my placing horns upon him, so long as no open scandal ensued. But he, and I, would have drawn the line at my consorting with a traitor."

"Then it might follow," Hoare said, "that Kingsley killed your husband, not because he feared discovery as your . . . er . . ."

"*Cicisbeo,* Mr. Hoare. Lover."

"Yes . . . but because of the cipher he allowed you to find."

"Exactly. I was foolish myself, perhaps, and must take some of the guilt for poor Adam's death, for I told Peregrine Kingsley what I had done with the message, and gave him his *congé* on the spot. I was right to do so, *nie?*"

With this question in her native tongue, Mrs. Hay definitely edged closer.

THE BUNCH OF Grapes, where Hoare knew he would either find Jaggery himself or learn of his whereabouts, was a known haunt of men who lived on the wrong side of the law. Yet it was not the filthy, dark lair a stranger would therefore expect. It did not reek of bad gin, used beer, or stale tobacco. It was full of neither drunks nor drabs, and none of the occupants were bedraggled. The small smugglers, illegal tradesmen, master crooked craftsmen, and other well-behaved criminals of Jaggery's sort had better taste than to frequent a den and enough money to support that taste.

So the Bunch of Grapes was a tidy if slightly battered place, well lit and smelling faintly of good ale. The only occupants Hoare could see were several groups of what looked like respectable workingmen and a small party of young sprigs.

The occupants all looked up when they saw an officer enter, then returned to talking—one quartet, quite openly, about last week's raid of the revenue men on a well-traveled smuggler's route. They seemed to think a rival gang had ratted on them.

"They better not start anything with us," one said. "We'll sort 'em out like we did last time."

"Wasn't us as done it," said a tidy man at another table. "Must have been Ackerley's boys stung 'em out."

"They didn't do no such thing," said Jaggery, whom Hoare now sighted in a corner, accompanied by a very small, wan girl child with enormous black eyes that seemed to look him through and through. "I 'appen to know."

The child caught the man's attention with a yank on his sleeve. Upon sight of Hoare, his eyes went wide.

"An' how the 'ell would *you* know, Mr. Jaggery? It's not your line o' trade," the tidy man commented.

"Softly, softly, friends," said a middle-aged man behind the bar. "There's gentry present." Though he wore a scar across his nose, he also wore a clean green cloth wrapped about his waist and a polite expression on his ruddy face. Jaggery sat back with a resigned look and glanced at his young companion.

"We haven't seen *you* here for a bit, Mr. Hoare, sir," the scar-nosed man said. "Have you been at sea, then?"

"Not really, Mr. Greenleaf," Hoare whispered. "Just working for His Majesty and taking a bit of a journey now and then, in *Serene.*"

"So. She's *Serene* these days, sir?"

"Not now. I turned her into *Alert* as soon as we got into harbor today."

Several of the other guests laughed knowingly, but Jaggery's little companion looked perplexed and dared to speak up. "What's a lert, Da? A neel, like, or a sole?" she asked, to more laughter. She blushed and hung her smooth ash-blonde head.

"I'll buy you a pint," Hoare said to Jaggery, "if you'll introduce me to your friend and give me some news."

Jaggery hesitated, looking for a way out of this, then resigned himself to the broadside to come and looked heavenward.

"For what we are about to receive, may the Lord make us truly thankful," he said. "Two pints, then, Mr. Greenleaf."

"And a glass of Madeira for . . . ?" Hoare added.

"Me dorter Jenny," Jaggery said.

"Just a minute, then."

Greenleaf disappeared through a door behind the bar and returned with a black cobwebbed bottle. He took a corkscrew and bent to open it, holding it between his knees in the old-fashioned way. The cork came out with a soft pop, and the heady tropical fragrance of a superb Madeira replaced the homely scent of ale in the atmosphere of the Bunch of Grapes.

"I'll change my mind," Hoare whispered. "I'll take Madeira, myself. That stuff smells like nectar."

"She orter, Mr. 'Oare," Greenleaf said as he poured the dark wine into two clean, coarse glasses. "She's been layin' there in the dark, in me back room, for nigh onto ten years, with 'er friends an' relations." He poured Jaggery's pint. "There you are, Mr. 'Oare," he said.

Hoare paid him and brought his purchases to the table where the old gunner and his daughter, Jenny, were waiting.

Ordinarily, Hoare would have described Janus Jaggery as an oily faced man as well as a two-faced one. Every time Hoare saw the man he was peering out from under his mop of greasy hair and whining through his gray-brown beard about the pain of his deformed left hand, his warped legs, and the buffets fate was forever dealing him. Here with his daughter, though, he certainly wore the better of his two faces. He now looked sly, but benign. Jenny Jaggery would be five or six years of age, Hoare guessed. In a threadbare frock that would have covered her twice, she was a wisp. But someone other than her father must have the care of her, for she and her frock were clean, though drab.

" 'Ere's to yer good health, Mr. 'Oare." Jaggery took a deep draft of his ale and wiped his mouth with his sleeve.

Hoare's first sip of the Madeira told him that, like a fortunate butterfly, he was sipping nectar.

"Is the man really named 'Ore,' Pa?" Jenny asked.

"Mind yer manners, lass," her father said. He tensed visibly where he sat, but seeing that Hoare was not about to knock him down or call his daughter out, eased back again and gulped down a draft. "An' to what do we owe the pleasure of yer presence here with us, Your Honor?" he asked warily.

"The late Peregrine Kingsley. You sent him this." Hoare held out the misspelled letter, keeping it firmly in hand and watching for Jaggery's reaction.

Jaggery read it as Hoare held it before him, moving his lips as he read. Did he seem relieved?

"Aye, Yer Honor. I can't deny it, seein' as it's got me own name on it in me own 'and."

"Tell me what's behind it."

"Saw nothin' wrong with pickin' up a bit o' blunt from the fancy Mr. Kingsley. The cove's captain wouldn't 'a' been 'alf tore up to find 'is wife had been makin' free with 'is lieutenant, would 'e, now?"

"He already knew, Jaggery."

The gunner's jaw dropped.

"And," Hoare said, "you could have gotten yourself spending the rest of your life in Botany Bay for extortion. What would have happened to your wife and young Jenny then?"

"Ain't got no wife. Slicer Kate sliced Meg's gizzard two years ago, and she took sick of it and died. Got 'anged for it, too, Kate did, in Winchester, at 'Ampshire assizes. My Jenny's a norphing, she is.

"Besides," Jaggery went on, "the captain went and died on me, 'e did, the thoughtless bastard. And there ain't no one will bother me now, now that other bastard Kingsley's been put out of the way. So there, Mister Hoare."

No connoisseur, Jenny had tossed off her Madeira in one gulp. Now she giggled, gave a small belch, let her eyelids drop, and fell asleep leaning against her father's shoulder.

"There. Now see what ye've done," Jaggery said reproachfully. He looked down at the child and laid his maimed hand on her glossy head.

"And what else was Kingsley about, Jaggery, that he should be afraid of the law as well as his lady's husband? And you referred to 'friends' that he had lost and you had kept. What were you and he engaged in together?"

Jaggery shook his head and looked at Hoare out of wide, innocent-looking eyes. "Mr. Kingsley 'ad a way about 'im,

Yer Honor. Much against me will, 'e persuaded me to take on some bits of nautical merchandise, like. Bits of ship chandlery. Scuttles, patent blocks, things like that, that might have gone adrift. Jom York's a good friend of mine. Ye know Mr. York, Yer Honor?"

Since York had found Kingsley's Marine uniform for Hoare, he could hardly deny it, nor, indeed, did he wish to. He nodded. "And Kingsley was no longer 'friends' with Jom York?"

"Never said that, Yer Honor, did I now? Mr. York's an up-right man, he is. . . ."

By calling him an "upright man," Jaggery meant, Hoare knew, that York claimed membership in the notorious Thieves' Guild, sworn to mutual confidence and trust. Hoare also knew that even though the outside world might be sure of its existence and its secret power, the Thieves' Guild was a fraud, a figment, and a fairy tale. But if Jaggery thought that he, Hoare, believed in it, let him.

"I'm not satisfied, Jaggery," Hoare said. "You're hiding something. You may be in far more shoal water than you know. Spit it out."

"As Gawd's me witness, Yer Honor, ye know all me sins," the man said. "Yer persecutin' me, and it's not right."

Hoare knew well that Jaggery had more to spill but, without any clue about what it might be, was at a loss as to how to get it out of him. Try as he would, the old boatswain hid and dodged behind a barricade of reproachful words. Hoare was missing the key to his secret fortress.

"Keep your hands off the King's property, man," Hoare said at last. He rose from the table and gave the sleeping Jenny a pat of his own. "And start combing those sly brains of yours about your friend Kingsley and what *he* might have been up to, beyond having at his captain's wife. I'll have my eye on you, and I never sleep."

He stopped on the way out to haggle with Greenleaf about

buying his entire stock of Madeira. Hoare left the Bunch of Grapes the owner of six dozen, having promised payment in full once they should have been delivered to the Swallowed Anchor and he had tested a randomly selected bottle from the consignment.

"It's not that I don't trust you, Mr. Greenleaf," he said, "but who's to say that some land pirate might make a midnight switch?"

Back at the Swallowed Anchor, Hoare found Mr. Watt fast asleep with his face in a copy of one of the enciphered messages to Ahab from Jehu. His candle had guttered out. Hoare picked the little man up in his arms and carried him up to the garret room he had been assigned by Mr. Hackins, the landlord.

Chapter VIII

❧

IN THE morning, Hoare found Mr. Watt despondent. He must have crept back into Hoare's sitting room at dawn or before, for a crust of bread and an empty teacup lay on the worktable. He had almost finished copying the last mysterious message.

"I have been unable, sir, to break the code—or rather the cipher," he said. "It may be one of those in which the key is to be found in certain pages of a book owned by all parties to the secret. The Bible is commonly used for that purpose, as I am sure you know, and if you consider the biblical names of writer and addressee, it is likely that it has been so used here.

"Often the encipherer gives in the first group or two the chapters or pages to be used in deciphering; that each of the three messages commences with two series of numbers suggests that to be the case.

"If this is the case, Mr. Hoare, we are lost without a key to what pages of what edition are used and how. However, I propose to you that I take with me the fair copies I have made and work on them during *Vantage's* passage south. I can inform you by fleet mail of any successes I have.

"But in all fairness, I must remind you that I lay no claim to expertise in the art of the cipher. There are men in Whitehall who spend their entire lives on the subject. I believe you should present these messages there."

With this, Mr. Watt stood and prepared to take his leave. "*Vantage* is about to weigh anchor," he said, "and I would not commit the crime of desertion, even if only inadvertently. She is, after all, only my second ship, and I still have my name to make."

"I'll put you aboard myself," Hoare replied on an impulse.

Thereupon the two men betook themselves to *Alert's* berth, where Hoare cast off and set sail to work down the Solent to Spithead. The little clerk's efforts to bear a hand scarcely hindered Hoare at all.

Indeed, *Vantage* showed every sign of imminent departure. As Hoare brought *Alert* to under her lee, the frigate's fresh new anchor cable was inching its way aboard to the "stamp and go" at the capstan and the squeal of the ship's fiddler. Her access ladder had already been drawn up, so he had to use his boatswain's pipe to signal the people on deck that it must be replaced if Captain Kent was to get his clerk back.

"Calm seas, and a prosperous voyage to you!" the envious Hoare said to Mr. Watt in his best whisper as he helped his passenger aboard. He would miss the clerk, and the exclamatory little Mr. Prickett as well.

Hoare said to himself that he owed it to *Vantage* to see her off to war, backed the yacht's jib, and hove her to. *Vantage's* anchor stock rose into the morning sun; her topsails thundered briefly and filled in their classic curve to take her out of the Spithead anchorage. She began to gather way in the light morning breeze, fair, gleaming, and virginal. *Alert* kept pace with her less than a cable length to leeward, on a parallel course. A light shower passed over the two vessels, and the sun broke through again.

Hoare heard a soft *poof. Vantage*'s wheel and her helmsman spun into the air in a fiery cloud, taking part of her main topsail yard with them, and plunged into the water between *Vantage* and *Alert*.

"Away, the fire party!" came faintly across the water. "Man hoses! Flood magazines!" Hoare swung his vessel's tiller to leeward and hauled in fore- and mainsheets, bringing her hard on the wind so as to close the frigate.

A blaze of yellow-orange light dazzled him; a deep concussion shook the whole roadstead. *Alert* heeled heavily away from the burst, nearly set on her beam ends. A last, stupefying thunder and *Vantage*'s magazine went up, and she came apart.

Fighting through a hideous rain of wood, cordage, metal, and body parts, Hoare rammed *Alert* into a cable-wide circle of roiled, wreckage-filled water. The air through which he drove her reeked of burnt powder, as if he were sailing into a fleet action once again.

He reached down into the cluttered sea to grasp a reaching hand. The arm attached to it was, in turn, attached to nothing. He dropped it.

Here was a hat, floating upside down like a merry little boat. Here was part of what must have been *Vantage*'s maintop; a naked black man was clinging to it. As Hoare passed him a line and the cooked skin peeled off the hand that took it, he saw that the man was not black by nature. The barge's low rail peeled more skin loosely from the man's body as Hoare drew him aboard. He coughed up bloody water and died there, on *Alert*'s deck.

Hoare drew another raw, pulpy thing inboard instinctively but then cast it overboard again like a trash fish. *Alert*'s deck had small enough space for the living; she would have no more room for the dead.

He heard someone croaking, "Oh, Jesus, oh, Jesus, oh, Jesus," and realized that the cry had been going on for some time. From the raw agony in his throat he knew that the voice had been his.

Hoare pulled in twelve more, plus the roasted man, before he was joined first by the few nearby harbor fishermen and then—too late to save anything but the dead—by a flotilla of ships' boats that had pulled double-banked out of the anchorage to save life. Of *Vantage*'s company, 327 souls in all, the other rescuers recovered only another 9.

Returning, heavy-laden, to Portsmouth, Hoare unloaded his castaways on the Hard, where a crowd of the curious and the anxious waited to succor the living and bewail the lost. When the other boats had all returned, the harried officer who had taken charge told Hoare that he had counted twenty-four survivors all told. Most were topmen who had been thrown clear, most of them frightfully burned, broken, or both. Of *Vantage*'s afterguard Hoare heard no names he knew.

Within the hour, Patterson, Sir George Hardcastle's secretary, called at the Swallowed Anchor Inn. He brought Sir George's compliments, and would Mr. Hoare kindly attend on him without delay?

The Admiral's pet rabbit had been warned, for he opened Sir George's inner door the moment Hoare presented himself.

"I had not expected to request your attendance again so soon, Mr. Hoare," the Admiral said, looking up from a disordered mass of papers. His face, usually impassive, was filled with weariness and sorrow.

"I trust you have made some progress with the matter we discussed at our last meeting?"

"No, sir, I have not, I regret to state," Hoare said. "Mr. Watt received orders to return aboard *Vantage* before he had any success. He left the enciphered messages with me, which was fortunate in the circumstances, given this morning's disaster."

"Indeed. God rest his soul, and those of his shipmates. It is about that incident that I wish to talk with you. Go away, Patterson, and close the door after you. Come back in ten minutes."

When Patterson had closed the door firmly and resentfully behind him, the Admiral continued.

"What I am about to reveal to you, sir, must not leave these four walls. You know, of course, of the loss of *Scipio.* Your recent visit to Weymouth had to do with that. But are you aware that that, and the explosion in *Vantage,* are only two out of several similar events?"

"No, sir."

"Good. The matter is most secret. If news of it were to get abroad in the Fleet, I shudder to think of the consequences. Spithead and the Nore would be nothing in comparison.

"On 2 June the schooner *Mischief,* 18, blew apart in the middle of the Channel Fleet. She had just made her number to *Vengeance,* 84, flag, having newly joined from this station. *Megara,* 32, also out of Portsmouth, is four weeks late in reporting to Calder in the Bay of Biscay."

"This is dire news indeed, sir," Hoare whispered.

"Moreover," the Admiral said, "news has just reached me from Their Lordships that Oglethorpe of the *Royal Duke* has died. It is no surprise. He was seventy-six, after all, had just lost his wife, and could scarcely walk. You knew of Oglethorpe?"

Hoare shook his head. He was in puzzlement. What had the dead Oglethorpe to do with him, or he with Oglethorpe? Perhaps he was to replace the late captain? Hardly. A lieutenant did not step directly into the shoes of a post captain unless the latter fell in battle.

"No, sir."

"Or of *Royal Duke,* perhaps?"

"No, sir."

"Good. Then *that* secret, at least, has held. *Royal Duke*'s an Admiralty yacht—mounts six . . . never mind. She bears an exalted name, even more exalted than *Inconceivable,* perhaps, or *Insupportable,* or *Alert.* Oh, yes. Young Gladden, who keeps sniffing after my poor fat Felicia like a hound after a bitch in heat, has told me about the ghost fleet you keep hidden. So have others. Oglethorpe and his command serve—served, I should say—under Admiral Abercrombie."

Hoare knew, at least, of Sir Hugh Abercrombie, KB, Vice Admiral of the White. Sir Hugh held no seagoing command, and Hoare had no idea of his role in the Navy. He had the impression that he held office in the Admiralty. In any case, Sir George did not seem ready to enlighten him.

"At present," Sir George said, "you need know no more about Admiral Abercrombie, Captain Oglethorpe, or *Royal Duke.* At some suitable time, you may have occasion to know them all—except, of course, poor Oglethorpe, that is. The present point is that Oglethorpe's talents are lost to us at a crucial moment.

"Now, sir, while I can hardly expect you, at your tender age, to be able to fill poor Oglethorpe's shoes, you have demonstrated similar talents."

"Sir?" Hoare had no notion of what Sir George was telling him, and his perplexity must have shown.

"Snooping, Mr. Hoare. Snooping, sneaking, and ferreting about like a damned bloodhound, with your tongue hangin' out. Tucking facts away, as a squirrel does with nuts. You rooted the man Kingsley out as if you'd been a pig sniffing for truffles. Before that, of course, there was the *Amazon* affair."

All things considered, Hoare thought, Sir George could call him a squirrel, a pig, or an illegitimate mud turtle for that matter, whenever he wanted, as long as the insults accompanied what sounded like praise. Was this the grim flag officer he had come to know and fear?

"I want you to find the cause of these explosions, Mr. Hoare, forthwith," the Admiral said. "I am issuing you orders to that effect.

"Patterson!" he bellowed. "Bring your writing gear!

"Now, Patterson," he said, "take this down. Put it into proper form; make a fair copy for my signature. Log and file the original.

"Until further orders, Mr. Hoare," Sir George continued, "you are to devote your fullest attention to determining and uprooting the cause of these losses.

"In the furtherance of this task, you are authorized to draw any reasonable funds from the authorities at Portsmouth and commandeer such manpower and equipment as may be ready to hand. You may refer to me any member of the service who cavils at providing such aid as you may require.

"Patterson, make sure that Hoare also has a general travel warrant and a supply of forms. That will be all. Wait outside until Patterson here has finished his scribbling."

The orders Patterson handed him at last defined neither "reasonable" nor "ready to hand," but Hoare was of no mind to quibble. Duty would have made him ready to begin rooting without ado; curiosity would have added urgency. Admiral Hardcastle's words just now were a spur for an already willing horse. If Hoare so chose, he could have taken them to mean that if he, at the end of some unstated period of servitude, had—like Heracles—cleaned enough stables and killed enough monsters, the Admiral might find him a berth at sea. Situated as he was, Hoare *did* so choose. Besides, he wanted to make someone pay for the flayed and mangled men he had pulled out of the sea that morning.

He left the Admiral's place of business, feeling quite as merciless as Sir George himself.

Chapter IX

⟫◆⟪

WHILE HOARE knew that some of his fellow officers were as happy on horseback as they were on a quarterdeck, he himself despised horses. Unlike those who claimed to find parallels between Noble Steeds of the Field and White-winged Chariots of the Sea, he found the beasts disorderly, disobedient, unpredictable, and happy to shit and fart about wherever they pleased, leaving their nasty doings underfoot to be trodden in. At least, though, his father had seen to it that, like them or not, he learned to handle the silly things without making an utter fool of himself.

So here he was, aboard a perfectly decent bay cob, trotting comfortably along in a light mist toward Wells, like any stupid squire on his way to Sunday matins. He had hired the thing instead of taking the regular *Racer* coach from Portsmouth to Bath and thence doubling back to Wells. He had felt that he would rather go at his own pace than be jammed into a rocking box at the mercy of some drunken, rapacious coachman. However awkward the cob might be, he—Bartholomew

Hoare—was in command. He needed only to make it clear to the cob that mutiny would have dire consequences.

The beast pecked at a stone, and he brought its head up, just as if he were helping *Alert* through a gust in the Solent. It made him feel rather pleased with himself. For once, he felt grateful to Captain Joel Hoare for making him spend so many mornings falling from the creatures' yardarms.

The horse slopped through a puddle, then stopped, straddled, and pissed hugely. That was exactly what irritated Hoare; no ship would have taken it in mind to heave to like this of its own volition, in midvoyage.

The horse's behavior gave Hoare's bladder an idea of its own. He dismounted and held the bay's reins while he added his own much smaller stream.

It began to rain again. Pulling an oiled-cotton cover over his second-best hat, he remounted and got the cob under way again. Not for the first time in this passage to Wells, he began to wonder what he had done. He hoped—devoutly, of course—considering his reason for being on it in the first place, that the catechism he planned for the soon-to-be-Reverend Arthur Gladden would bear fruit. After all, by the time he had journeyed to Wells and back, he would have taken four days out of his available time. To compensate, he must needs forgo as many days of relaxation on the water, in *Alert*.

The mist darkened as Hoare jogged into Wells. A few heavier drops began to spatter on the cob's forequarters and his own hat. With a few questions of passers-by, he found the Mitre Inn, which his own landlord, Hackins, had recommended. Hoare told the hostler's boy to have his beast made comfortable and readied for the homeward journey tomorrow. He gave no detailed orders, nor did he offer to care for the animal himself, as Hoare senior had told him every proper horseman made it a matter of honor to do. It was not his horse but a hireling, and the boy would know infinitely better what maintenance it needed.

Hoare needed no direction to Wells Cathedral the next morning, for its tower loomed over the old town like a first-rate among a fleet of shallops. Besides, its soft-toned, power-ful bells began to toll the hour, all too early in the day. He was happy not only to find that Arthur Gladden was known to the verger-gatekeeper at the door to the cathedral close, but also to catch sight of the man himself. The former lieutenant came pacing thoughtfully toward him along a cloister, well out of the rain, head in a small black book, unaware of his sur-roundings. The deacon?—ordinand?—was already clad in the uniform of his new service. In his cassock, he looked much more comfortable than he had in naval uniform—holy per-haps, it seemed to Hoare, instead of harried. Certainly the breeches under the cassock would be unsoiled.

Gladden looked up to see who was blocking his way, blinked, and smiled in recognition. He grasped Hoare's hand in a soft, clerical grip.

"Mr. Hoare! I hardly hoped you would be able to take leave from your duties in Portsmouth, but I had prayed you would come, and lo! my prayers have been answered."

Hoare had never thought to hear anyone actually say, "Lo!" out loud. For the sake of whatever flock Gladden was destined to lead, Hoare hoped that the man would become less godly once he was ordained.

"To tell the truth, Gladden, I am here only to ask you a question or two, if I may."

"Anything, Mr. Hoare, anything. After all, I owe my life to you. Come, sit beside me on this convenient bench."

Hoare took the indicated place. "First, though, I fear I bring bad news. Did you know that *Vantage* blew up and sank a few days ago, carrying all but twenty-four of her crew with her?"

"My God." Gladden turned white to the lips. "Only twenty-four saved? Who? How?"

"She blew up somehow, within half an hour of setting sail. I saw it all, from my yacht."

Gladden bowed his head—in prayer, Hoare supposed, in light of his calling. The astonished Hoare saw a pair of tears drop onto the cassock, where they rested and twinkled in the sunlight before sinking into the fine black wool.

At last, Gladden looked up. He reached into a pocket of the cassock and drew out a handkerchief, with which he blew his nose thunderously.

"Forgive me, sir," he said. "I have always been prone to tears in moments of stress. And, while I cannot claim to have found any bosom friends among my fellow Vantages, they were my shipmates, after all, as well as fellow Christians. Mr. Wallace, the Marine?"

"Lost."

"Mr. McHale? Mr. Courtney? Hopkin? The child Prickett?"

"Lost . . . all lost."

"I do not ask about Mr. Kingsley. I have heard of his capture and death. May God have mercy on his soul." Hoare saw Gladden actually shake himself, like a wet dog. "But you had questions to ask me?" he said.

"Yes. About Kingsley, in fact. You are the only surviving member of *Vantage*'s afterguard, and the only one who can give me an impression of him."

"What do you want to know?"

"Anything that comes to mind."

"It is not easy to speak of him, Mr. Hoare," Gladden said. *"De mortuis,* you know. I knew him before we were both seconded into *Vantage.* He had the experience to be a good officer, I believe, although he spent little time on his duties. How he managed to obtain his captain's approval of as much leave from *Vantage* as he took I could never understand. After all, she was fitting out. Perhaps Mrs. Hay persuaded her husband?

"For he was an arrant womanizer, as you know. But he also busied himself as much with the commanders and post captains of the vessels at Spithead as he did with their sweethearts and wives. It was almost as if he had appointed himself an ambassador of good will from the Port Admiral to new arrivals, for within hours after one of His Majesty's ships had made her number, there would be Mr. Kingsley in his hired shallop, bearing gifts.

"I often wondered why. Perhaps . . . he had little interest, to be sure, and knew what its lack could do to his career. There were those in *Vantage*'s wardroom who sneered at his encroaching ways, his fawning upon every post captain he could reach. His private life was licentious, his public life dissolute, his behavior in society obsequious, his treatment of inferiors overbearing. May God forgive me, I did not like him.

"That is all I can tell you, Mr. Hoare. We were a new ship, and for the most part her officers were still practically strangers to one another. Kingsley was sinfully deluded. That is all I know."

"Did you know of Mrs. Hay's liaison with Kingsley?"

The mouth of the priest-to-be primmed. "I did not *know*, exactly, but I confess I found their behavior somewhat suggestive. In fact, I . . . but no, surely not."

"What?" Hoare pressed.

"I wondered if Captain Hay knew something was going on between them.

"I am sorry," Gladden concluded, "that you found it necessary to come so far for my small crumbs of intelligence, but I hope it means that you will attend tomorrow's service? There will be a small reception following the ceremony." He looked up at Hoare, almost shyly.

"With the greatest of pleasure, sir," Hoare whispered. From Gladden's cool but understanding analysis of his late shipmate's character he, Hoare thought, might have the makings of a priest, after all.

THE CEREMONY OF ordination was new to Hoare—no churchgoer as a rule—and he observed it with interest. The bishop was, as Hoare thought the late Mr. Kingsley might have put it, the lead player, but he was supported by a choir and no fewer than four other clergymen. When all five laid hands on Gladden's bowed head and then upon the heads of the two other ordinands, Hoare had to suppress a smile. Gladden's head, he thought, was more crowded with hands than the gun deck of an 84 on her first night in port, after the hands' women had boarded. On this occasion, at least, no women were involved, so there were none of those rhythmical grunts and squeals from the hands and their guests in the double-shotted hammocks.

Hoare had found himself a modest place toward the rear of the cathedral, where its peculiar reversed arch separated him from the proceedings at the altar, so the prayers, psalms, hymns, and other goings-on up forward came only faintly to his ears. But he had ample opportunity to inspect the entire godly crew as it passed him in stately double line ahead, singing a measured recessional hymn and accompanied by the profound rumble of the cathedral organ. Tears came to Hoare's eyes. Organ music and a choir, with the trebles in descant, always did that to him. Perhaps that was why he was no longer churchly.

It seemed to him that the newly Reverend Arthur Gladden's face showed a special exaltation, raised as it was above a brand-new strip of embroidered silk freshly draped over his shoulders. What was the thing called? A crope? A style? For the life of him, Hoare could not remember. He was certain of one thing: When it came to pomp and circumstance, even the Navy could learn a lot from the Church. Of course, he reminded himself, the Church had been at it quite a few years longer than the Navy.

He said as much to the former third in *Vantage* when he made his way up the line of well-wishers in the cathedral close to congratulate him. Gladden smiled vaguely, then turned to the older couple beside him.

"Papa? Mamma? May I introduce my Savior?"

Lady Gladden's eyes opened wide. Had her son just capitalized the word?

"I mean, of course, Mr. Bartholomew Hoare, the man who saved our name from disgrace and me from death."

Hoare made his leg and bowed over Lady Gladden's proffered hand. "The Navy's loss is the Church's gain, I am sure," he whispered. The simper she returned would have made a honeybee gag.

Sir Ralph Gladden was a wealthy, idle half-pay captain waiting his way comfortably up the ladder to Admiral of the Yellow, a strapping prizewinning specimen of the squire breed, flaxen-haired like his sons. He took Hoare's hand in both his own and gripped it hard.

He cleared his throat, as if embarrassed. "Let me introduce you to my daughter," he said. "Anne, may I present Mr. Bartholomew Hoare of the Navy?"

Forever afterward Hoare thanked his gods—whoever they were—for not looking about him in search of the young lady. He could never have forgiven himself for the insult. Happily, he looked down instead, to see a bonneted face looking back up at him out of amused periwinkle-blue eyes. The young person should still have been in pantalettes. Certainly she was too young to be out—but no; the figure, in pale blue lutestring, had breasts. She was a well-formed young woman, not a child. But she was wee.

Hoare bowed over the upstretched, gloved hand. "I am charmed, Miss Gladden."

"Both my brothers have told me of your service to the

Gladden family, sir," she said. "We are grateful to you today, as well as proud of Arthur."

Sir Ralph took up the thanks of his daughter. They went on and on. They were heartfelt, perhaps, but Hoare found them onerous and begged to be excused as soon as the knight stopped for breath.

Released at last, Hoare had found the ham and the syllabub when a soft masculine voice spoke into his ear.

"So, sir. Our neophyte priest believes a *whore* was his savior? Or—heresy of heresies—that his savior was a whore? I could not help but overhear the words of the hero in our recent little liturgical drama."

It was the Graveses' acquaintance from Weymouth, Mr. Edward Morrow, as swarthy and sardonic as before.

"Forgive my coarseness, Mr. Hoare, as well as the highly improper play on your name," Morrow said. "I am doubly guilty and must make my confession to one of the exalted ladies of Bath. But I was so pleased to see you that I let my tongue run away from me. Will *you,* instead, grant me absolution, sir?"

The smile that accompanied the Canadian's words seemed oddly forced, which made the man himself all the more mysterious.

Looking beyond Mr. Morrow, Hoare saw Dr. Graves in his wheeled chair, deep in conversation with his wife and the forgettable Miss Austen. At the sight of Mrs. Graves, his heart leapt unaccountably.

"Well-met, Mr. Hoare," Dr. Graves said. "What brought you to Wells, of all places?"

Hoare explained he was there by invitation from the Gladdens. "And you?" he asked.

"Two purposes," the doctor said. "First, we are actually visiting Bath and not Wells. Miss Austen was kind enough to reciprocate our earlier invitation to her. It has been over a year since we came to Bath, and we were commencing to feel a trifle dull in Weymouth.

"Then, too, I had reports of a Dr. Ellison's having considerable success with problems of palsy such as my own and wished to consult him. It appears, however, that my lower half has atrophied too far for his regimen to take effect."

"And Mr. Morrow kindly offered us his carriage," Eleanor Graves interjected. "It is more commodious than our chaise. Then he offered to drive us, and how could we refuse?"

"So there you are, sir," Morrow said.

Hoare accompanied his acquaintances to Mr. Morrow's carriage, escorting Miss Austen. As they walked, the lady explained that she had dragged the doctor and his wife to this morning's ceremony in order to have comfortable transportation at no cost to herself. Lady Caroline Gladden had been a childhood friend of her late mother, and a match between Miss Austen and Peter Gladden had once been mooted.

Hoare only pretended to listen, for he was trying to eavesdrop on the trio ahead of him. Their conversation mystified him. It sounded as if Morrow was pressing some action upon the doctor, for Hoare heard Dr. Graves say, in a voice that displayed more than a little irritation, "No, no, Morrow. No more than I could the last time you urged me. I can still do no such thing. I pray you, sir, oblige me and refrain from mentioning the subject again."

In the absence of Mrs. Graves's girl Agnes, Hoare helped Morrow boost the doctor into the Canadian's carriage and hitched the wheeled chair to it. Hat in hand, he stood to watch his four acquaintances bowl away toward Bath. The chair followed along, looking like a jolly boat being towed behind a sixth-rate. He retrieved his horse and his saddlebags from the Mitre and set out on his own return journey to Portsmouth. He had barely exchanged a word with Eleanor Graves.

As THE COB jogged easily along, Hoare chided himself for having chosen to come to Wells at all. The voyage had wasted four days. He had learned only that Kingsley had been a bot-fly of a man, ever looking for a place to light and bite. With women, he had been avid for their bodies; with men, his avidity had been for interest. He had been wont to bear gifts about in eternal hope of achieving one goal or the other.

Not an attractive man, to be sure, but still, what had Kingsley done to deserve being shot in the back of the head when he was already as good as sentenced to hang? Admiral Hardcastle had wondered aloud what important secrets that rakehell lieutenant had owned that could have required his silencing. Hoare had as yet come no closer to an answer.

His mind turned and writhed like a cluster of earthworms, squirming and getting nowhere. He forced it into another channel, an intriguing one, but nothing that called for his formal involvement: the matter of Mrs. Graves and those two mysterious attackers. At Wells, she had made no reference to her adventure or to the death of one attacker at her hands, which had so clearly disturbed her at first.

Morrow had brought a peculiar little party to Bath and thence to Wells. Not the least peculiar was Morrow himself, with his insinuating approach to Mrs. Graves and the near-malice that he showed to Hoare. What had Morrow been pressing upon Dr. Graves so persistently that the doctor had needed to chide him?

Restless and dissatisfied with himself, Hoare decided to bait at Warminster, some eighteen miles on, change horses there, and continue to Portsmouth through the night.

THE NEW HACK was a sorrel instead of a bay. Its home stable must have been in Winchester, if not Portsmouth itself, for it was quite ready to have its sleep interrupted. As it jogged along, Hoare found himself reexamining his earlier reveries. He felt as a master weaver must, trying to unravel an apprentice's botched work. There had to be a common thread in the case, or a repeated knot.

Captain Hay's murder? Kingsley's murder? He dozed and—dozing—dreamed. Something about Mrs. Graves, about the anker. Alternately waking and dozing, as he had taught himself to do during long, uneventful night watches at sea, he let the sorrel hack carry him homeward.

FOUR DAYS LATER, on arriving at the Victualling Office, Hoare found a letter lying on his flimsy desk. He remembered the hand from his evening in Weymouth with Dr. Graves and his lady. His heart gave a palpable thump. What was happening to him?

My dear Mr. Hoare [he read]:

Even though it can hardly concern you as a naval officer, I have been told that you are also a skilled investigator, so I make bold to inform you of my husband's death the night before last, and to beg your assistance, as a friend, in bringing his killer or killers to justice.

Here is a summary of the facts as I know them. On Tuesday night I had retired, leaving Dr. Graves to his correspondence. I was awakened by the sound of an explosion in the street outside; this was followed by a crashing noise below stairs. I took the candle which I keep at my bedside in case my husband required assistance and descended to the ground floor.

I found my husband in his study-workshop. He had fallen forward out of his chair. His head had struck the table before him, and the blow had cut open his forehead. He was quite dead—not from the blow, but from a bullet which had penetrated his chair and continued into his back.

I sent our manservant to Sir Thomas Frobisher posthaste

with the news of Simon's death. He arrived within the hour, and was followed shortly by Mr. Morrow.

Both gentlemen are justices of the peace, so they will, of course, attempt to discover the murderer of my husband. However, I am less than confident than either their time or their inclinations will lead them to do so with the dedication the inquiry will certainly demand. For I am frankly not without suspicion that one of the two gentlemen—I have no notion of which—may not be devoid of self-interest in the matter.

When my husband died, he had evidently been engaged with a small, indecipherable document which I saw myself, beneath his hand. It is not now to be found. Neither Sir Thomas not Mr. Morrow could recall having seen such a paper. In fact, Sir Thomas suggested that the shock of finding my husband dead had left me subject to delusions.

I know myself, Mr. Hoare, and I know what I saw.

Dr. Graves was a kindly, gentle, and talented man. I will have his killer brought to justice, and I will not be denied. I would therefore deem it more than friendly of you if you were to come once again to the aid of your sorrowing friend and obedient servant,

Eleanor Graves

Chapter X

———◦———

*H*OARE ADMITTED to himself that the devices that had produced the explosions in the fleet had probably been loaded in Portsmouth. But, he told himself now as he had told Sir George Hardcastle before, Mrs. Graves might, after all, be able to decipher the message that had defeated Mr. Watt. She had seen "a small, illegible document" on her husband's desk, and it had disappeared. Moreover, he reminded himself, the mysterious anker—the keg that had brought him to Lyme Regis—had come ashore on Portland Bill. Old Dee had told him so. Thus, his decision to point *Unimaginable* westward to Weymouth once again could have had nothing directly to do with the widow's appeal.

He had not seen the late doctor's house by daylight before. Standing in the early summer sunshine, it was a graceful brick structure, suited to the successful physician who had owned it. The door and ground-floor windows were draped with black and purple swags. So was the sorrowful maid Agnes, who ushered Hoare into the drawing room where Dr. Graves had demonstrated his listening device and where he had first raised and then destroyed Hoare's hopes of recovering his voice. Mrs. Graves already awaited him there, seated on her tuffet. This morning, in her glossy black weeds, she looked not like a partridge but like a rook or a small raven. Her expression, even more than Sir George Hardcastle's, was grim and merciless. His heart did not thump, but went out to her.

Mrs. Graves cut off Hoare's whispered condolences before he had properly begun them. "Thank you for coming in answer to my letter, Mr. Hoare," she said. "I shall not take up your time with empty courtesies. Tell me, sir; what can I do to advance your inquiry?"

"Tell me in the fullest detail what happened on the night of Dr. Graves' death."

"But I put everything into my letter, sir."

Hoare shook his head. "No, Mrs. Graves. That would be impossible, even for a professional observer. For instance, you did not tell me the time of night that the shot awakened you. How was your husband dressed? How was his office lit? And so forth."

He stopped to rest his whisper. "In fact," he continued, "would it disturb you to reenact the event itself, at the place where it occurred?"

"If by 'disturb' you mean 'arouse painful memories,' Mr. Hoare, not in the least. My memories of my husband transcend place."

She seemed to choke, recovered, and went on. "And I am not afraid of ghosts. Besides, I am sure that Simon's ghost, if there were such a thing, would be a gentle one . . . to me, at least. So let us proceed as you ask." She rose from her tuffet and began to lead the way into the front hall.

"Do you wish us to commence in my bedroom," she asked over her shoulder, "where, of course, the shot awakened me? Or will it be sufficient for me to begin at the foot of the stairs?"

Hoare felt strangely disturbed at the idea of seeing the lady's chamber. "We can begin here," he whispered.

"Very well. You asked me what time of the night it was. I can only estimate it, for while this clock under the stairs must have chimed, I fear I was too distracted to notice it. It rang four just as Sir Thomas entered, so I would judge that it was about three in the morning."

Hoare nodded.

"As I believe I wrote in my letter," she went on, "I was awakened by a shot. With it came the sound of something below me, falling. When my husband is working below stairs, I keep a candle burning, so that I will not need to grope about for flint and steel if an emergency should arise. I used the candle to light my way downstairs. I could see light coming into the hall from my husband's study-workshop."

Mrs. Graves walked into the study, which lay diagonally across the hall from the drawing room. Hoare now saw it for the first time. It was a peculiar place, half-library, half-laboratory. On one side, low counters supported a variety of instruments and vessels that Hoare, at least, found quite daunting. He could recognize retorts, measuring glasses, microscopes. A handsome Herschel telescope stood in a corner in its glowing mahogany case, awaiting its departed master. He could not imagine the use of some of them; he found some oddly beautiful. They glittered in the sunlight like a small trove.

Set apart in one corner, under a high north-facing window, a table bore a multitude of clean, tiny instruments including what Hoare believed was a miniature lathe. A few possible products of this machine lay in clean white porcelain saucers—tiny gears and pinions that could only be portions of clockwork mechanisms. Several mounted magnifying glasses stood about. The center of the table was clear, as if to provide the experimenter with ample work space.

"Was it at this table that he did his experiments?" Hoare asked.

"No. The table is an addition of the last three months," said Mrs. Graves. "My husband had taken to the study of Mr. Whitney's principle, as it might apply to watchmaking."

"Mr. Whitney's principle?"

"An American by the name of Eli Whitney, Mr. Hoare. I know little about him, except for what Simon told me. He has apparently found a way of producing the locks of muskets in considerable volume, by somehow making components that are identical. I remember Simon saying that the man astonished a group of gunsmiths by assembling complete locks from several heaps of parts.

"To tell you the truth, I know no more than that."

The other, literary half of the room looked more familiar to Hoare. The rows of filled bookshelves lifted all the way to the plain ceiling. The shelves, however, were unusual. Being unable to walk, let alone climb the usual rolling library steps, the doctor had devised a pair of endless chains, between which the bookshelves hung on gimbals so that they remained forever upright.

Apparently, the doctor could control these chains from his chair, so that he could make them present him with the shelf or shelves he needed at the moment. Hoare was tempted to try the mechanism himself, but now was hardly the time.

Between the two parts of the chamber were a low cot with gleaming brass handrails that the doctor could grip when moving from chair to bed and back, and his writing desk. Except for a magnifying glass and the usual writing materials, the surface of the desk was quite bare. The doctor's empty wheeled chair faced it, some three feet away. The floor between chair and desk bore marks of the doctor's lifeblood, and spots of blood marred the desk's top.

"I found Simon slumped forward in his wheeled chair," Mrs. Graves went on. "His forehead had been thrown forward onto the desk. There were drops of blood from his forehead on his papers. I knew immediately that he was dead.

134

"But his death was not due to the wound in his forehead. As I had thought, the sound that awakened me was a shot. Someone standing in the back lane outside behind the house had taken aim at my husband as he sat at the table with his back to the open window and fired a single bullet at him. It penetrated his chair . . . here—you can see the hole it made—and continued into Simon's back. It was the shock of the bullet hitting him that drove his face into the table.

"I ran into the back hall and called out to waken the servants. Then I sat down on the floor beside my husband and took his poor head in my arms."

"The message you mentioned?" Hoare prompted her.

"It was not in Simon's handwriting. As I remember it, the words were very even. Beside it was the paper on which Simon had been writing when he was killed, with a splash of ink where he had dropped his pen. But to tell the truth, Mr. Hoare, I barely noticed the arrangement of the desk at the time. My mind was elsewhere. When the servants entered, I sent our man Tom to Sir Thomas and Mr. Morrow with the news. The two arrived within minutes of each other."

"Which gentleman arrived first?" Hoare asked.

Mrs. Graves shook her head. "I fear I do not recall, sir. They both said all the proper things, I suppose, and did what must be done, but by then I had begun to be a trifle confused. One of them—Sir Thomas, I suppose, as the senior magistrate—took charge of affairs. It must have been he who had Simon's body removed from the chair and laid out decently on his bed.

"I am ashamed to say that from that moment until the next morning—the Wednesday—I remember nothing. I awakened in my own bed, with no knowledge of how I got there. In fact, I was hard put to it to recall any of the previous night's events. It seems that Agnes, who I am sure meant well, administered a draft to me, unaware that Mr. Morrow had already taken it upon himself to do so."

"Mr. Morrow? How would he have found . . . ?"

"Mr. Morrow has become quite familiar with my husband's workplace. I believe that is to be laid at *your* door, Mr. Hoare."

This brought Hoare up all standing. "I do not understand you, ma'am," he protested.

"Simon had little to say to me about the project in which he was engaged with Mr. Morrow," the widow said. "He was always very closemouthed about his doings, both as a physician and as a natural philosopher or mechanician—whichever term you prefer. But he gave me to understand the two were experimenting with nonmedical uses of the listening device which so caught Mr. Morrow's interest when you and he dined with us a fortnight ago."

That explanation was as good as any. Hoare himself had noticed the American's interest in the instrument. He went on to the matter of most immediate interest.

"And the message? When did you notice it was missing?" he whispered.

"After I came to my senses on Wednesday morning," Mrs. Graves said. "I returned to where we are now standing, to greet my dead husband. The servants had had mercy on me, for his body was cleaned and decently laid out on his cot.

"I sat down beside him once again for a moment, to share with him a few last memories. Then I recalled myself to duty and went to his writing table to begin informing those who should be informed . . . his sons, of course, and a few more distant relatives.

"That was when I realized the document that interests you so much had disappeared from the worktable. So, too, had the sheet upon which Simon had been writing. The Bible, though, was still there, right where it is now."

"The Bible?"

"Did I not tell you, sir? Here." She took the familiar black volume and offered it to Hoare, who leafed through it.

"But it's in French!" he exclaimed.

"Which makes it doubly peculiar," she said. "As a rule, Dr. Graves would hardly have been reading his Bible at all, let alone in French. He was no more godly than myself, I fear. We have not been well regarded at St. Ninian's. In fact, I was surprised when Mr. Witherspoon consented to pray over him. Nonetheless, my husband's knowledge of Scripture was as great as any bishop's. And he speaks—spoke—French as well as you or I speak English.

"In any event, I felt it important to know what Simon was doing in those last minutes before he was killed, so I took the occasion of his burial to ask Mr. Morrow and Sir Thomas if they knew anything of the documents. Neither gentlemen could tell me anything. In fact, it was then that Sir Thomas suggested I had imagined them. He reminded me, ever so gently, that I was already in a state of confusion and that I had subsequently swooned. Mr. Morrow—the two gentlemen were together—agreed. I did not swoon, Mr. Hoare. I never swoon. I was drugged."

"Drugged, ma'am?"

"Yes. As I told you just a minute ago, Mr. Morrow had administered a calmative draft from my husband's shelves, and my well-meaning abigail followed suit. I . . . did . . . not . . . swoon."

"I understand, ma'am," Hoare replied, trying to make his flat whisper sound as placatory as he could.

To his surprise, Mrs. Graves smiled. It was the first time Hoare had seen her dimples since that first evening, in this very house, when she had displayed her writing tricks.

She looked at him quizzically. "Has anyone ever told you, Mr. Hoare, that you could make your fortune on the stage? Your facial expressions—and, indeed, the motions of your entire body—give a remarkably clear picture of your state of mind. Perhaps it is a subtle way of communicating what a whisper such as yours cannot convey . . . a compensation, do you think?

"Forgive me, sir," she said. "I grow ever more impatient with men who assume that, because I am a woman, I am *mere* . . . not only feeble but foolish. I am neither.

"To return to the matter of the message: despite Sir Thomas and Mr. Morrow, there is clear evidence that there had been papers on my husband's table when he was killed, which were no longer there by the time I returned to this room.

"Look." She pointed to the table. "The spatters of blood have been wiped from its surface, but not before they left these stains in the wood. They were hard to see by candlelight, I suppose, against the polished mahogany, but there they are. Do you see what I see?"

Hoare nodded. Now that Mrs. Graves had pointed them out, he could see that several of the dark spots were not perfectly round. They were semicircles, as if part of the blood had fallen on another surface, which had then been abstracted. The ghostly outlines of two pieces of paper met his eyes, as clearly as if the sheets were still there.

"Shall I tell you what I think, Mr. Hoare?" Mrs. Graves asked.

Hoare nodded again.

"I believe one of my two callers that night removed the message for reasons of his own. And, since Edward Morrow had the most to do with my husband, I think I now suspect him of being the more likely culprit.

"Why he might behave in such an underhanded way can only be a matter of speculation, but it might have to do with the inquiry he and my husband were carrying out together. Perhaps the message related to some valuable discovery, which Mr. Morrow decided on the spot to arrogate to himself alone. But that, as I say, is only speculation, and in suggesting it I may be blackening the reputation of a blameless man."

Hoare made a mental note. He had long since decided he

must question both Mr. Morrow and Sir Thomas. His inquiry of Mr. Morrow, at least, would now have added substance.

"Would your witchcraft with the pen extend to a description of the message?" he asked.

"I have no witchcraft, Mr. Hoare," Mrs. Graves said sadly. "No broomstick could bear me; I am too stout."

Once again, a forthright remark of the widow's left Hoare at a stand.

"Let me try to show you, however," she said. "If you will be so kind as to bring me a chair . . . No, no, Mr. Hoare, not my husband's wheeled chair. Choose another, if you please."

The summer sun caught her hair as she settled herself down at the writing table. Hoare noted a few more white strands in it than he had seen when they first met on Portland Bill. She drew a fresh sheet to her and began to write.

"I cannot recover the words," she said. "In fact, I doubt they *were* words in the usual sense, for they were singularly uniform."

Looking over her shoulder, Hoare saw the "words" take shape. He had seen the selfsame formations not so long ago, on the tissue-paper messages Mr. Watt had studied so fruitlessly.

"The only word I could decipher was this last one," Mrs. Graves said as she wrote.

"Jehu!" Hoare's exclamation was a strangled grunt of triumph.

"Did you sneeze, sir?"

Hoare laughed. A woman of his acquaintance had described his laugh as the sound of a dropped eyelash. "No, ma'am. I said, 'Jehu,' as you were writing it down."

"Yes," she said. "The wild driver, you know. Second Kings, chapter 9, verse 20, I believe."

"I did not tell you, Mrs. Graves, but a series of documents with the same signature has come into my possession under suspicious circumstances. Tell me, are you also gifted at ciphering and deciphering secret codes?"

She shook her head. "No, sir." She paused. "Of course!" she cried. "The document was a ciphered message, and Simon had begun to translate it into readable form!"

"I do believe . . . ," Hoare began, but Mrs. Graves overrode his whisper. She handed Hoare her re-creation, and he pocketed it.

"Why, pray, would Mr. Morrow have abstracted it? And why would Simon have had it in his possession in the first place?"

Hoare shrugged. "We cannot even guess now, ma'am. Let us see how matters unfold."

"There is more, Mr. Hoare. Let us remove into my drawing room, where it is more comfortable and the memories are less painful."

When Mrs. Graves had resumed her tuffet, she continued.

"I have decided that since you are not only a naval officer but also evidently deal with confidential matters from time to time, I shall do England no harm by informing you of an activity in which my husband engaged himself on behalf of our country. He was sworn to secrecy. So, therefore, was I."

Hoare sat forward.

"An agent of the English intelligence service approached Simon several months ago. He had learned that Simon, besides being a physician of some standing, was also skilled in the contrivance of novel mechanisms of a scientific kind—not only clocks and watches with unusual properties but also orreries, for instance, and the like.

"He asked my husband if he could devise a sturdy, accurate mechanism that would sound a small signal bell at a preset time, as far ahead as a year from the time it was set. It would be used, the man said, as a check upon a vessel's longitude as determined by conventional means. I admit I do not understand how that was to be done, but then I am no navigator. Undoubtedly it will be obvious to you, Mr. Hoare."

"It is not, ma'am, but that is of no consequence. I was never a close student of the arts. As any midshipman must, I learned to fix my ship's position with clock, quadrant, and line of bearing, but no more. And even that experience is nearly ten years out-of-date."

"In any case, Simon built a first trial model, then a second improved design. I believe he constructed five or six of them all told."

"Do you know who the English agent was?" Hoare asked.

"No, Simon kept that information to himself, and I never spied on him."

"Of course not." Hoare's heart sank. "Thank you for telling me. I shall treat the information in the confidence it deserves."

At his request, Mrs. Graves now assembled the other witnesses at hand—the small staff of household servants—and withdrew to the drawing room so he could question them without her possibly disturbing presence. He quickly found that the maid, Agnes, and Mrs. Betts, the cook, had nothing to contribute save tearful words of woe.

Tom, the Graveses' manservant, had more interesting things to tell him.

"I thought I heard a shot like in the night, sir, but I was that tired, I rolls over and goes back to sleep till the mistress woke us by callin' up back stairs.

"Well, then I gets me breeches and shoes on, sir, and goes downstairs to Master's rooms. There Mistress is a-settin' on the floor in the middle of the room, a-holdin' of Master's head.

" 'Go quick, Tom,' she says, 'an' knock up Mr. Morrow an' Sir Thomas.' So I goes to Sir Thomas, who was abed, and then I goes uphill to Mr. Morrow, and then I comes home."

"Had Mr. Morrow also been in bed?"

" 'E were in shirt and breeches, sir, so I dunno."

"Thank you, Tom. You did quite right," Hoare whispered.

He followed Tom out of the doctor's workplace and made his way into the drawing room.

"I think I have finished my business here, ma'am," he said. "It only remains for me to call briefly upon Mr. Morrow and Sir Thomas, and to question the examiner . . . Dr. Olney, is it not?"

"Mr. Olney, sir," she said. "He is a surgeon, you will remember, and not a physician. As to the two gentlemen, may I speak a word of caution?"

"Please."

"Mr. Morrow is a very deep man, and proud. He built the competence left him into a fortune. He was not the first to discover the distaste our English gentry have for money earned in trade, as he earned his, instead of inheriting his wealth. He is therefore proud of having made his way into acceptance in our modest country society, and he is likely to resist anything that puts his hard-bought standing at risk.

"I have known Sir Thomas longer than I have Mr. Morrow. He is as proud of his ancestry as Mr. Morrow is of his accomplishments. He believes, I think, his blood to be a brighter blue than that of some of the nation's governors at Windsor and Whitehall, and is convinced that he is being refused the higher rank which he therefore deserves. He will brook no interferences in his reign over Weymouth and its environs. But there. You will laugh at my presumption."

"It is no presumption, ma'am. It sounds very much like keen perception."

"Thank you, Mr. Hoare," she said. "Be frank with me, then. You are prepared to help me in my pursuit of my husband's killer?"

"As far as my service duties permit, ma'am. The matter of the ciphers leads me to believe that there is, in fact, some connection between your late husband and the work of some less savory characters in Portsmouth."

At once, Hoare regretted these words, for Mrs. Graves's eyes grew cold. "Surely not, sir. Not only was he a cripple; despite his education in France, he was the most honest of Englishmen. Will you not explain yourself?"

"I had not known Dr. Graves was educated in France."

Mrs. Graves's voice was now far less cordial. She showed no dimples at all. "At Lyon, Toulouse, and the Sorbonne. He studied with both Dupuytren and Laënnec, as you already know. That is general knowledge.

"But I fear I keep you here under a misapprehension. I had hoped to enlist your help in tracking down my husband's killer, not in blackening his name as a loyal British subject. You know your way out, I believe. I bid you a good day, sir."

Hoare would not leave matters like this. He would not slink away. "I understand your concern, ma'am," he whispered. "I cannot believe him to have been a conscious party to any un-English action. But the cipher which you saw on his worktable, bearing the signature 'Jehu,' clearly ties him in some way to the late Lieutenant Kingsley, and Kingsley was less than an honorable man."

He cleared his throat painfully.

"In fact, it now appears that Kingsley, whom I knew as a debauchee and nothing more, may have been far more than that. He may have been involved in a plot of some nature. Possibly someone made use of him, and also of Dr. Graves' talents under some pretext. It is my duty to find out if that is, indeed, the case. If it is, I will see the culprit or culprits brought to justice."

By now, Mrs. Graves was also on her feet. This was no partridge; it was a kestrel that looked so fiercely up into Hoare's eyes.

"If you succeed in this mission of yours without sullying Simon's good name, well and good, sir. I shall be your debtor. But if you drag that name in the mud, you will have his widow to deal with. I shall be your enemy. Do not let me detain you. Good morning."

Her voice broke. She collapsed onto her tuffet and buried her face in her hands.

"You have no right," she sobbed. "No right. Kindly go away, Mr. Hoare, and leave me to my lonely grief."

"Go away now, zur," echoed Tom the manservant from the door. He watched with a stony face as Hoare sadly let himself out.

Chapter XI

⟸⬩◆⬩⟹

SHAMEFACED, HOARE trudged a long mile north out of town, past Gloster Row and Royal Crescent. He paid his penny at the turnpike and plodded on up the steep slope to Mr. Morrow's comfortable house on the hill crest. At the doorway a saddled horse stood waiting, hip-shot, in the spring sun. He wished the beast had been in his charge, for the walk, nearly an hour long and all uphill, had left him sweating heavily, though not out of breath. He named himself to the manservant and was admitted. Mr. Morrow appeared after a short delay, booted and spurred. To him, Hoare stated his errand.

"Frankly, sir," Morrow said, "I am at a stand as to your purpose here in Weymouth in the first place, let alone your curiosity about my affairs. Forgive my bluntness, but have you nothing better to do with your time than bother peaceable men who would prefer to be about their own business?"

"I am not troubling you out of idle curiosity, Mr. Morrow,"

Hoare replied in the mildest whisper he could summon, "but on a matter of serious concern to the Navy."

He sat expectant.

Morrow waited in vain for him to amplify what he had said. At last he said, "Well, then, Mr. Hoare, I see no harm in telling you I had asked Dr. Graves to determine whether the listening device with which he entertained us when first we met could be put to use in my quarry. It has long been known that stone with flaws or faults gives off a different sound when struck than clear, workable marble. It was my notion that with the doctor's device my men could make better selection of workplaces."

"Then you are familiar with Dr. Graves' own workplace, sir?" Hoare asked.

"Moderately, sir."

"Mrs. Graves tells me she saw some documents on her husband's worktable when she first came into the room . . . documents which she says were not present when she returned there the next morning."

"Aha. So that is where the land lies, eh?" Mr. Morrow said in a bleak voice. "The widow accuses me of abstracting one of the good doctor's discoveries for purposes of my own. At least, I trust that to be the explanation, sir, and that the accusation does not originate with you. For I hope I may be sure, sir, that, as an officer and a gentleman, you do not insinuate . . ." He paused significantly.

"I doubt neither your word nor your honesty, Mr. Morrow." At present, you prickly bastard, Hoare added to himself.

Morrow looked at him severely, as if to stare him down. "This interview is continuing longer than I had expected, sir," he said. "If you will excuse me for a few seconds, I have an urgent message I must send to the quarry. Please to make yourself comfortable."

Morrow was as good as his word, for he returned within

minutes. "As a matter of fact," Morrow went on more blandly, as if he had not interrupted himself, "I fear blame for Mrs. Graves' delusion may, indeed, lie in part at my door. For when I saw the distress under which she was laboring, I took the liberty of drawing a scruple of laudanum from the doctor's apothecary shelf and administering it to her. It produced some noticeable confusion in her mind.

"I was alarmed to learn later that the maid Agnes foolishly did the same thing, so doubling the dose and rendering the poor woman unconscious for some hours. Fortunately, the effect was transient, and she is none the worse for it—except for her confused conviction that I stole some of her husband's secrets. It may interest you to know Sir Thomas Frobisher is of my mind."

With this, Mr. Morrow rose to his feet with a meaningful look. Hoare must needs follow suit.

"And now, sir," the American said, "I must ask you to excuse me. As I said, there is a matter of considerable urgency at the quarry, to which I should be attending at this very moment.

"Let us not forget our engagement to match our yachts, Mr. Hoare," he added at the door. *"Marie Claire* and her crew stand ready, at your convenience. See? There she lies."

Mr. Morrow's voice was filled with pride. And justifiably so, Hoare thought. Schooner-rigged and half again the length of *Unimaginable, Marie Claire* gleamed as she lay at a mooring close inshore, easily visible from Morrow's hilltop house.

"Next time, sir," Hoare said. "I'll need a hand or two aboard if my craft is to do herself justice."

HOARE MUST NOW retrace his steps back into the town that lay displayed before him, its harbor twinkling in the sunlight. Sir Thomas Frobisher's dwelling would not have been out of place among the mansions of London's Mount Street. It must be staffed accordingly, for the big front door was opened by a bewigged footman in livery and pimples. Hoare named himself to the man, handed him his hat, and let himself be ushered into a large room to the left of the hallway, decorated in the latest French style. It was more than a trifle dusty.

Hoare had ample time to examine the mixed lot of ancestral portraits set on the walls to entertain the waiting visitor. The male Frobishers were almost uniformly froglike, the females weedy.

"Pat Sprat could eat no fat; her man could eat no lean . . .," he hummed to himself, paraphrasing Dr. Graves's ditty about his wife and Hoare himself.

Hoare had reached a Frobisher in half-armor—at the Battle of Naseby? If so, on which side?—when Sir Thomas himself entered.

If anything, Hoare soon discovered, his host would be even less enlightening than Mr. Morrow had been. Could Morrow have sent a man with word of his likely advent?

Sir Thomas did not offer refreshment or even invite him to be seated. Instead, he stood in the doorway, managing despite his lower stature to look down his nose at him coldly. Hoare could think of nothing to do but to fall back on an equal formality.

"I am here, Sir Thomas, to inquire into the recent death of Dr. Simon Graves."

"Eh? Speak up, man. I can't hear you."

Hoare repeated himself as loudly as he could.

"Why?"

Hoare could feel his face reddening. "The Admiralty has reason to believe, sir—"

"What? Speak up, I told you."

"You hear me well enough, sir, I believe. The Admiralty—"

"Has nothing to do with me. Nor I with the Admiralty."

"Admiralty business, sir," Hoare persisted. "On His Majesty's service. I require your written authorization to question the coroner who sat on Dr. Graves' death."

"Is that all, fellow?" asked Sir Thomas in a voice that oozed contempt. "Then wait here. If you should need to call at my house again, the tradesmen's entrance is at the back." He turned as if to leave the room.

Hoare rarely flew into a rage. When he did so, he turned white. Now, he barely restrained himself from seizing the baronet by the shoulder, in his own house. It would have been disastrous.

Instead, Hoare put his fingers to his mouth and blew a piercing blast into Sir Thomas's ear. It must have nearly deafened him, for he turned back to Hoare in a rage of his own. On his catching sight of the death that lay behind Hoare's face as it loomed over him, the rage turned into something approaching fear.

"The written authorization, Sir Thomas, if you please. *Now.*"

Frog-shaped the baronet might be, but he was no less valiant in defending his position. "I found you an offensive jackanapes, fellow, when first you pressed yourself upon my acquaintance by seducing Eleanor Graves into effecting an introduction to me. My opinion remains unchanged. The tradesmen's entrance next time, remember, or I'll have my men take a horsewhip to you."

With this, Sir Thomas left the room, making a peculiar grinding noise. Hoare had read of people gnashing their teeth, but he had never before heard one actually do it. In the midst of his own fury, he was delighted at the sound.

Hoare now had another opportunity—long, long—to catch his breath, recover his temper, and further his acquaintance with the baronet's ancestors. He had now gotten as far as a flat-chested maiden of twenty, done in the style of Mr. Gainsborough, when a footman entered. He was not the same footman who had ushered Hoare into the ancestral gallery, for his pimples were pink instead of purple and were located elsewhere on his face.

" 'Ere," he said, and thrust a sealed paper at Hoare, then turned to leave the room. "This way," he added over his shoulder.

Hoare followed him, opening the envelope as he went. This at least would serve.

The footman's livery was threadbare and much too big, Hoare noticed with secret glee. At the door, the man pointed to the left, toward the town hall.

"That way," he said, and gave Hoare a little shove. Hoare's blow to the footman's belly carried his pent-up wrath with it and knocked him back through the open doorway.

Hoare marched down the street, seething. He had been twice a fool, he told himself. Despite Mrs. Graves's warning, he had totally failed to foresee how Sir Thomas would react to the invasion of his manor. The baronet must have had advance warning of his coming and his purpose and had already worked up an impromptu strategy for putting Hoare in his place. In that, at least, the man had failed.

For his own part, Hoare knew, he had been wholly unprepared for the baronet's attack on him through his handicap. As it was, he was lucky even to have gotten the scrap of paper. With it, of course, he had gotten Sir Thomas's enmity.

And most unforgivably, he had deeply offended Mrs. Graves without justification or reason.

Hoare would not have put it past Sir Thomas's flunky to have misdirected him out of excess malice borrowed from his master, so he was relieved to find a decrepit half-timbered cottage within a stone's throw of the town hall, with a sign over its door:

JOSIAH OLNEY
SURGEON AND APOTHECARY
WENS REMOVED

While Sir Thomas had, of course, sat behind Olney as the coroner presided at the inquest on his colleague's murder—the jury had, as instructed, brought in a verdict of "murder by person or persons unknown"—it was Olney to whom he must turn for professional information about the killing.

Hoare more than half-expected that Sir Thomas had kept him waiting not only from simple ill will but also so he could send word ahead to the coroner to make himself scarce. But there Mr. Olney was, seated in a cobwebby nook and rotting quietly. He rose to greet his visitor, hastily brushing the snuff from his waistcoat. Hoare could read his thought: *Could this be a patient? One, perhaps, with money?*

Mr. Olney, Hoare suspected, was a former naval surgeon. At least, while respectable enough to have been made medical examiner for the Weymouth Assizes, he was not the professional peer of the late Dr. Simon Graves, physician, artificer, correspondent with Laënnec and Dupuytren. Nonetheless, he showed himself willing to help Hoare as best he could. Hoare did not even have to show Sir Thomas's paper. He had, then, made a new enemy for no reason.

"I am calling on you, sir," Hoare whispered, "to inquire into the circumstances of Dr. Graves' death."

Olney was manifestly disappointed to learn that Hoare was not a patient, but he obliged. He summarized the inquest on Dr. Graves; there were no surprises here. The surgeon was unaware of any particular efforts on the authorities' part to track down his colleague's killer. Certainly Sir Thomas had issued no orders to anyone concerning the murder.

Was Sir Thomas too self-important to have been bothered? The baronet had seemed to be a good friend of Dr. Graves and his wife. Why had he done nothing to track down the physician's murderer? Why, in fact, had he taken such an intense instant dislike to Hoare? Hoare feared that his impatient jape about bats, when they were first introduced, lay at the root of the matter.

"But forgive me, sir," Olney was saying. "I altogether failed to offer you a drop. I usually take a bit of port at about this time of day. Will you join me in a drop?"

At Hoare's nod, Olney reached up and opened a cabinet from which he drew a decanter and two glasses. Apparently observing that one of them was dusty, he wiped it out with a large polka-dot kerchief, and began to pour.

"Was there an autopsy, sir?" Hoare asked.

"Why, shame on me," Olney said, and spilled some of the muddy wine on his desk.

"Bless my soul, I clean forgot, I did. Of course I did. I made an autopsy on my poor colleague. I knew he would have wanted me to. Shall I tell you about it?"

"Please," Hoare whispered.

"And by the bye, sir, I have an excellent emollient *linctus* for the throat, should it interest you. My own concoction."

Hoare explained his whisper as briefly as he could, then paused expectantly to hear about Dr. Graves's autopsy.

"As you probably know," the surgeon said, "the cause of death was not the contusion on Dr. Graves' forehead. That occurred when the impact of the bullet in his back threw him forward against his table. No, the immediate cause was that ball itself. It penetrated the wooden back of his chair, broke through his rib cage from behind, and buried itself in his heart. It carried into the wound a few splinters from the chair and some threads from the doctor's shirt. He was not wearing his coat—because of the warm weather, I suppose. The ball killed him instantly, of course. Here it is."

He rummaged in a drawer and pulled out a distorted leaden object, still encrusted with blackish red.

Hoare took it eagerly, got the folding knife from his pocket, and scraped away carefully at the reddish deposit.

"This is no musket ball, sir," he said at last, displaying it to the surgeon. "If you look closely, you will see it bears raised lands. It was fired from a rifle. This is the second time within three weeks that I have seen one."

"Why, so it is. I should have noted that. It has been many a year, sir, since I have seen a ball which was fired from a rifled musket. They were not common in the Navy in my day. But you would know that, of course."

"May I have it, sir? I think it could be very important."

"Certainly, Mr. Hoare. You would not mind giving me a receipt, would you? Sir Thomas is a great stickler for the paperwork."

"Not at all, Mr. Olney. And perhaps, in turn, you would write down a description for me? 'Rifled bullet,' perhaps, 'removed from the body of Simon Graves,' and so forth."

"Delighted, sir." The surgeon handed Hoare a pen.

The two set to their scratching in a companionable way and then exchanged documents. Thereupon Hoare tossed off the surgeon's awful port, pocketed the rifle ball, and said goodbye to Mr. Olney. Hoare left a half-guinea on the cluttered desk, beside the empty glass.

One more task remained to him. He wanted to learn more about the discovery at Portland Bill of the anker that had first brought him to Weymouth. Was this a unique discovery? Had anything else of interest been discovered at the same place and time?

The Weymouth station of the Coast Guard was no more than a short walk away. He had passed it upon leaving *Unimaginable* at her berth in the harbor. The cutter *Walpole* lay alongside the station. Hoare invited himself aboard, handed the anchor watch one of his self-explanatory leaflets, and while awaiting an officer inspected the cutter with a keen naval eye.

"Cutter" she might be named in the Coast Guard, but *Walpole* was a brisk-looking brigantine of about one hundred tons, armed with several popgun four-pounders. Her bewigged figurehead showed she was properly named, not for His Majesty's present prime minister, but for William Walpole the elder. Her commander, who was fortunately aboard, came on deck himself to invite Hoare below. The red-haired Mr. Popham would have been Hoare's own age, small, spare, and brisk like his command. Hoare envied him.

"We Coastguardsmen have to make do with ourselves as clerks," Mr. Popham explained as he cleared a clutter of papers from the table and the extra chair.

"Give me your opinion of this burgundy, sir, will ye? Took it off *Rose* just last week."

It would be one of the Coast Guard's quiet perquisites, Hoare knew, and it was worth every penny the smugglers would have gotten.

As soon as courtesy permitted, Hoare brought up the matter of the sandy "anker." In doing so, of course, he dutifully distinguished between anker, a vessel for holding liquids, and "anchor," for holding a vessel, and joined Mr. Popham in the obligatory laugh.

Mr. Popham remembered the anker well. He also knew well Dickon Dee, the sand-loving fisherman, and was amused at Hoare's description of their encounter.

"It did, indeed, come ashore just where he told you it did," he said. "I would have told you that had you asked me . . . but then, I think you really wanted to meet Dickon Dee and test his powers."

Hoare smiled acknowledgment.

"It was an interesting little object," Popham said. "Did you notice what I noticed?"

Hoare looked inquiring and waited.

"We're accustomed to seeing French cooperage, of course—ankers, demi-kegs, kegs, barrels, even a tun now and then. They come ashore as well as being brought ashore, if you take my meaning. But you could tell from the scarfing and rab-

154

beting that this was a good, stout English anker, not French. The French coopers contrive it differently, Mr. Hoare."

"I had not known, sir," Hoare said.

"Now, sir," Popham went on, "what puzzles me is why an *English* anker would be cast adrift in such a fashion, with the contents that puzzled you.

"What did you make of the message?"

"What message?" Hoare asked.

"The message in the anker, with the clockwork, of course."

"There was no message in the anker . . . at least, not when it passed through my hands. What was it like?"

"A cipher, or I'm a lizard. On gray waterproof paper. . . ."

Mr. Popham might be describing either the message Mrs. Graves had described or the ones Hoare had seen with his own eyes. Here was another piece in the puzzle, but where did it fit?

"I'll be damned, Popham," Hoare said. "This is *most* interesting information. I'm greatly obliged to you for it—as well as the burgundy.

"But now, I must be under way, or I'll miss my tide."

Popham rose to usher his guest from the cutter. "You'll have ten minutes to get out into the Channel and catch it. It's been a pleasure, sir. Come visit *Walpole* again, next time you're this way."

"And let me offer you a glass of Madeira, Mr. Popham, when you call in Portsmouth. The Swallowed Anchor will find me."

UNIMAGINABLE IDLED ALONG under the slowly circling summer stars on a broad reach, her high mainsail and full clubbed jib drawing her gently toward Portsmouth at no more than a knot. The flowing tide, Hoare reckoned, would give her perhaps four knots over the ground. At this rate, she would reach home by noon tomorrow. He sighed, leaned back against her taffrail, and mused about Dr. Graves's clockwork. Had the doctor possessed enough leisure and enough talent to keep not just one but two inquiries in the air at a time—the clockwork project and his undertaking with Morrow? More distressing: Dr. Graves could have built his clockwork devices for an English agent, as he had told his wife. But Hoare could not understand why an Englishman would have been so havey-cavey about the arrangement. Unwittingly—or wittingly—Dr. Graves could have undertaken the work for a man in French pay. If so, had he done so unwittingly? Had he known? Had he himself, perhaps, been the agent?

These thoughts interwove themselves in Hoare's brain with thoughts about the ciphered messages. Now, he was sure. There must be a link between the anker full of clockwork, Dr. Graves, and the late Mr. Kingsley of *Vantage*. What was it? And why had the two men—so different in ability and calling—been killed?

The fog's sudden onset caught Hoare by complete surprise. A slightly heavier breath of breeze, a brief gurgle under *Unimaginable*'s bows, and the stars vanished. With them went the wind. The pinnace slowed perceptibly. Hoare's view forward shortened, was gone. Within a minute, he could barely make out *Unimaginable*'s own mast, and she lay idle, sails slatting in a low, greasy leftover swell. Only the faint red and green glows of her running lights reached him now.

He went below to get out the conch shell he used as a fog horn. Back on deck again, he returning to his niche against the taffrail and blew a long, mournful hoot into the featureless gray-black. He repeated the blast about every minute, counting by his regular pulse. Between hoots, he listened.

There were no other hoots, though once he thought to hear a faint echo of his own.

Aft, a faint blur in the darkness. He aimed the conch toward it and hooted.

"Ahoy," came a quiet call.

Not being able to reply, he set down the conch, drew out his boatswain's pipe, and twittered.

A blaze, a *crack,* and a stunning blow across the back of his head, and the stars returned, flickering across his vision like so many fireworks. He slumped sideways. So this was death, he thought.

He could not have been unconscious for more than a minute. He could not understand, he could not see, he could not move . . . but he could feel, for he felt a soft thump against *Unimaginable's* larboard side. He could hear. He heard a man say something. He could not understand. As far as he could tell, he was sprawled against the tiller, looking upward and seeing only the fog . . . or nothing.

He felt *Unimaginable* lurch to larboard with the weight of someone coming aboard. Whoever it was—he could *see!*—leaned over him, picked him up by the shoulders, and shook him. His jaw lolled. Pain lanced through his head, and he heard the steady, slow drip of his blood on *Unimaginable's* quarterdeck. Damn him, he thought, and laughed at himself. I'll make the bloody bastard pay for bloodying my bloody quarterdeck with my own bloody blood.

"Mort. Bon." He understood this, well enough. "Aides-moi, louche. Mettons-le en bas."

Another man came aboard. Between the two of them, they hauled Hoare to *Unimaginable's* hatchway and dropped him below. He landed on his face and felt his nose crunch against the cabin table. He heard at least one of the men follow him, using the more civilized ladder. A light flared. A fist took him by the hair, picked his head up, and dropped it onto the floorboards.

"Vous devez lui couper la gorge, monsieur, pour la sûreté," said the second man. ("You'd better cut his throat, sir, to be sure.)

"Non. Il a été officer et gentilhomme. Viens; prends-toi les pieds. Vite, alors!" (No. He was an officer and a gentleman. Come on, take his feet. Quickly.)

Both men's French had an odd, eerily familiar accent. But Hoare was very tired. He decided to go away again.

HOARE'S RIGHT SIDE lay in water. The other side was cold and wet. The back of his head throbbed, and he could not breathe through his swollen nose, so he could smell nothing. But he could see again. A square of fog showed him the open hatchway through which the boarders had dropped him. And he could hear—the heavy slosh of seawater about him and the regular *bump, bump, bump* of some pot or other swanning about in *Unimaginable*'s bilges.

And he could move. He reached painfully up with one arm, gripped the edge of the table, and heaved enough so as to bring the other arm up in aid of its friend.

Had the boarders stove *Unimaginable* in, then? If they had, he thought wildly, he'd have their balls for breakfast. But she could not have taken on much water yet. If he knew where he was . . . He was sitting in water, not on the combined floorboards and trail boards that bore *Unimaginable*'s aliases, but directly in her bilges. The hard object intent on grinding him a new arsehole was her open seacock. Being a small, tight vessel, she only needed one cock. By being lightly impaled on it, he was keeping *Unimaginable* afloat by keeping it from doing its proper work of letting in the Channel. He apologized to the seacock, turned it off, vomited an ounce of bitter bile, rolled over, and fainted again in the bilges.

HOARE RETURNED TO his senses to see gray daylight outlined in the hatchway. *Unimaginable* still lay hove-to, swaying heavily in a slow, greasy swell. He summoned the strength to clamber up the ladder onto her deck, where he crawled forward and manned her pump. Stopping to rest after every few feeble heaves, he was able to summon a thin, intermittent stream of seawater from below to pour over the side.

Twice he had to make his way back below to clear floating debris from the intake. On the second of these trips, he thought to get a piece of soft tack from the waterproof cupboard over his stove. He picked up a soggy stocking, wrung it out, and returned topside. He wrapped the stocking around his throbbing head and sat himself beside *Unimaginable*'s idly swinging tiller while he devoured the bread. When he was through, he felt stable enough on his pins to get to his feet and look about him, holding onto her larboard shrouds.

Though the sky was still a dull gray, the fog had lifted, and he could see several fisherman in the middle distance, between *Unimaginable* and Anvil Point. Through the haze on the horizon ahead, he could see the Needles. *Unimaginable,* praise God, had carried him quietly with the flowing tide past the eddies of St. Alban's Ledge during the night, without his help. She had brought him more than halfway home.

Hoare found the strength to trim the two standing sails and set *Unimaginable* on an easterly course under the faint southerly breeze. Still too full of ocean for comfort, she wallowed but complied.

Hoare felt weary, dizzy, and languid. He went below and sloshed about among the flotsam until he laid hold of a half-empty bottle of *vin ordinaire* and a slab of braxy ham, which he brought back on deck. Since this soaked him to the crotch once more, he resolved not to return below until *Unimaginable* was home and dry. The trip had been worth it, however, for the meat and wine brought a bit of energy to his body. He went forward and worked the barge's pump in a desultory way, while she idled on toward the Solent, helped along by the last of the flood. As the tide went slack, the breeze picked up, as often happens in these waters, until *Unimaginable* began to leave a gurgling wake. Hoare's deadened mind began to function again.

Obviously, the two men who had boarded his craft in the fog and left him for dead were French or Channel Islanders. More likely the latter, for they were scattered all over the south coast of Britain, making their living as fishermen, workboat men, smugglers. Searching his memory, he found within a hundred miles of here only one Frenchman who was not a prisoner of war or an officer on parole—Marc-Antoine de Chatillon de Barsac, the *maître d'escrime* whose Portsmouth establishment Hoare haunted whenever occasion offered. But de Barsac was a friend and, moreover, suffered from violent seasickness. He had vowed never to set foot on a waterborne vessel again until he could return to France in triumph, with his King. He would hardly have been lying in wait for Hoare off St. Alban's Head on the sunniest of June days, let alone a foggy night.

Channel Islanders were another matter. Most of them were bilingual. They were scattered all over the Channel coast of England, earning their living as gardeners and as seamen of various types. More than one officer of the Navy—Sir James Saumarez, for instance—was a Channel Islander. Yes, his assailants could easily be Channel Islanders.

Hoare gradually recovered his energy as the sun broke through, but for the most part, he left *Unimaginable* to find her own way home with only the most necessary guidance, her captain brooding as she sailed. By the late sunset of late May, she eased into the Inner Camber, still listing slightly and lying heavy in the water. She rolled like a woman about to give birth. Hoare made her fast with the help of Guilford the watchman and betook himself up the strand to the Swallowed Anchor. Here Susan the pink girl took him in hand, binding up his head and putting him to bed with a hot toddy.

Chapter XII

—⟫•◆•⟪—

"TELL ME more about Kingsley," Hoare said to Janus Jaggery two mornings later. They were basking in the sunny kitchen garden of the Bunch of Grapes. The bench was out of earshot of Mr. Greenleaf's other customers, and the garden was ablaze with blossoms whose scent overbore the mild rotten reek of the kitchen's wastes. Nearby, young Jenny served "tea" to herself and three creatures that her da had just cleverly twisted out of straw to keep her company.

"Ain't nothin' to tell, Mr. 'Oare. 'E was always a cove to try an' buy 'is way into favor with presents what 'e give to anyone 'e thought might 'elp him to advancement.

" 'E was a bum-sucker, yer worship, and a wild spender. Where did 'e get his blunt, then? 'E was too well-known in the Navy to try the gentry-lay, an' those bits of 'ardware we traded was as nuffin'. 'E was a bully. An' that's what set me off the Navy in the first place, Mr. 'Oare—the bullyin'."

"And what else did you do to help him?" Hoare asked.

"Well," Jaggery said reluctantly, "sometimes I'd put 'im in

the way of a bit of fine goods from t'other side the Channel—
a length of silk, like, for one of 'is morts. Then there was the
brandy. In ankers. Lots of *them*. 'E got 'em himself and tended
to 'em 'imself, most particular. Wouldn't 'ave me lay me 'ands
on 'em, no, not at first."

"And where did you meet to do these bits of nefarious
business?"

"I've a friend, Yer Honor, what 'as the night watch at Arrowsmith's ware'ouse. You know—the ship chandler? 'E let us
use it, so long as we never took none of Arrowsmith's wares.
Didn't take much space no'ow."

"Space or no space, Jaggery, that's cappabar, as well you
know—disposing illegally of His Majesty's property. Get taken
up for that, and off they pack you to Botany Bay, before you
can whistle. And what will happen to your little Jenny then?"

Upon Hoare's words, Jaggery instinctively searched the
tiny garden. No Jenny.

Through the wall behind them came a squeal. Silent as
any cat, Hoare got to his feet and, stooped over, threw open
the door into the inn kitchen. There was a yell of pain, a crash
of crockery, and the clatter of fleeing feet. Hoare went through
the door in a rush, almost tripping over Jenny as the child
darted back out into the garden.

"I *bit* 'im, Da!" Jenny shrieked. "I *bit* 'im!" In her pale face,
the child's eyes sparked like black fire.

For a fraction of a second, a dark figure was silhouetted in
the doorway beyond, leading into the barroom. Another crash
followed, and a shout of rage from Greenleaf. Hoare raced
across the barroom and thrust his head out the front door.
Down the cobbled lane he saw the fugitive dodging through
the throng, running like a started hare toward the water. The
object the man carried in one hand caught against an awning
pole, and he dropped it, continuing his flight. Hoare caught it
up. It was a tapered, flexible tube, like the one Dr. Graves had
demonstrated that night in Weymouth.

It brought certain memories together: Morrow's interest in it; the enciphered messages in Kingsley's correspondence and the similar messages whose appearance Mrs. Graves had sketched; Morrow's birthplace; the oddly familiar accents of the two French-speaking men who had boarded him and beaten him a few nights ago; Janus Jaggery's admissions just now about Kingsley's ankers of "brandy." Put together for the first time, these assorted facts melded into a certainty: the man behind the mystery was Mr. Edward Morrow.

Hoare stopped in his tracks. At forty-three, he had no hope of catching the eavesdropper himself on foot. Moreover, he sensed a far greater opportunity to forestall the fugitive in his rush to escape and report to his master. If he were to seize opportunity as well as device, there was not a moment to be lost.

But how? True, the fugitive *seemed* to be making for the harbor, suggesting that he would make his escape by sea. He could, however, have been laying a false track and would change course for some inshore spot where a horse awaited.

Hoare felt himself on the horns of a dilemma. Should he pursue by land? He had no idea how long it would take a troop of horsemen to ride from Portsmouth to Weymouth, but it had to be an eighty-mile journey. He doubted that horsemen would be able to change mounts en route, as a solitary postboy or a scheduled coach could do. And they would not want to travel at night, he supposed. It could be two days before they reached their destination. By then, the fugitive— traveling every minute except to change horses—would have long since reached Weymouth and alerted Morrow. If Hoare traveled by land, the race was lost from the start.

No, his only chance was to go by sea. With today's northerly wind likely to endure, *Inconceivable* could make the passage in less than a day, but she would arrive with an inferior force. Given the terms on which he stood with Sir

Thomas Frobisher, Hoare could hardly hope to recruit a force in Weymouth or its environs. Yet if his *Inconceivable* were to make her best speed, she could accommodate no more than two besides himself. Well then, they'll have to be the best fighting sailors in Portsmouth, Hoare told himself. He hastened to the Admiral's offices to gather his trivial reinforcements.

With two experienced, intelligent-looking tars in tow, Hoare was about to work his way back through the town to where *Inconceivable* lay when it occurred to him to search the harbor first from a spot on the Common Hard, to see if he could catch sight of the fugitives among the waterborne traffic. With a whispered apology, he seized a telescope from an elderly nautical-looking gentleman and set to examining every small craft he could see working its way southward toward the Solent.

"See, Cyril!" came a woman's voice at his side. "Only see how our nation's guardian bends his eagle brow in search of one of His Majesty's enemies on which to swoop!"

Hoare could not help himself. He glanced in the speaker's direction, to see a plainly dressed woman of about his own age, bending to address a child of perhaps six. Seeing that she had caught Hoare's attention, she simpered and moved away, looking over her shoulder widowlike. Hoare returned to his search.

On the low southern horizon, about to disappear behind Gosport, a sleek schooner was just hoisting her flying jib to the soft northerly wind. She was too glossy for a fisherman; her masts were daringly raked. Besides, no mere fisherman troubled with little handkerchiefs like flying jibs. Hoare recognized her as the yacht Morrow had proudly pointed out to him from his own doorstep outside Weymouth—his *Marie Claire*.

Hoare clapped the pilfered telescope to with a snap and returned it to its nonplussed owner with an unctuous, apologetic smile. He beckoned to his two men and set off again at a run across the dockyard. By the time he reached *Inconceivable, Marie Claire* would have thirty minutes' lead on him. On a broad reach, the schooner would be at her best. Nonetheless, Hoare thought as he panted along, it was over ninety miles to Weymouth by sea. With the low sea and the favorable breeze, *Inconceivable* had a fair chance. Morrow—or his yacht, at least—would have his race after all, it seemed. But there was not a moment to be lost.

With the very possibility in mind that he would have other naval men aboard her, Hoare had rigged *Inconceivable* Navy fashion throughout. In pitch dark, any able seaman could find any of the lines cleated to her tiny pin rail without fumbling. His two men turned to as though they had been aboard her for a month. Within minutes, with the aid of the docker-watchman Guilford, they had all shore lines inboard and had turned her end for end. *Inconceivable*'s tall triangular mainsail gave his new crew pause for a moment. But since the whole rig could have been grasped by an eight-year-old—let alone men like these—in no time, *Inconceivable* was under way, her bow wave beginning to chuckle softly as if she were confident of her race's outcome.

By the time *Inconceivable* had reached the Solent proper, *Marie Claire* was well on her way to Cowes. Hoare saw her change course to larboard, ease her sheets, and straighten up slightly. She had a good three miles on *Inconceivable*. This would be the schooner's best point of sailing, so it would be a long, stern chase, devoid of maneuvers unless—as seemed unlikely—the wind veered westerly.

Hoare eyed his scratch crew unobtrusively. Though one was ruddy and the other black, the two were cut from the same human cloth, tough, horny-handed, pigtailed men in clean frocks. Both had kicked off their heavy buckled shoes immediately on coming aboard, showing big, almost prehensile feet as horny as their hands. As soon as her two simple sails were drawing to Hoare's satisfaction, both had turned to and begun priddying *Inconceivable*'s already-spotless deck. Hoare beckoned them to join him beside the tiller.

"My name's Hoare," he whispered. "Don't trouble to laugh, either of you. I've been known to wipe the laugh off a man, together with the rest of his head." He smiled to show that he was not wholly serious, and the two men relaxed visibly. "We're too small a ship for formality, men, so make yourselves at home. I can't talk in more than a whisper, so you'll want to keep one eye on me and one on *Inconceivable* here."

He stopped to catch his breath, and went on.

"And one eye on that flash schooner up ahead. I want to take her if I can, sink her if I can't. She's carrying at least three Frenchmen, maybe more. I think they are the ones that have been blowing up so many of His Majesty's ships. At least, I believe so, and the Admiral thinks so, too, so that's all you really need to know. But I want to tell you a bit more. Bear with me if I must stop to wet my whistle once in a while."

With this, Hoare began to expound his suspicions. When he had brought the two up-to-date with his discovery of the listening device, he asked them about themselves.

"Now, tell me who you are, and your ratings."

"I'm Bold, sir," said the black man. "Cox'n of Sir George's barge. Bold's me name, and bold's me nature. *Har har har.* An' this smart lad Stone here, 'e's just been named stroke oar. We knows who *you* are. You're the gentleman what found all of *Amazon*'s mids."

"Yes," Stone said. "An' you 'auled me aboard thicky little barky of your yerself, zur, when *Vantage* blew up t'other day. For which I says 'thanky,' zur."

"Which one of you should I rate as 'sailing master,' for now, and which as 'gunner'?"

"Well, sir, Stone was capting of one of *Vantage*'s carronades."

"Then that's that. Bold, you're master, and Stone, you're gunner. Take turns at her tiller for a bit, and get used to her. I'd have you both take her 'round the compass, but we haven't time now, if we're to catch *Marie Claire* up there."

When Stone had had his turn, Hoare left Bold at *Inconceivable*'s tiller and took the gunner below. He wanted the craft's odd armory overhauled.

"First, Stone," he said, "draw the charges in all the weapons. Here's a worm. They must have all been wet when she took on water awhile back. Reload the lot from this barrel."

Stone rolled up his sleeves and set to. Hoare returned on deck.

After a bit, Stone's head looked up at him from below. He was carrying the powder keg.

"No good, zur. She be started in the 'ead. Soaked through, she be."

"Clear through?" Hoare's whisper was filled with dismay.

"To the very core, zur. All twanty pounds of 'er. Look 'ere. This lump, she be from the very center of the keg."

"The pistols? The swivel?" Hoare asked piteously. "The crossbow?"

"Dunno about the crossbow, zur. Never seen one of 'em before. But like you said, the powder in the other weppings was all damp."

"The grenades?"

"Can't tell, zur. Un be all sealed up, you know. But the fuses . . ."

Stone went below, where Hoare heard him rummaging about.

"No good, zur. Fuses be all wet!" he called at last.

Hoare could gladly have beaten his head against *Inconceivable*'s mast. As soon as possible after bringing his waterlogged vessel home the other morning and drying her out, he had replenished her fully. He had replaced hardtack and soft tack. He had made certain that the coal for his galley stove was dry, and likewise the kindling and tinder. He had also been quite confident that his little keg of red large-grain powder and his flask of priming powder were secure. He had failed to make sure. He had not kept his powder dry. Without firearms, how were *Inconceivable*'s three men to take *Marie Claire?* There could be no question. There were at least as many "Frenchmen" aboard her, and they would be well armed—with pistols, if nothing else.

For a long instant, Hoare contemplated temporarily abandoning the chase and returning to Portsmouth, there to resume it in some more conventional manner. He would certainly not actually abandon it. He looked ahead to the schooner. Even if the fugitives were only Morrow's minions, he wanted at least one of them. If Morrow himself was aboard, all the better.

From the respectful tones one, and only one, of his two midnight boarders had used on that misty night—just about here, Hoare realized—he was certain the other boarder had been Morrow. That put Morrow in his debt. Hoare thought no more about turning back.

He had seen how *Marie Claire* gave the Cowes headland a wide berth, so as to clear the nasty heap of submerged rocks just offshore of it. *Marie Claire*'s sails gleamed ivory in the sun of late morning, until she disappeared behind the minor cape on which Cowes lay. She had not dodged south into the Newport estuary. The odds were, then, that she would make a straight run for Weymouth.

So Morrow, or whoever was conning Hoare's chase, knew the local waters. He himself would hoist *Inconceivable*'s sliding keel halfway and shave the rocks, accepting the additional leeway this would give her in exchange for the cable-length he would gain. The tide was just past full.

The rocks now behind her, *Marie Claire* hove into sight again, making for the Needles, heeling slightly less than before and slicing scornfully through the light offshore chop. She had set her gaff topsails. Little good that will do her, Hoare thought; *Inconceivable*'s plain mainsail overtopped the schooner's main topmast by a good two feet.

Morrow might be a traitor, but nonetheless he had chosen his yacht with an expert eye. With every rag set and gleaming golden in the afternoon sun, throwing an occasional rainbow of spray across her long bowsprit, *Marie Claire* was beautiful. And since the wind held steady, it promised to be a straight run to Durlston Head—clear in the distance—thence to St. Alban's Head and Weymouth Bay. There was little likelihood that, even if Morrow were not in command, the crew of "Frenchmen" would commit any blunders that would bring *Marie Claire* within reach of *Inconceivable*'s jaws. And in any case, to Hoare's shame, those jaws were all but toothless.

"I think we're over'aulin' the chase, sir," Bold said behind him. "I can see her crew—some of 'em, anyhow."

In the glass Hoare thought to see four figures. He handed it to Bold for confirmation.

"Looks like four of 'em to me, sir," Bold said. "And we're 'aulin' up on 'em good and pretty, like I said. Thicky crazy rig of yourn. . . ."

"Just the same," Hoare said, "it may well be dark before we come up on her. And there are only three of us. Shall we see if it's true that one true British tar can whip any three Frogs?"

"Har har har," Bold said.

His comrade was more forthcoming. "Lost 'most all my shipmates in *Vantage*," Stone said. "If it's true, that idee of yourn, I wouldn't mind payin' the bugger off for that."

"Well, then," Hoare said, "here's what we'll do."

MARIE CLAIRE HAD passed the Needles and had been briefly silhouetted by the setting sun when Hoare and his crew learned that they had come up within pistol shot of her. The ball thumped harmlessly against *Inconceivable*'s mast, just above her toy pin rail, dropped to the deck, and rolled into the scuppers. Hoare suggested that his men take shelter behind *Inconceivable*'s narrow cabin trunk.

"They won't 'ave that much ammunition, zur, will they?" Stone asked. "Mebbe if we annoys 'em enough, they'll shoot it all off afore we gets within killin' range." So saying, he rose to his feet, flourished his hat, and delivered a terrible yell. There was another shot from the chase. Stone's hat flew from his hand, and he joined his companions behind the cabin trunk.

"*Har har har,*" Bold said beside him.

HOARE FELT UNFAIRLY treated, whether by himself or by the fates. Foot by foot, in slow motion, *Inconceivable* was drawing up on *Marie Claire*—and his teeth were drawn. The chase became silhouetted in the westering sun. Her stern was ample enough that four Frenchmen lining her taffrail, side by side, could deliver a steady, slow harassing fusillade. A fifth man stood boldly at her wheel. The enemy must have long since guessed that since she had yet to open fire, *Inconceivable* had no means of doing so.

The tapping of pistol bullets on her hull and the *pop* they made when tearing through her canvas was a constant thing. As the gap between the two vessels narrowed, the taps grew sharper. Hoare and his crew stayed crouched in the shelter of *Inconceivable*'s cabin trunk.

Slowly, slowly, the sun reached for the horizon beyond *Marie Claire*. Slowly, it began to drown itself. A last rare green flash, and it was gone. At the water's surface, the wind all but died except for an infinitesimal cat's-paw every now and then. The two craft lay all but idle on the gently heaving water, commencing to box the compass as they lost steerage way. *Splat,* as a ball struck the water beside Bold and threw up a trivial spray. *Rap,* as another stuck the front of *Inconceivable*'s cabin trunk. *Tang.* That would have been her anchor. By now, Hoare thought, Eleanor Graves and her sling could have brought down every man in *Marie Claire.* But Hoare had no sling, and if he had, he would not know how to use it.

The Frenchman must have fired a hundred rounds by now in this futile target practice. Surely, as Stone had said hours ago, they would have begun to run short of ammunition.

Apparently the French skipper had the same idea.

"Cease firing, Fortier," came a quiet voice in French over the water. "You haven't hit anything but the water and the wind in all this time."

Hoare recognized the voice instantly. Edward Morrow was aboard, in command of his own yacht.

"Give me your pistols. You can load for the rest of us," Morrow added. The other Frenchman whined.

Time passed, interminable minutes while the gap between the two vessels barely narrowed. If we don't catch them soon, Hoare told himself, we'll lose them in the dark.

"We'll sweep up on 'em," he whispered.

Stone blanched at the idea of standing erect under fire to work *Inconceivable*'s sweeps; Hoare suspected that Bold did as well, though he could not be sure, given the growing darkness and the coxswain's natural hue.

"Jest as ye say, sir," Bold said. "Odds are ye'll lose one of the two of us though. There goes half yer boardin' party."

Hoare was silent, at a stand. At last he said, "Here's what we'll do."

HOARE AND STONE ducked below to put Hoare's plan into effect, leaving Bold at the tiller in the growing dusk.

A hammering and banging began below decks. Only seconds apart, the two amateur carpenters broke through *Inconceivable*'s thin strakes. The blades of her sweeps thrust out from these jury-rigged scuttles. Hoare doffed his uniform coat and laid it neatly on his cot; the two carpenters turned galley slaves and began to heave.

The firing from *Marie Claire* had fallen off as the darkness gathered. Now it redoubled, and the pistol flashes were near enough to reflect off *Inconceivable*'s sails.

"Mr. Hoare wants to know: are we showing a wake yet?" Stone grunted from below.

"Tell him 'just,' Jacob," Bold replied in an undertone. "We might be makin' half a knot. The chase, she might as well be swingin' at anchor."

"She's put out sweeps of her own now, sir!" Bold called below after another minute.

"Mr. 'Oare says, 'They can't row and shoot at the same time, any'ow,' " Stone answered.

Now, *Inconceivable*'s taller mast began to tell, for somewhere above the lesser reach of *Marie Claire*'s main topsail, a breath stirred.

"She's answerin' 'er helm again, sir," Bold said.

"Good. Head about two points to windward of her, and we'll bear down as soon as we come abreast. Meet her now. Dyce."

Shortly, *Inconceivable*'s sweeps stopped and lifted, dripping audibly, into the quiet air. Then they withdrew into their crude ports. Hoare stuck his head out of the companionway and crawled into the cockpit, keeping low. He reached back, pulled his sweep out of the hatch, and handed it to Bold. Bold made the tiller fast, thrust the sweep into its socket dead aft, and began sculling, slowly and strongly. Under her own sweeps, *Marie Claire* seemed to make no headway. She would have rated double *Inconceivable*'s tonnage, so this could be no surprise to Morrow.

Hoare leaned down into the cabin and said in his loudest whisper, "Bring up the crossbow and the quarrels, Stone."

" 'Quarrels,' zur?"

"Arrows, Stone. They're alongside the crossbow. They look like bolts."

More rummaging sounds followed.

"Got 'em, zur." Stone handed up the weapons and hoisted himself out of the cabin with a single thrust of his powerful shoulders, disdaining the ladder. "You orta been mannin' that there oar, Loveable, not Mr. Hoare," he said.

"I does what my orficers tell me to, Jacob."

"You be a lazy bugger, that's what you be," Stone said. He hauled a grapnel up from below and began to splice it to the bitter end of a lanyard.

Under a steady, slow, harassing fire, Hoare and his crew blacked their faces and hands with soot from *Inconceivable*'s galley stove. Cradling the cocked crossbow in his arms and dragging the bag of quarrels behind him, Hoare crawled forward in the dusk, under cover of *Inconceivable*'s rail, into her very bows.

He had procured the crossbow only last year, when he happened to stop at an inn outside the ruins of Corfe Castle. The weapon had to be centuries old. Although he had bought it on a whim, he felt obliged to try it out. He had chosen a meadow outside Portsmouth, where he at least had had a chance to retrieve the bolts.

Hoare had found at once that the crossbow worked. In fact, it was surprisingly powerful. While his first shot went into the blue somewhere to the north of the tree at which he was aiming, his second, fired from a hundred yards, buried itself so deep in the trunk that he could not withdraw it. He would not have cared to be one of the steel-clad men-at-arms who had faced the thing, and he understood why crossbows had been outlawed by chivalry and Church alike.

He had also learned that the crossbow was extremely slow to load—slower, even, than his lost Kentucky rifle, which, in turn, had taken him twice as long as one of his pistols or a smooth-bore musket. To cock the bow, he would have to stand upright, press his foot into a combination stock and stirrup, and heave mightily on a steel lever. The notion of doing this under fire from *Marie Claire*—sporadic though it was—gave him a grue. And his accuracy would be laughable.

Sheltering behind *Inconceivable*'s jib, Hoare shouldered the awkward weapon, making sure that it cleared her forestay. By now, the chase was less than a hundred yards ahead, a few points off *Inconceivable*'s larboard bow. Hoare had ordered Bold to come up on her from windward, so as to take her wind with *Inconceivable*'s towering mainsail. He leveled the crossbow and waited for a target to show itself.

He did not have long to wait. The silence of *Inconceivable*'s pursuit would certainly have convinced the other vessel's crew by now that she was without firearms—as, indeed, she was. By now, they were close enough to distinguish one from another, even in the dusk. Now he could see five of them, no fewer. Short of extreme heroism and the most extraordinary luck, any attempt at boarding her was doomed. And so, in all likelihood, was Bartholomew Hoare.

Two of *Marie Claire*'s crew were standing on her taffrail now, one reloading his pistols and the other taking aim. Hoare too took careful aim, held his breath, and squeezed the crossbow's strange long trigger.

With a sharp, soft *snap,* the crossbow kicked back against Hoare's shoulder. His target uttered a croaking cry, clutched at his leg, and fell backward against the helmsman, knocking him away from the schooner's wheel. *Marie Claire* drifted gracefully into the negligible wind, athwart *Inconceivable*'s bows, where—had she been armed with cannon—she could have murdered *Inconceivable* with a raking fire.

Now! Hoare cried to himself. He whistled an ascending banshee note. In response, Stone raced forward to stand beside

Hoare. He twirled his grapnel as though he were swinging a dipsey lead—*or a sling,* flashed through Hoare's mind. The three Inconceivables braced for the impact, grasping any shroud or timber within reach.

Stone let fly with his grapnel. Instead of catching in *Marie Claire's* rigging, it caught in the clothing of a second Frenchman, who jerked like a jigged salmon. Stone heaved at the grapnel line. The jigged man clutched at a shroud, missed, fell forward into the Channel. Stone's grapnel tore away.

Inconceivable rammed *Marie Claire* just aft of her starboard main shrouds. Her bowsprit thrust across the schooner below her main boom before grinding to a near-halt. *Marie Claire* heeled heavily away. There was a crash below—perhaps, Hoare hoped, from Morrow's best yachting china. Carried along by the schooner's momentum, *Inconceivable* began to swing to starboard, pressing against *Marie Claire* and braying the jigged man between the two hulls like an ear of Indian corn. He squalled. One arm waved briefly in the narrow gap before he was drawn down into the welcoming water.

The blow into *Marie Claire's* midships must have caught another enemy wrong-footed, for he spun and went overboard on the side away from *Inconceivable.* The others—two were still on their feet—were nimbler. One chopped an axe into *Inconceivable's* forestay as it tangled in the schooner's main shrouds, and cut it apart just as Hoare clutched at the nearer of the paired shrouds. *Inconceivable* rebounded. Caught wrong-footed himself, Hoare felt his feet leave her. He dangled in *Marie Claire's* shrouds, first by one hand, then by both, when *Marie Claire* drifted away from his own precious pinnace, his first and only command.

Behind him, *Inconceivable's* jib came down with a run over Bold and Stone. There was another grinding sound. Even where he hung, Hoare knew the two craft had parted company.

By the time Hoare's sailors had struggled out from beneath the jib's hampering folds, *Marie Claire* and her involuntary stowaway were a cable or more off, steadied again on a course for Weymouth. She was as good as home free.

He did not dangle long. Two of Morrow's men hauled him out of the schooner's shrouds and dragged him to her little quarterdeck, where their master stood waiting.

Chapter XIII

———————

*H*OW DID did you get onto my traces, Mr. Hoare?"
Morrow asked. "Take your time in replying, and rest
your voice as often as you wish. The wind is still light, and we
have several hours to while away before *Marie Claire* makes
port. As for your amusing little jury-rigged row-galley . . ."

Morrow gestured toward Hoare's pinnace. *Inconceivable* lay
motionless less than a cable away, a shadow in the dusk, her
forerigging all ahoo where forestay and jib halliard had been
cut, her high mainsail drooping unattended, the sweeps dangling from the raw holes Hoare and Stone had chopped into
her tender sides. She looked a floating wreck. Hoare's heart
went out to her. Meanwhile, *Marie Claire*'s sails had filled, and
she was under way again, ghosting toward Weymouth and
leaving the smaller craft behind.

Moreau saw Hoare's expression. "Perhaps I'll return tomorrow, tow her in, and add her to my fleet. You just used her
to kill my man Lecompte, after all. You are my debtor. What
you Anglo-Saxons call 'blood-geld,' eh?"

He smiled and cracked Hoare across the face with his open hand. Instinctively Hoare struggled to strike back, but the burly men holding his arms restrained him with ease.

"Be seated, pray," Morrow said. He gestured to his men, and Hoare found himself flung onto the deck with stunning force.

"I repeat: How did you find out what I was doing?"

"I put two and two together, Mr. Morrow," Hoare said.

Morrow leaned down and cracked him across the face again. This time, he used his closed fist.

"You mispronounce my name, Mr. Hoare," he said. "My name is Moreau—baptized Jean Philippe Edouard Saint-Esprit Moreau."

"A long name for the *métis* son of a fur trader, Monsieur Moreau."

Crack came the hand.

"Fur trader, m'sieur? My father was no fur trader. He would not have soiled his hands with trade. No, no. My father was Jean-François Benoît Philippe Louis Moreau, nephew of the archbishop and seigneur of Montmagny. His seigneurie stretched from the river south to St.-Magloire and east to St.-Damase des Aulnaies—many, many *arpents,* m'sieur. When *Monseigneur mon pére* died, I inherited half that land. It is still mine.

"And Lecompte whom you just murdered, and Dugas to whom I had to give the quietus after Madame Graves crippled him for you, and Fortier here grew up together with me," he added proudly. "Almost as brothers. I even permit them to address me as 'monsieur' instead of 'monseigneur.' Only they had—have—that honor. Now, for the third time, tell me how you sniffed me out."

Crack.

"I was in Weymouth in the first place," Hoare whispered when his head cleared, "because of the infernal machine the Revenue picked up inland from there. Then I could not help but note your interest in Dr. Graves' avocation of clock-making.

"I was impressed, by the way, with the simple, clever reason you gave when you asked him to make up pieces of clockwork—'for the *British* secret service,' quotha!"

He braced himself for another *crack*. When it did not come, he was bold enough to ask a question of his own.

"What led you to leave your estate, then?"

"Because I am métis, m'sieur, as you know very well. The peasant folk care nothing that a man has Indian blood. Why, Bessac here is a quarter Naskapi, and as proud of it as I am of being the son of a Cree chieftainess.

"But the *grands seigneurs*—ah, that is different. With them, blood's the thing! No, I was not received in the neighboring seigneurs' manors, and I must not pay court to their daughters."

Morrow's—Moreau's—voice took on more than a trace of a French accent. "And when the English came! Ah, M'sieur Hoare, it was you English that made life intolerable for us! You scorn Holy Church; you have stolen our trade; you have debauched our women."

Hoare barely contained himself. He had not "debauched" his dear, dead Antoinette; he had wooed and won her as a gentleman should.

"It was worse still," Moreau went on, "when *Monseigneur mon pére* decided that since the English were here to stay, one of his sons—I, the younger—should be educated as an Englishman, and sent me to the English school in Québec. I need hardly tell you, English officer that you are, the beatings, the bullying—treatment no gentleman should have to endure. But *I* endured it, *m'sieur!* I learned to be as English as any milord! Why, even you thought me English, did you not?"

But nobody, Hoare told himself, had thought to teach the young Moreau the rhymes and nursery tales English children learned in the nursery. Hence Moreau's perplexity when Dr.

Graves had recited his harmless trope about "Jack Sprat, who could eat no fat" as he took his guests in to dinner that first evening, when Hoare first met Eleanor Graves. It had been then that Hoare had begun to suspect that Edward Morrow was other than he presented himself to be.

And it had also been that evening, he realized, that he—Bartholomew Hoare—had already begun to fall in love with the wife of his host.

"I should have recognized your accent as soon as I heard you speak French," Hoare said.

For the first time, Moreau looked startled. "French? When did you hear me speak French?"

"When you and your man—Bessac?—boarded me, thinking you had killed me, with my own rifle, at that," Hoare said bitterly, and decided to press his luck further. "As you suggest, I, too, have been an English schoolboy. I assure you, sir, that a lad with a name like mine faces unusual problems, too. And yet, hating us English the way you do, you chose to come into our midst." He paused inquiringly.

Upon learning that Hoare could not speak, many people concluded wrongly that he could not hear and talked with each other, or with him, as if he were a useful piece of furniture—a side table, perhaps, with a compote on it. Hoare sometimes found this attribute useful, if sometimes insulting, and encouraged it. He did so now, by remaining silent and trying to look like part of *Marie Claire*—a fife rail, perhaps, or a mop.

Moreau bit and, having bitten, swallowed the bait all the way down.

The year 1794, he told Hoare, was when representatives of the new French Republic made their way covertly to Canada. They found young Moreau, feeling as he did about the English, a ready recruit. Any cause that advocated the recapture of the lost New France was a cause for which he felt himself ready to die. This, and his perfect English, suited him to the role of undercover agent in England. So Jean Philippe Edouard

Saint-Esprit Moreau became Edward Morrow, and off to England he went.

As Hoare already knew from Dr. Graves, from his wife, and, indeed, from Moreau himself, Edward Morrow, with his manners and his money, had had no difficulty in establishing himself in Dorset society.

Moreau stopped in middiscourse to take flint and steel from his pocket and light the binnacle. His face bore a reminiscent expression.

"And Kingsley?" Hoare prompted.

"Kingsley?" Moreau paused, then smiled wryly and shrugged. "Ahhh, the light-minded lieutenant." Moreau, he said, had met Peregrine Kingsley at a Portsmouth gambling house, long before that officer was seconded to *Vantage* and while he was still on half-pay. Moreau had seen Kingsley take certain liberties with the cards. On making inquiries of his own, Moreau had also learned that the lieutenant was intensely ambitious, unscrupulous, heavily in debt, and deeply involved with several women simultaneously, women of low degree and high. Whenever it became time to use him, Moreau knew he would have Kingsley in his pocket, ready to be used.

At about the same time, Moreau had discovered Dr. Simon Graves's inventive gifts and put them to use, leading the doctor to believe that in doing so he was advancing the Royal Navy's ability to locate its ships and unaware that, instead, he was helping Moreau to blow them up. Because he could not always communicate with the doctor directly, he had made him privy to the cipher that he himself had been given.

"A permutation cipher, Graves called it," Moreau went on reminiscently. "A *temurah,* or some such word. Out of the Jewish Cabala, as I remember. It was fortunate that he, like . . ." He caught himself.

Of course. That explained to Hoare why Dr. Graves had a French Bible at hand when he was killed. Perhaps, too, it explained why Mr. Watt had failed to break the cipher; it had not been written in English but in French. But . . . what had Moreau stopped himself from saying?

"He, like . . . ," he had begun. Like whom, or what?

But, Moreau continued, when Dr. Graves had balked at making any more identical devices for him, he had seen the danger the physician posed. To ensure himself a more reliable supply, he had diverted one of the machines, in its English anker, to France—as he thought—to be copied in larger numbers and returned to him. This perfectly natural move had, so to speak, blown up the entire affair.

"It was an understandable mistake, Mr. Hoare, I think. As far as the smuggling gentry are concerned, barrels do not leave Britain—they and their precious contents come *into* your peculiar country."

So the anker with the clockwork samples Dr. Graves had unknowingly made for the Continental watchmakers was on its way back inland when one of the smugglers had the notion of checking its contents. When they found that it held, not the brandy that their customers were expecting, but a confused mass of springs and gears, they must have discarded it.

"And Dr. and Mrs. Graves?" Hoare whispered.

"I needed more power over the cripple, if I were to control him as I must. I had yet to find an alternative source for my clockworks, so I still needed him alive to supply me. I sent Dugas—my good Dugas—with a local rough to take the woman while she was wandering foolish and alone along the beach at Portland Bill. I would not have harmed her, of course. I thought her an estimable lady, if fat. I would simply have sequestered her at my quarry or here aboard *Marie Claire,* and held her hostage against the doctor's continued service to me.

"I misjudged her. She was not gentle, but vicious. With her damned stones she wrecked poor Dugas' face and, with your meddling to help her, caused him to fall into the hands of the English. Even Frobisher . . . but there. Dugas knew too much

182

to be left in enemy hands. He had to be silenced. I owe penance for that, and for the death of the honest doctor. He, too, was well-meaning—"

"Mais qu'est-ce que vous dîtes, monsieur?" came Fortier's appalled voice in Hoare's ear. Moreau fell silent for a moment.

"There," he then said. "I've told you all this so you can meditate about it while you drown. Overboard with him. Now."

Each of the men holding Hoare was well-muscled, and their grip was unbreakable for a man of Hoare's age and condition. He found himself swinging by his arms and legs between two pairs of powerful arms. Helped along by a light, disdainful push from Moreau, they tossed Hoare over *Marie Claire*'s low rail. He barely had time to draw breath before he struck the water.

Chapter XIV

⟨⟩◆⟨⟩

*I*RISH PENNANTS—the occasional tag ends of line left by careless crewmen to drag along over a vessel's side—had always spelled slipshod seamanship to Hoare, and, like his fellow officers, he had suppressed them wherever found, as if they were so many signs of sodomy. Now, however, he thanked fortune that Moreau, at least, cared nothing for them. From a cleat below *Marie Claire*'s toy stern gallery a good three fathoms of half-inch line trailed sinuous in her wake. One of Hoare's flailing hands found its bitter end. It might have been the painter of a poorly minded skiff, for it was frayed and not whipped. Whatever else it may have been, it was a blessing.

Hoare kicked off his shoes. As silently as he could, he hauled himself up the line in the dark, hand over hand. As silently as he could, he hoisted himself far enough out of the water to shift his grip to the rail of the stern gallery. The carven structure was a mere flourish which Moreau must have installed to make his little schooner seem bigger. It was rugged enough to carry part of Hoare's weight, but when he tried to hoist himself as silently as he could out of the water, it creaked softly, alarmingly, out of the vessel's own rhythm.

His gently searching feet struck against something vertical beside them. It was *Marie Claire*'s rudder, its gudgeons groaning gently in the pintles as the helmsman adjusted her course. There Hoare squatted, secure, but seized by occasional chills, and waited in the night to discover what fate might bring his way.

Above him, he could hear French being spoken. The voices came and went.

"I must . . . London as soon . . . close down . . . You must go . . . Jaggery in Ports . . . Dispose . . ." This voice was Moreau's.

". . . in London, sir? . . . Louis-. . . ?"

This was one of Moreau's men. To Hoare's straining ears it had sounded as though the Frenchman was naming someone, presumably Moreau's man—or master?—in London. "Louis." How agonizing not to have caught the rest of the name.

"Never mind who. Tend to your own business. Get forward, you lubber, and trim the fore-staysail. . . ." Moreau's words came loud and clear. Yes, the other had, indeed, been naming someone. Damn.

Silence fell on deck. Hoare resigned himself to clinging where he was while his destiny worked itself out. *Marie Claire* ghosted on toward Weymouth. He clung, schemed, dozed.

"HERE." AFTER THE long silence, Moreau's sharp command struck hard on Hoare's ears. "No, we won't anchor. I must get ashore, and since you, you cretin, let our skiff go adrift, you must put me onto the quay. There, beside that interfering revenue cutter. Then take her out again. I'll send two or three men out in a skiff.

"Stand off and on offshore of the Bill until I signal you. It may be three or four days. If you don't see my signal by Wednesday, make for Douarnenez and report to Rossignol.

"Now, repeat my orders."

Mumble.

"Very good. Now come up, Bessac! D'you want to put our bowsprit through the cutter?"

The rudder swung over to port. Hoare took advantage of the *Marie Claire*'s concentration on setting Moreau ashore to part company. He slid silently back into the water and swam to the strand as quietly as he could, to cast himself on the mercy of Eleanor Graves. The east was red.

"WELL, MR. HOARE, what next?"

Eleanor Graves had heard enough of Hoare's whispered story. The manservant Tom had at last assured himself that the coatless, unshod, bedraggled figure that had roused him out of his bed and to her doorstep was, indeed, Mr. Hoare. Tom had awakened his mistress and sent the maid Agnes off to help Cook prepare an early breakfast. Now he sat, a mute Jack Horner, in a corner of the drawing room lit by the early morning sun, on guard.

Eleanor Graves was seated on her tuffet. From beneath a sensible, sexless flannel nightgown ten small straight sallow toes peeped out. They made Hoare think of so many inquisitive hatchlings. He felt impelled to comfort them but answered the lady instead.

"It would be futile," he said, "to try persuading Sir Thomas to lend me men to hunt Moreau down."

Eleanor Graves snorted. "Rather, *he* would hunt *you* down, pop you into one of his dungeons, and torture you to death. Mr. Morrow—Moreau, I suppose I should call him now—will have spun him an enticing yarn about you by now. And Sir Thomas is sure to have been inveigled. He has taken you into a strong aversion, you know. Any *posse comitatus* he calls up will be on your trail, not Moreau's. And so?"

Hoare had no handy plan to offer up in reply. He excused himself to himself by reflecting that he had, after all, been awake all night, either towing behind *Marie Claire* like so much shark bait or hanging from her counter like a six-foot simian. And he was, after all, forty-three years old.

"Think a bit, Mr. Hoare, while I remove my improper person from your sight and make myself as ladylike as I can. Agnes will bring you a breakfast in a moment."

Eleanor Graves rose from her tuffet and went upstairs. She took her toes with her. Hoare was left alone with Tom.

"You could 'scape by hidin' in the mistress's shay," Tom said.

Hoare started out of a doze. "I don't drive. Can you?"

"Not me, Yer Honor. I were no plowboy afore I went into service wi' Doctor, and no ostler. I were a sweep's boy. Doctor saved me balls, 'e did."

Hoare understood. He had learned during one of his snooping ventures that the tarry dust from the flues, up which their masters sent them, coated the orphan lads' immature scrota, generally remaining there, eating away, for months or more between baths. The children generally succumbed to cancerous ulcers before puberty, dying as little eunuchs.

The silence that ensued was broken when the maid Agnes entered with steaming porridge and a plate of crisp bacon for Hoare's breakfast. She set the tray down on her mistress's tuffet.

"There be a man at kitchen doooor," she announced. "Sailor man like. 'E be askin' for Mr. 'Oare." Maidenly, she blushed as she spoke the dirty word. " 'Is name be Stone, 'e sez."

Stone?

"Will you go and inspect him, Tom?" Hoare whispered. "Ask him what Bold looks like. Then come back and tell me what he says."

Tom nodded, preceded Agnes from the room. Too late,

Hoare saw what he had just done. Whoever the man at the door was, he would know now that Hoare was within. Damn his sleepy mind.

" 'E says Bold be black." In the doorway, Tom looked puzzled.

"Bring him in then, if you please, Tom. He's on my side, and the mistress's."

Stone's face lit up when he saw his officer. He knuckled his forehead. The officer in question was quite sure that his own face lit up as well.

"What fair wind blows you here, Stone?" he asked.

"Me an' Bold, zur, when we sees you left aboard thicky schooner, we sez to each other, we sez, 'Mr. 'Oare'll be off to Weymouth with 'er, and 'e'll be in shoal waters an' on a lee shore.' So we stops up the sweep-ports what you an' I jes' finished a-carvin' in yer yachtet, an' gets 'er under way again. We didn't want to go a-drivin' into Weymouth 'arbor like we owned the place, not wi' thicky schooner already in port, so we sets a course for Ringstead Bay instead.

"Me bein' a native of these 'ere parts," he added.

"Why, you'd be Jonathan Stone's boy Jacob!" Agnes exclaimed. "I be Agnes Dillow. Remember me? Yer ma and mine was gossip!"

"Why, so ye be, miss." Stone knuckled his forehead again. Agnes simpered.

"What then?" Hoare asked. This was no time for courtship on the part of either Hoare's man or Hoare himself.

"Well, zur, we 'auls 'er up on Ringstead shingle, safe as can be, an' then we argies summat about 'oo were to come into Weymouth. I sez I should be the one as coom in, but 'e wants to coom tu, 'e does. But when I tells 'im a black man 'ud stand out in Weymouth town like a negg in a coal'ole, 'e agrees to stand watch by yer yatchet for a day. Then, if nor you nor me shows oop, 'e'll 'aul 'er off, make for Portsmouth, an' make a report to the Admiral. So 'ere I be, zur. I 'opes we done right."

"You have indeed, Stone. God bless you. Tell me, can you drive a carriage by any chance?"

"None better, zur. An' thread a four-in-hand through a needle, fine as any Corinthian up in London."

By the time Eleanor Graves returned below, the three men—Hoare, Stone, and Tom—had devised a plan for the first two to elude Sir Thomas's men, whom Stone had reported were already buzzing about Weymouth like so many bees. No one, it seemed, had been ready to believe that Hoare had obligingly drowned. Hoare wondered why until he thought to inspect his raw, bleeding hands. As soon as the crew saw the scarlet evidence of his secret ride in tow of *Marie Claire,* they would have gotten word ashore to their master, and Moreau would have run to his crony Sir Thomas.

Mrs. Graves completed the charade for them.

"Stone shall be a messenger from my friend Mrs. Haddaway in Dorchester, with an urgent request for me to come to her aid. He shall drive us in the chaise, and a spare horse can follow us on a lead. It will be the animal on which Stone came to Weymouth. You, Mr. Hoare, shall hide beneath me. There is ample space for you under the seat. Outside town, we will divert to Ringstead, leave Mr. Hoare and Stone, and find a local lad to take us on to Dorchester."

"Then ye'd best name yer friend to me again, ma'am," Stone said. "An' gi' me 'er likeness, tu. If I'm to be ridin' postilion, some'un might be askin' me questions."

Mrs. Graves nodded. "Of course. Haddaway. Mrs. Timothy Haddaway. Emily Haddaway. She's a real person, Stone, my age, twice my size all 'round . . . two children, little Timothy, the babe, and Arethusa."

Outside the town, the unwelcome batrachian voice of the knight-baronet brought the chaise to a halt. Hoare—reasonably comfortable, though coiled like an adder beneath the woman he had come to love—held his breath.

"Why, Sir Thomas!" Mrs. Graves cried. "What are you and

your men about, pray? It looks like a *posse comitatus,* sir, indeed it does."

"About that, Eleanor, my dear. Mr. Morrow brings news that your acquaintance Hoare is a wanted man, a fugitive from the King's justice for the forcible drowning of one of Mr. Morrow's Channel Islanders, seen hereabouts just last night. We're out to take him up. Have you seen him, Eleanor?" Sir Thomas's voice was stern.

"Not for this age, Sir Thomas. Not since we encountered each other after poor Simon—"

"Best take my advice, Eleanor. Should you catch sight of him on your way to—"

"Dorchester, Sir Thomas. Emily Haddaway—you know Emily, of course—sent word that her poor little babe Timothy has the croup, and she wants my advice. I'm sure I don't know why," Eleanor Graves gushed.

"You are a wise, wise woman, Eleanor," Sir Thomas said. "After a proper interval of time, I hope I may wish—"

The listening Hoare never had a chance to learn what Sir Thomas wished for Mrs. Graves, for Stone broke in: "Pardon me, ma'am, but we must get under way if we are to make Dorchester by dark."

" 'Under way,' my man? Why, you sound like a seaman and no postboy."

"Seaman I was, zur, before I swallowed the anchor and took service wi' Mr. Haddaway. But, excuse me, zur. . . ."

Hoare was jarred as the chaise started forward on its delayed way to the pinnace. He gloated quietly at the picture of the chaise, with Stone at its helm, leaving Sir Thomas Frobisher at the post.

AT PORTSMOUTH, THE sighting of *Inconceivable,* creeping cautiously across Spit Sand with her sliding keel fully retracted, was instantly reported to Sir George Hardcastle. The Admiral showed himself as merciless as ever. Hoare was to betake himself forthwith to the Admiralty offices, where he was to report his progress—if any—to Sir George. Wrinkled and unkempt though they were, the second-best uniform and hat he carried on *Inconceivable* would have to do, if he was to persuade the Admiral that he was not habitually slow to obey orders. In that, he failed.

"Late again, Hoare. And filthy, too," Sir George said. "I am quite out of patience with you, I declare."

Hoare quickly summarized for his Admiral his glacial chase of *Marie Claire,* his brief capture by her owner, his escape from Weymouth. Moment by moment, the Admiral's face grew grimmer.

"No more now, sir," he growled at last. You shall bring that man back here, to justice, dead or alive. Lose not a minute."

"May I enlist reinforcements to bring him in, sir?"

"I have sent my secretary Talthybius to you a number of times, young Hercules," Sir George said, "with one task or another. You are given those tasks because I am confident you will carry them out to my satisfaction. I do not expect you to turn to me with whimpers about how you are to execute each task. I have neither the time nor the inclination to hover over you like a mother hen. I have other tasks of my own to perform, which is why I give yours to you in the first place. Take yourself off, sir and do your duty."

The Admiral's verbal lash notwithstanding, Hoare had another lash to inflict on himself before he was ready to obey his instructions—to take Jaggery. With Jaggery in hand, he was sure, he could complete the investigation with which Sir George Hardcastle had charged him.

Jaggery was not at the Bunch of Grapes. Mr. Greenleaf believed he might be at work in Arrowsmith's warehouse. He gave Hoare directions. To reach the warehouse, Hoare had to pass his own quarters on the way.

The warehouse was nothing more than a series of inter-connected sheds that reached from Eastney High Street to the shore. Hoare found no one in the first two sheds and squeezed through a narrow passage into the third. He pulled out his boatswain's call and piped "All Hands!" in the hope that Jaggery, if he was there, would respond by instinct.

The man himself appeared in a crooked doorway at the far end of the enclosure. He looked bewildered.

Anything he might have been saying to Hoare was drowned by a thunderclap behind him, a blast that threw Jaggery forward and Hoare backward. A cloud of fire followed the burst. Behind Jaggery, the shed roof collapsed, and the flames began to get a grip on it. Jaggery lay still, face up on the floor, half-buried in debris.

The choking battle reek of burnt powder filled the place. Hoare coughed, wheezed, and wept as he struggled over the fallen beams in the smoke toward the other man.

Jaggery lay supine, facing what had been the ceiling. From his waist down he was hidden under a massive joist that lay almost level with the bricks of the room's floor. He was breathing hard. From the ruins of the shed Hoare could hear the soft roar of flames as the fire tightened its grip.

"Help me up, Yer Honor. Somethin's holdin' me poor weak legs down an' I can't move 'em. Get it orf me, can't yer?"

Hoare freed a lighter beam and began to search for a spot that offered him leverage room. He found one, set the beam's end under the joist, and heaved down on the beam with all his weight. For all his frantic prying, the joist would not budge. Outside, he heard the jangling of a fire bell. The engine's feeble streams and bucket brigade would do as much good here as two old men in a pissing contest.

Another, smaller explosion sounded in the ruins. A flickering of fire reflected itself in Jaggery's wide eyes, and those eyes filled with fear.

"Smartly, man, can't yer? 'Eave!" he gasped. " 'Eave!"

He choked and grabbed Hoare's shoulder with his free hand. It was the mangled one, but it could still cling to Hoare like a cargo hook.

Five minutes later, the heat of the fire was scorching Hoare's hair. Jaggery blew a pink bubble. It burst in Hoare's face as he stooped, chest heaving.

Jaggery was breathing hard. "I'm a dead man," he said. Hoare could not bring himself to deny it. He rested his hand on the other's shoulder.

"Yer a decent cove, Yer Honor," Jaggery said at last. "I've no . . . no mind to be roasted alive. Will yer put me down?"

"If you tell me who 'Himself' is. Morrow's boss."

"As Gawd is me witness, I dunno, Yer Honor. Morrow, 'e's the only one what knows his name."

"Why did Kingsley bring one of Morrow's ankers aboard his own ship?" Hoare whispered. "He might as well have shot himself."

Jaggery shook his head. "Kingsley, Yer Honor? 'E didn't take no anker aboard *Vantage*. I did. Like all the other times, I thought I was slippin' brandy to 'im, for 'im to give to officers that might 'ave interest, to get 'em on 'is side."

The heat was beating on Hoare's face.

"It was only when Kingsley was dead, and Morrow weren't comin' into town no more, that I dared tap one of them ankers. Wouldn't do no 'arm now, I thought, to have a bit of 'is oh-be-joyful. 'Twasn't as though it belonged to no one anymore, bein' as 'e was dead.

"An' look what I tapped into instead. Oh, well, I guess I was dis- . . . dis- . . ."

"Dispensable?"

"Aye. That's the word. Oh, 'urry, sir, 'urry! I can feel the fire on me toes." By now, Jaggery's voice was as faint as Hoare's own whisper.

Hoare could not believe the man, dying though he was. At least one more layer remained in the Jaggery onion.

"You're lying, Jaggery. Tell me the truth, man, or I'll leave you to burn, all by yourself."

Jaggery grunted, was silent. Then he sighed. A pink bubble formed at his mouth and broke. "All right. I knew first thing 'e were up to no good, and I found out what was in them ankers first off. Then I thought, well, I never thought that much of the Navy, and there's me Jenny to be kept safe, so I went along with it. That is the truth, Yer Honor, the whole truth, and nothin' but the truth, so help me God."

At last his words rang true.

"Will ye take care of me Jenny, Yer Honor? She's a good girl, she is, and she'll be a double orphing tomorrer." His eyes stared intently into Hoare's. "We puts up with Greenleaf at 'is Bunch of Grapes."

"I'll do it," Hoare said again. "She'll be brought up a lady."

"Lady, me arse. She's Wet Meg's get, she is, with no lines spoke between us. Just teach the lass to read an' write, will yer? Ye promise?"

"I promise, Jaggery."

"Give her a kiss from her ol' da, then. *Uh*. Now, do it. Hope it won't be so hot where I'm goin'. Oh, *Jesus.*" Another pink bubble formed and broke.

Apalled at what he must do, Hoare took out his knife, tested the point against his thumb. Leaning away from Jaggery so the man's blood would strike the advancing fire instead of him, he slipped the point between Jaggery's ribs. Jaggery hissed, jerked like a salmon. Soon, the fire already charring his uniform, Hoare closed Jaggery's eyes and backed out of the wreckage. Time was pressing, but his new obligation pressed more heavily.

JENNY JAGGERY REMEMBERED Hoare. When he told her her Da was dead, she stood thoughtful for a minute.

"I'm a norphing, then, for truth," she said.

194

"I'm afraid so, child," Hoare replied.

She went to the pallet where she slept and took a small threadbare purse from under the pillow. "Ain't enough here to pay the rent," she said, after counting the contents. "So I might as well start doin' it now. 'Ow do yer want to do it to me, Yer Honor? Be easy on me, will yer? I never done it before."

"You'll not have to 'do it' for anyone till you're grown-up, Jenny," Hoare said, "and not then unless you really want to. I promised your Da I'd take care of you, and that I'm going to do. Get your things together now, and we'll be off."

At first, Mr. Greenleaf appeared reluctant to see Hoare about to vanish with the child, but when Hoare had explained the circumstances and assured him that she would only be moving to the Swallowed Anchor, where he and his good wife could readily reassure themselves of her well-being, he released her into Hoare's keeping with a smile and a ha'penny.

Hoare turned his tubular charge and her pitiful bundle of belongings over to the pink girl Susan at the Swallowed Anchor, telling her to feed the child and find her a corner she could call her own. Jenny took Susan's hand readily enough but looked over her shoulder at Hoare.

"Wait," he whispered. "I forgot. Your Da gave me a packet of kisses for you, and told me to give you one every night when you go to bed.

"Here's for tonight." He bent over and kissed Jenny's cool, round forehead. It was a new experience, for him at least. "Off you go, child."

Susan came downstairs after a while. "She's sleepin' peaceful, sir," she told Hoare. "She didn't even 'ave no dolly, so I give her the one I had when I were her age, an' she cuddled up with it as nice as could be."

She paused and looked down at Hoare.

"If it ain't presumptive of me to ask, sir," she said, "what are yer plans for 'er? She seems like a good little mite."

195

"To tell the truth, Susan," he replied, "I haven't thought it through. She's Janus Jaggery's child, you know."

"Well, Janus Jaggery may have been a bad man, but he weren't a *bad* man, sir, if you catch my meaning. Now, you don't really want to set up to be a da to her, do you? You never struck me as a marryin' man, an' she orter have a mam." Susan's look grew speculative.

"We'll just have to see, Susan," Hoare said thoughtfully. "Meanwhile, take good care of her."

THAT DONE, HOARE was ready to see that Edouard Moreau was brought to the King's justice. For this, there was again not a moment to be lost—though, Hoare confessed, he himself had wasted several precious hours in dealing with the Jaggery child.

The arrest of Moreau would be a personal pleasure, but Hoare would be exceeding his brief by thinking to command the expedition it would apparently require. Besides his disaffected French-Canadians, Moreau could well have other English renegades at his disposal as well—Irish irredentists, too, perhaps, ready to avenge Wolfe Tone. Yet, whether he would be exceeding his brief or not, Hoare wanted to be in on the kill, in person. The stink of the vanished *Vantage* was still fresh in his nose.

How was he to go about it? A more tactful officer than himself—one who had kept on good terms with Sir Thomas Frobisher instead of near-hostility—could simply call on the baronet for a force of his watch, march up the long slope from Weymouth town under the eyes of Moreau, cut him out from among some sixteen men, and haul him away. In doing so, this more tactful officer would, of course, have no difficulty in persuading Moreau not to put an end to him with the Kentucky rifle he had stolen, as he had done with at least two victims—Kingsley and Dr. Graves.

Moreover, the man behind Moreau—Fortier's and Jaggery's "Himself," lurking in the shadows of the case—might still be in the offing with reinforcements for the defense of his man Moreau. Then again, maybe not.

The Marine division headquartered in Portsmouth, Hoare remembered as he went, included—as well as nearly fifty companies of infantry and batteries of artillery—a troop of hybrid creatures. Half soldier, half sailor, half cavalrymen, they were called "Horse Marines." These military chimeras served as outlying guards on the landward side of Portsmouth. On their rounds, they kept an eye peeled for seamen and fellow Marines seeking to disappear into the countryside. They were a despised laughingstock—military bastards—about whom ribald jigs had been circulating for years.

Hoare had met two of their officers, including their captain, not so long ago and taken their part in a dispute with certain regular hussars. It was to their corner of the Marine barracks that he went. He hoped their captain—a John Jinks, if he remembered correctly—would be at hand and that he would respond to Hoare's appeal for armed support.

Captain Jinks was both present and complaisant. "It'll give the lazy rascals a jaunt," he said. Within minutes, Hoare was jouncing out of town on a borrowed charger beside Captain Jinks, his troop of Horse Marines jingling behind him.

A DAY AND a half later, the troop trotted through a mizzle of chilly rain and crested the Purbeck Downs beside Morrow's quarry. There a dozen men or more, variously armed, blocked the narrow paved roadway into Weymouth, up and down which Hoare had plodded before, to be insulted and rebuffed by Morrow and Sir Thomas Frobisher. At their head, Sir Thomas himself sat a handsome eighteen-hand horse—an Irish hunter, Hoare hazarded to himself. Another horseman flanked Sir Thomas.

"Halt right there, you troop of sleazy imitation soldiers," Sir Thomas Frobisher said. "How dare you trespass on Frobisher land without my say-so?"

"I don't know that I care for the way you describe my Marines, sir," Captain Jinks retorted. "In any case, we bring a warrant for the arrest of one Edouard Moreau, alias Edward Morrow, on charges of treason, et cetera, et cetera. Stand aside, please."

"Show your warrant, sir," Sir Thomas said. His bandy, froggy legs barely reached below his mount's barrel.

Captain Jinks turned to Hoare, as did Sir Thomas, who looked at Hoare with extreme distaste.

"You again, fellow," he said, his voice oozing contempt. "I told you I'd have you horsewhipped if I laid eyes on you again on my manor."

"I think not, sir," Hoare whispered. "Here is the warrant. I think you will find it quite in order." He held the document up.

"Well, fellow? Give it to me," Sir Thomas ordered.

"I think not, sir," Hoare repeated. "You may advance as far as you must in order to read it."

"Never mind," Sir Thomas said. "I did not sign it, and I am the law of this land. You can go to hell, and take your fornicatin' document with you."

"The warrant is signed and sealed by the Marquess of Blandford, sir, as you can plainly see. As I need not tell you, he is Lord Lieutenant of this county." Hoare hoped that Sir Thomas would stop arguing and decide either to resist this troop of mounted Marines or to obey his Lord Lieutenant. He felt himself running out of whisper.

Sir Thomas muttered a few words to his fellow horseman, who spurred his animal at a furious, foolhardy pace down the hill toward the town. With no good will, he gestured to his other followers to clear the road. He himself sat his horse, fuming, while the red-coated troop filed past him like a martial hunt passing in review before their Master of Fox Hounds. At the tail of the last trooper, Hoare doffed his hat and bowed silently in his saddle to the baronet. He was crotch-weary and glad to be ending his eighty-mile journey. It had rained all the way.

Moreau was not at the offices of his quarry. At the door of the house at the top of the zigzag road that led down to the town, Moreau's manservant shook his head.

"You'll not find the master here," he said. " 'E's gorn."

"We'll see about that," Captain Jinks replied grimly. "Sergeant MacNab!"

"Sah?"

"Take four men. Station one at each door of the house. Search the house for our man. You'll remember the description given you last night by Mr. Hoare."

"Sah!"

One of the troopers failed to suppress a guffaw. Sergeant MacNab turned on him.

"Silence, man! Twa days o' muckin' oot the stables forrr ye!"

The rest of the troop jogged carefully on down the turnpike, behind Hoare and their captain. They spurned the outraged tollbooth keeper and proceeded into town.

Waving frantically, the maid Agnes stood at Mrs. Graves's front door as the troop clattered up.

"She's gone to keep an eye on Mr. Morrow on the shore!" Agnes cried. " 'You'll find him at Portland Bill,' she says I was to tell you, 'where you and I drove off his men together'!"

Once off the smooth blocks of the street and down on the shingle, Jinks set the troop to a canter—but not for long, as first one horse and then another went lame, victims of the treacherous cobbles.

"It ain't the 'untin' that 'urts the 'orse; it's the 'ammer, 'ammer, 'ammer on the 'ard 'ighway," Captain Jinks reminded Hoare out of the side of his mouth.

When they rounded a small point of the cliff, the troop's leaders could see Moreau, alone, heaving a shallop toward the surf. It might well have been the very shallop that had sheltered Eleanor Graves from her assailants that first afternoon. The wind was easterly and gusty, the clouds heavier than they had been on that first occasion. Perhaps a quarter-mile offshore, *Marie Claire* lay hove to, her foresail backed, tossing in the first line of breakers. Hoare handed the warrant to Captain Jinks. Let him do the shouting.

Jinks deployed his men. A sudden rain squall hid *Marie Claire,* then swept across the waves toward them.

"Edouard Moreau, alias Edward Morrow," Jinks cried, "I have here a warrant for your arrest on charges of treason! Advance and surrender!" He gestured to his men to spread out along the stony beach and take aim.

"I'll be damned if I do!" Moreau shouted.

"Surrender, or we fire!"

Moreau continued to shove at the skiff. The curtain of rain squall struck. *Marie Claire* vanished behind it. It drove down on the waiting troop, bent on soaking the carbines' priming powder.

"Fire!" Captain Jinks cried.

Two carbines went off. Three misfired with faint, wet sounds. Hoare dismounted and began to plod wearily toward Moreau along the shingle, turning an ankle at every third step.

"You'll never make it through the surf, you fool," he whispered to the métis, knowing well that his words would be lost within inches of his mouth.

Moreau did not even turn. He had the shallop afloat at last. He heaved it into the sea until the first surf foamed around his knees, drew himself aboard it, and set the oars in their tholepins. Looking over his shoulder every few strokes to see that he was on course for *Marie Claire,* he began to pull for her. The Canadian handled his oars as well as any Coastguardsman.

In the offing, Hoare saw a pair of men clamber over the schooner's side into a small boat and cast off, towing a light line behind them. They were still beyond the breakers.

Hoare reached into one deep pocket for his first pistol. He hoped it was dry. Using his left arm as a rest, he took careful aim at the oarsman and fired. Hoare could not see where his ball went. He found his second pistol, took and held a breath, and squeezed the trigger. The weapon sputtered, hung fire, and destroyed a wave top. Taking another stroke, Moreau grinned mirthlessly at him over his oars.

There came a *whicker* overhead, and a sling-stone clipped a wave top beyond Moreau's shoulder. Turning, Hoare saw Eleanor Graves on the low cliff above him, astride a Downs pony. She was bareback, her thighs exposed to the rain, her hair mingled with the beast's shaggy mane. She had loaded another stone into her sling.

The second stone took off one of the shallop's starboard thole pins. Moreau caught a crab with his starboard oar. The shallop swerved and broached to, just in time to catch a breaking sea broadside. The sea poured aboard it over the gunwales. She swamped and lurched heavily to leeward.

Moreau went overboard into the boil. He was out of his depth, for his head disappeared. When he came to the surface again, his clutch missed the shallop's gunwale by no more than a finger. A crosscurrent caught the boat and began to edge it away, leaving Moreau to struggle after it, losing a tantalizing inch or two with every stroke.

In his mind's eye Hoare could see the burnt and mangled men of *Vantage,* with those of *Scipio* and the other vessels Moreau and his minions had destroyed. The man had put paid to upward of a thousand loyal English sailors. Hoare would be damned if he would let him drown peaceably. He kicked off his shoes and waded into the surf until he was waist deep. He looped his belt knife's lanyard over his wrist and dove forward into the surf, his hat carrying away somewhere into the windy darkness. He let the knife drag behind him so that he could put the full force of both arms into his stroke.

As Moreau struggled seaward toward his schooner, he had turned his back to Hoare, whose sudden grip on his coat took him unaware. Hoare climbed up the other's sunken back and forced his head into the water.

Moreau twisted in Hoare's arms, gripped both ears, and pulled his head forward. His teeth gnashed at Hoare's nose, clenched into it hard. Hoare let him gnash. He let go of the métis with both hands and pulled the sheath-knife into reach by its lanyard. He jabbed it forward and felt it sink into some soft part of Moreau's midsection.

Moreau's mouth opened in a gasp, releasing Hoare's nose and sucking in water. Hoare shook his head and twisted the knife in Moreau's body, withdrew it, stabbed again at random. Moreau rolled over. His eyes opened wide, staring into Hoare's. The métis gave a choked cry and grimaced, spewing bloody water through his teeth into Hoare's face. Hoare let go of the knife, pulled his enemy's head underwater by his coarse, clubbed black hair, and bore down on top of him. Moreau sank under him, bubbled, and died—whether by drowning or from his knife wounds Hoare never knew and never cared.

Hoare could see the shallop rocking, logy and tantalizing, still just out of reach as if it were alive and viciously teasing. He took a firmer grip of Moreau's hair, rolled over on his back, and began to tow him ashore through the surf.

Beyond the breakers, the hands left in *Marie Claire* hauled their shipmates back aboard. Before Hoare had struggled ashore with his captive's body, the schooner was under way under reefed fore- and mainsails, making seaward toward France.

Eleanor Graves clambered off her pony and down the cliff-side path, to look down at Hoare as he gasped above his victim, bleeding from his torn nose.

"Well done," she said. "I would happily have crippled him

and delivered him to the Navy's mercy, but I would not have wished another man's death on my conscience. The one—Dugas, the leader of my attackers—was enough."

"You didn't kill Dugas," Hoare whispered. "Someone smothered him to death."

Her eyes lit up. "Then I could have killed Morrow after all," she said. "He came to my house in the rain after you and your man Stone left in the chaise. He stunned poor Tom with a club, forced himself into my presence, and threatened to kill both Agnes and Tom if I did not hand over Simon's papers. So I did.

"He leafed through them, but found nothing. Could he have supposed I would have given him them all without a fight? It did not come to that, for one of his men stormed in to warn him of your coming and he fled without harming any of us further. I followed him on Rosie here.

"Take him away now, with my compliments to the Navy."

She turned away, climbed slowly back up the cliff path to her waiting pony Rosie, while Hoare, with the help of one of the Horse Marines, loaded the body onto a spare mount.

Chapter XV

———⟫◦◦◦⟪———

$\mathcal{H}$OARE FOUND the journey back from Weymouth with the Horse Marines almost insupportable. He was weary, weary to the bone—from his struggle to save Jaggery, from the forced march to arrest Moreau, from his hard swim and the death in the surf at Portsmouth Bill, from the necessity of traveling nearly a hundred miles in company with Sir Thomas Frobisher. It was quite enough.

For no sooner had Sir Thomas got wind of Moreau's death than he marched his miscellaneous men up to the Moreau quarry offices and obtained the surrender of the twelve leaderless Canadians who had not escaped to France on *Marie Claire*. With this victory to boast of, he elbowed Captain Jinks aside by claiming that, the Frenchmen also having been taken on Frobisher land, they were his prisoners. The journey to Portsmouth became a Frobisher parade, led by Frobisher's men, with the Horse Marines bringing up the rear—and Bartholomew Hoare nowhere.

Delancey, the flag lieutenant, cut Hoare out from the troop and brought him, travel-worn and dusty, to his master.

Sir George ordered Hoare to summarize his transaction in Weymouth, chided him for having greatly exceeded his authority in abstracting Captain Jinks and his men, and—only when Hoare's whisper broke down completely—mercifully released him with instructions to prepare a written report and deliver it to him within twenty-four hours.

In the Admiral's anteroom, Hoare found Sir Thomas Frobisher, triumphant, purple, and goggling. The baronet glared and brushed past him on his way in to demand of Sir George the peerage he deserved for frustrating the Frogs' latest knavish tricks.

Before leaving for the Swallowed Anchor, Hoare stopped to extort supplies from Mr. Patterson: ample paper, fresh-cut quills, and enough of Patterson's finest India ink to carry him through this latest Herculean task. Patterson needed Hoare's threats, pleading, and finally the promise of a bottle of the precious Madeira to release it all. He also persuaded Patterson to promise that when Hoare had finished he would have one of his clerks make a fair copy for Sir George's eyes.

Sounds of disputation began to come through the door to Sir George's sanctum. By the time Hoare left the anteroom, laden with his loot, they had risen to acrimonious shouts.

As he came out the door to the street, the voices of the two enraged knights rose to a roar, culminating with a thunderous croak from Sir Thomas: "Damn the Royal Navy, and damn you, too!"

Upon this, Hoare fled for home, bath, bird, and bottle.

THE FOLLOWING MORNING, Hoare felt quite refreshed in body, but not in spirit. He did not look forward to putting his actions down on paper. The act had a sense of finality about it. Nonetheless, now finding all was in readiness, he was ready to begin.

First, however, he must move his parlor table to a particularly well lit part of the room. He doffed his uniform coat and hung it carefully on the back of the chair. He turned back his right sleeve.

Now, feeling perfectly comfortable, he was ready to begin.

First, however, he needed to make sure his poor throat would not run dry in midvoyage. He slipped downstairs and had the pink girl Susan prepare a pitcher of her mild, soothing, lemon-flavored tisane. He chatted idly with little Jenny Jaggery as he waited for Susan to finish, sighed, and took the pitcher back upstairs. He placed the pitcher where it would be handy but not in the way of any sudden flourish of inspiration.

Now fully prepared, Hoare was ready to begin. He selected a pen, dipped it in Patterson's ink, and wrote down the necessary prelude.

Portsmouth, 19 August 1805

Admiral Sir George Hardcastle, KB, Commanding
at Portsmouth
Sir:

So far, so good. He paused in meditation, reread what he had written, then began to set down his next words. His stupid pen had dried out, and he must dip it again in Patterson's precious ink before he could continue.

You have had the kindness to instruct me to prepare a report which you propose to forward to Their Lordships of the Admiralty. This report, you have directed, should include such of those events surrounding the recent sequestration of infernal machines on HM ships as cannot be substantiated and would therefore be of no value in court. In other words, I am to narrate what I believe to have happened, as well as what is known to have happened.

Hoare was properly under way now, all sails drawing. He went on to set forth the details of the case. He told of Morrow's French-Canadian origin, his hatred of the English, and his recruitment as an agent of Bonaparte.

He described Morrow's approach to Dr. Graves, the latter's manufacture of clockwork for him in the belief that he was doing so for their use in His Majesty's ships—as, of course, they were,—and the doctor's growing suspicion of Morrow's motives.

He informed the Admiral of how Morrow had sent two of his men—one Dugas and another—to abduct Mrs. Graves and hold her as surety against her husband's obedience.

He reported how Morrow, with Jaggery's assistance, had inserted the mechanisms into powder-packed ankers and used others such as the treasonous Kingsley to sequester them in vessels of the Navy. How Kingsley had had in his possession no less than three of the still-undeciphered messages from the person Jaggery had known only as "Himself." That person, he suggested, was the same one spoken of by Morrow's man Fortier as *lui*, the two terms being equivalent.

After a ten-minute period, which he took to stretch and pace about his parlor, Hoare now enumerated for his Admiral the individual deaths which must be laid at Moreau's door—those of Kingsley and Dr. Graves, and perhaps that of Jaggery as well—although another must have smothered Moreau's man Dugas. He pointed out that several matters must be of grave concern to the Navy. The one of most immediate urgency, he wrote, was the elimination of any armed ankers that remain unexploded.

The second major concern, however, as Hoare advised, was the unmasking of "Himself," the anonymous figure who directed Morrow, Kingsley, and Jaggery and may well have an unknown number of other agents at his command. In Hoare's opinion he was probably 'Jehu,' the author of the captured texts. "As long as a man of such caliber is at liberty, His Majesty's Navy remains imperilled."

Except for the proper closing courtesies, this concluded Hoare's report to Admiral Hardcastle. Thereupon, he rested.

THE NEXT MORNING, Hoare bore his blotted masterpiece to Admiralty House, where he cajoled the Admiral's rabbit into making a fair copy. This done, he signed it, sealed it, and ordered the rabbit to place it before their common master with all possible speed. Then he returned to the Swallowed Anchor to await the consequences. He whiled away the time by returning *Inconceivable* to a full state of readiness, having taken the liberty of keeping Bold and Stone at hand for a day or two beyond what was proper.

"GO FIND SOMETHING to do somewhere else, Delancey," Admiral Hardcastle said from behind his mountain of papers. "And close the door after you.

"Take a pew, Mr. Hoare. A glass of Madeira with you, sir. Pour me a glass, if you'd be so kind, and take one yourself. I'd like your opinion of it. I think you will find it a superior product. Your good health, sir, and a prosperous future to you," he went on, raising his glass. "And the thanks of the Admiralty for having put a stop to that Frenchman's capers."

Hoare could have been tasting a wine from his own stock. At the second sip, his suspicions hardened. "Excuse me, Sir George, for asking," he said, "but . . . where did you procure this nectar?"

"From Greenleaf, at the Bunch of Grapes," the Admiral replied. He sounded a trifle smug. "I'll warrant *you've* never stooped to a place like that. I was past there just yesterday. Hasn't even settled properly yet."

And that bastard Greenleaf swore he sold me the last of his stock, Hoare snarled to himself. I'll have his guts for garters.

"Now, about the man Moreau's nationality," the Admiral continued, sailing on, all unconscious of Hoare's outrage. "He was a Canadian, even if of French extraction, and therefore a British subject. He would have been hanged for treason."

"Yes, sir," Hoare said. "But he would have come to the same end in any case, would he not? Hanged for treason, or hanged for a spy?"

"Obviously, sir. Nonetheless, this puts a different complexion on things. We can't have the nation looking over its shoulders for traitors in our midst, coming from lower Canada, or the Channel Islands, for that matter.

"No. Our people—*all* our people, whether English, Scottish, Irish, or Canadian—must be seen as loyal subjects of our poor mad Majesty. No. The man was a Frenchman, one of Boney's deluded fools. I'll have Delancey put that about. Delancey!" Sir George bellowed, and the flag lieutenant reappeared as if by magic.

"Good," Sir George said. "I do like promptness in my officers."

In a few paragraphs, he dictated an aide-mèmoire to the Lords of the Admiralty in Whitehall, describing how Royal Navy forces had rooted out the French agents who had been responsible for the Portsmouth explosions but mentioning the names of neither ships nor men—nor the name of Thomas Frobisher, knight and baronet. He dismissed Delancey.

"Very good," Sir George said. "That'll quiet the damned scribblers. And give that self-important blatherskite Frobisher no comfort either." He cast a sardonic eye over Hoare's untidy garb. "You need a wife," he stated. "Go and find one."

Hoare could only nod, and Sir George continued.

"Your tale, Mr. Hoare, draws too heavily for belief upon the history of classical warfare. Crossbows, slings, and now ramming. . . . I declare, I don't know what the world is coming to. Fill our glasses again, sir.

"Ahem. Since you persist in acting in a classical mode: you accomplished your labors for 'Eurystheus,' young Heracles; even Talthybius the Dung Man—my clerk Patterson, that is—has had the impudence to say so. Furthermore, you apparently impressed Abercrombie's man."

"Abercrombie's man, sir?"

"Yes." The Admiral was commencing to sound restless. "Sir Hugh Abercrombie. He had somebody observing you, it seems, during that triumph of yours after the *Vantage* affair. You should remember; I certainly don't. I wasn't there. Besides, the less I know about Abercrombie's people, the happier I am. *I* don't care to be yellowed because I told secrets I shouldn't have known.

"However, that is neither here nor there. What I can tell you is that Their Lordships of the Admiralty, in their infinite wisdom, have instructed me to order you into *Royal Duke* as master and commander when she makes Portsmouth from Chatham. I am pleased to obey Their Lordships, of course. Here are your preliminary warning orders. I understand she weighed for Spithead on Tuesday, under her present lieutenant. *Your* lieutenant, perhaps I should say. I took the liberty of keeping him in his post. I think you will not be displeased with my decision."

"He is a man," Sir George went on, "whose powerful voice more than balances his . . . well, you will see. In any case, you will be able to relay your orders through him. I'm surprised no one ever thought of that before. Pity; a promising naval career has been held back unnecessarily, in my opinion."

"May I ask, sir, who . . . ," Hoare whispered.

"You may ask, sir, but you will receive no answer. I exercise my privilege of being irritating to my subordinates whenever I choose. Let you unveil the man yourself when you read yourself in. I drink to your health and continued good fortune, Captain Hoare."

"*Captain* Hoare." Bartholomew Hoare had never really hoped to hear that glorious prefix attached to his name. He glowed within.

Sir George, suiting his action to his words, waited until Hoare's expected expressions of shock and joy ran down and then continued.

"Your appointment will not be gazetted yet, of course—not until you've read yourself in—or had Mr. What's-his-name do it for you. But you may mount your swab as soon as it pleases you to do so. And, since I'll wager you're going to be rushing off to Weymouth anyway, you may as well take this copy of the *Chronicle* with you while you're about it and read it to that widow who interests you so greatly. There's a bit in it about her late husband.

"But steer clear of Frobisher, though, d'ye understand? I can't have you in the same room with him. He's too important in that part of the countryside, and in the House, for you to get embroiled with him. Understand?"

Hoare nodded his assent, whispered his heartfelt thanks, made his bow, and left to find the best tailor in the port. Later, he would invite his friends to help him wet his new swab. Tomorrow morning, he would rent an agreeable horse and betake himself to Weymouth. There was not a moment to lose.

When Hoare handed the article to her, Mrs. Graves read it silently. Then she looked up at him. "This is very gratifying indeed, Mr. Hoare," she said. "I now apologize most abjectly for having misunderstood your intentions toward my late husband, and I thank you from the bottom of my heart for having cleared his good name. Ask me for any reward it is in my power to grant."

Hoare had done this once before, in Halifax, at the feet of his sweet Canadienne. Nevertheless, he was trembling as he dropped to one knee.

"Mrs. Graves . . . Eleanor," he began haltingly, "I have now reached a position in the service where my future is more certain than it was. And I already command a small but sufficient income. I wish to ask . . . to ask you if you could bring yourself to share that future."

"Mr. Hoare," she said, looking down at him with those piercing brown eyes. "Or perhaps I should say 'Captain Hoare,' if I remember my naval etiquette. Bartholomew. I am thirty-four years old and—to be blunt—still a virgin despite my widowed state. Are you so besotted as to think that, at my age, I would be able to accommodate the attentions of a man? That I would be, or could become, a suitable spouse for an active gentleman in the prime of life? That I could bear his children—yours, to be precise?

"Come, come, sir! I am a mundane woman, and I know it. I am not interested in a lark. No," she went on. "I thank you, not only for your offer, but for the kindness which must have inspired you to make it. To be sure, my late husband's lands go to his children. But you should know that poor Simon . . ." She seemed to choke, but continued, "When we were wed, Simon made over to me the jewels he gave me, his house and its furnishings, and his practice is mine to dispose of as I see fit. I shall not be thrown upon the town for my living. I have no children of my own for whom I am responsible. I shall be reasonably prosperous, in fact."

"I do not make my proposal out of pity, Eleanor," Hoare protested. "I make it out of admiration, high regard, and the deepest affection. I . . . I love you."

"I wonder, Bartholomew," she said gently, "if you recall the evening you spent with Simon, Miss Austen, Mr. Morrow—Moreau, I suppose I should call him—and myself. . . ."

"Vividly."

"Then you will remember my saying something like this: 'I permit no one but my husband to listen to the music of *my* heart. It belongs to him.' I meant those words then, Bartholomew, and I mean them still. Perhaps it is too soon after Simon's death, but my heart is not yet mine to bestow."

"Then I shall not withdraw my proposal," Hoare whispered. "Your heart may not now be yours to bestow on a living man, but perhaps it will find its way back to you in due course. Meanwhile, you have the disposition of my own."

Hoare could say no more. He bowed over Eleanor Graves's hand, turned, and left her house. Once again, it was raining.

Glossary

—————❖—————

Nautical Terms Employed During the Period

ahoo: In utter disarray

anker: A small keg, containing about ten gallons

brow: A gangway between the shore and a vessel or floating dock. Also, the floating dock itself

cheerly: Briskly

gudgeons: Sockets, affixed to a vessel's stern-post, into which the rudder's pintles fit

havey-cavey: Slipshod or surreptitious

hoy: A small freighter with a large hatch, suitable for transferring supplies to ships at sea (e.g., blockading fleets)

interest: Influence, a principal means of advancement in the services and the government alike. Treated as a combination of credit and honor, traded and exchanged like a commodity

marines: A force of seagoing soldiers who served as landing parties, occasionally as ship's police, generally as guards against mutiny. Occasionally took part in the less-skilled aspects of ship-handling and gunnery. "Lobsters," "Jollies," or "Leathernecks," their relations with the hands were not always cordial

overhead: Belowdecks, the ceiling. Obviously, the upper side of the overhead is a deck

pintles: The downward-projecting male fittings of a rudder, which are inserted in the gudgeons. In combination, the two sets of fittings—male and female—permit the rudder to swing more or less freely

press: The sweeping up of hands—experienced, if possible, inexperienced if necessary—by gangs of sailors from undermanned vessels or the Impress Service. Each gang was commanded by an officer. Certain mariners, such as fishermen and East Indiamen, were "protected." As long as they could show papers to that effect, they were generally safe from impressment

quarterdeck: Designates the after-portion of the vessel's deck, generally raised five feet or so above the waist, and reached by companionways to port and starboard. The quarterdeck, generally speaking, was officer's country

quarter-gallery: Protrusions on either side of the stern cabin, containing latrines for the officers and the ship's captain

rifleman: One of a widely-scattered regiment of skirmishers and sharpshooters, clad in green after the American War, who used the accurate but slow-to-load rifle as their principal weapon. While called "swords," the bayonets attached to Riflemen's weapons differed little if at all from the ones used by infantry of the line

waist: The central half (approximate) of a vessel's upper deck, between the forecastle and the quarterdeck

waisters: The least-skilled class of seamen

yellowed: Active flag officers of the Royal Navy could hold three ranks: rear admiral, vice admiral, and admiral. Each of these ranks was divided in turn into three parts, identified by the color of the flags flown by their flagships and the vessels in their fleets. Red was the lowest in seniority, white the next, and blue the highest. A flag officer who was unemployed for whatever reason was designated as an admiral (or rear admiral or vice admiral) "without distinction of squadron;" he was "yellowed." Admirals of the fleet, being always on active duty, were never yellowed